T0294380

In Strange Places

Clare Porac

In Strange Places

©2021 Clare Porac

print ISBN: 978-1-09836-067-2
ebook ISBN: 978-1-09836-068-9

Contents

To Fred

1974

ONE

The office door was open halfway. Susan slid through the opening and leaned against the wall.

"Hi, Dan, you wanted to see me?"

Dan's head was bent over the pages of a manuscript. He did not look up but waved his hand toward the sofa across from his desk. Susan hesitated. She rarely came to Dan's office because his office and this piece of furniture were infamous. The other graduate students in the lab—all men—called it the seduction sofa. She had heard stories about Dan's extracurricular affairs almost from the first day he became her thesis advisor. Dan claimed he needed the sofa to rest his injured back before lecturing in class, but the graduate students scoffed at this excuse. Whatever the truth, his office unnerved her. She avoided it and met with him in the lab research rooms whenever possible. Today, she perched on the outer edge of the sofa on the cushion closest to the door.

Susan watched Dan's staccato motions blue-pencil the sheets in front of him. She was thankful he was not editing her dissertation with such intensity. Her final draft was written, and the date of her oral dissertation defense was set. Why had Dan insisted on a meeting this afternoon? Her work for a spring graduation was complete.

While Susan waited, she examined Dan's bent head and noticed a hint of a bald spot peeking through the strands of black hair. This sign of aging would make Dan happy. He was different from the other young male

1

assistant professors, who preferred the disheveled look of shoulder-length unkempt hair, denim shirts, and tattered jeans. Dan preferred formality, white shirt, black trousers, tie and jacket. His hair was short and cropped in a not-quite-military brush cut. He had exalted in the appearance of a few grey hairs at a recent research meeting. "I want to look older," he said. "I think it gives me and my research more credibility with journal editors if they think I'm more established."

The cluster of graduate students slouched around the conference table responded to Dan's announcement with a cynical stare. Most academics would relish their reputation as a young genius—PhD at twenty-five—his dissertation research published in a prestigious psychology journal—a grant from the National Science Foundation. But Dan wanted to appear middle-aged, and as far as Susan could see, he was succeeding in his quest. It was hard to believe Dan was in his early thirties, just a few years older than Susan and the other graduate students in the research group.

Dan's eyes remained glued on his work, but he grabbed a sheet of paper from the top of a stack of books on his desk and tossed it in Susan's direction. The paper fluttered to the carpet before she could catch it mid-air.

"I want you to apply for this job. I saw the ad when I was in British Columbia," Dan grunted.

Susan crouched to pick up the paper lying at her feet. Her eyes skimmed the print. It was an ad for a psychology faculty position in a university and in a place unknown to her. She sputtered, "I'm not going to apply for a job at," she peered at the sheet, "James Douglas University in Victoria, British Columbia. I don't want to go to British Columbia. It's in another country, and besides, it's too far from New York." She flushed when she saw Dan's jaw tighten. What a stupid blunder. Dan was going to British Columbia. In a few months he was leaving the Institute for Research in the Social Sciences for a faculty position at the University of Vancouver.

Dan threw his pencil on the scattered sheets of paper, stretched back in his chair, and glared at Susan across his cluttered desk. Susan cringed. She recognized that stare of demonic aggression used when he demolished the research presentation of a graduate student at a lab meeting. "Look, I'm not asking you to leave New York. I'm merely suggesting you apply for this job in Victoria." Susan stared down at the ad and struggled to read the details. A painful lump burned in her throat.

Dan leaned across the desk, his voice clipped. "I hate to be blunt, but I will be. What is it now, late March? How many job offers do you have? By my last count—none. It's time to think about applying to places that might not be at the top of your list." Her cheeks burned. Susan imagined tearing the ad into shreds and throwing the pieces at Dan's face. She resented the reminder she was the only graduating PhD student in the lab group who did not have a job offer for the next academic year.

Dan continued. "I was told when I was in Vancouver the universities in British Columbia are expanding and looking for research talent. You may have a better chance of standing out from the pack in a job hunt in Canada. Two of my PhD students last year got jobs in Toronto."

Susan ducked her head to avoid Dan's stare. An image of the thick file of rejection letters locked away in her desk spun before her eyes. *Thank you for your application…we had many qualified candidates…could only choose one…good luck with your search for a position…best wishes for your future success.* The formula rejection letters from psychology department heads always followed the same script.

"I've never had a PhD student fail at a job search, and I'm not going to spoil my track record with you. Shoot off an application to James Douglas. If by some chance you get the position, I'll add you as a co-author on the textbook I have a contract to write. I'm looking for a co-author because I don't have time to write all the chapters myself. Your name on a textbook will give you the recognition you need to make your job search easier the next time around."

Demoralized, Susan stared at the sheet of paper, knowing Dan was watching her and waiting for a response. She struggled to control her face and voice. She might cry later after she had fled to her tiny office but not here with Dan. It hurt to admit he was right. Her dream of a faculty position at one of the Ivy League schools had crumbled to dust. Her hopelessness intensified when her applications to several East Coast state universities met rejection. She had learned a harsh lesson these past months. Applying for a job did not mean getting a job. Susan needed a faculty position, and she needed a new strategy to find one, but Canada and British Columbia had never been part of her plans.

Susan realized she had to be strategic. There was no point in alienating Dan. Her oral defense was only a few weeks away, and she wanted her dissertation advisor on her side during the ordeal. This was not a good time to be viewed as a liability. The application for the position at James Douglas was a probable long shot for success. What did another rejection letter matter if Dan was placated?

"Okay, I'll apply," she muttered. She felt Dan's eyes follow her as she left his office. Susan raced down the hallway exhausted by the effort to maintain her composure. She was not sure she would like Dan after today.

* * * * * * * * * * * * * *

Julie grunted, "It's hard to believe you're moving to Canada in a couple of weeks. I hope you know what you're doing. Go to Boston or Washington or even New Jersey, but stay here on the East Coast, close to New York. Things are bound to get better now that the crook, Nixon, has resigned. You have a lot going for you. I know you'll find a job."

Susan studied her friend's pleading face and wondered whether her invitation to meet for a farewell cup of coffee was a good idea. Julie's ongoing disapproval of her decision to leave New York was eroding her confidence. She had shared every triumph and defeat during five grueling years of graduate school with Julie Edelman. The two of them had spent hours in this booth at the coffee shop on Fifth Avenue across from the Institute. They studied for their comprehensive exams, which they both passed, they dissected Susan's failed marriage and eventual divorce—one of the darker episodes of the last five years—and they drank coffee and shared gossip about the happenings at the Institute, especially those with a prurient twist.

"Julie, I sent applications to psychology departments all over the East Coast, and there were no takers. I took the *only* job offer I got." Susan frowned. She knew she sounded defensive, but Julie's attitude was making her tense. "Besides, I won't stay in British Columbia forever—just a couple of years until the book with Dan is published. He says co-authoring a textbook will improve my chances of getting a better job when I go out on the market again."

"You sound anxious. Are you getting cold feet about the move?" Julie's voice held a tinge of hope.

Susan rested her head against the faded padding of the booth. She took a deep breath and exhaled slowly. "I don't have the financial luxury of getting cold feet. I need a job." She was going to Canada and would not back out now. She was scared, but she could not share her anxiety with Julie who would pounce on her fears and launch another verbal assault to convince her to stay in New York. Instead she said, "James Douglas rescued me from the humiliation of being the only grad student in the lab who failed at their job search. Besides, I want a fresh start now that Paul and I are divorced, and leaving town's a good way to do that."

Julie's dark eyes narrowed. "It depends on how you look at it—whether you were rescued or not. You're taking a big chance—the West Coast *and* another country."

"Dan's students usually don't have problems getting job offers. I honestly didn't think it would be this hard to land a good faculty position," Susan mumbled.

"So, to save his ego, Dan arranged the job for you," Julie hissed.

Susan protested, "Dan suggested I apply to James Douglas, but he says it's a coincidence I got the job. He told me the universities in Canada are expanding so there are more faculty positions opening up there." Susan shrugged. "Everything happened so fast. I sent my application, and a few weeks later I got a call from the department chairman. We talked on the phone, and the next thing I knew the department made me an offer."

"Sue, don't be naive. Of course, Dan got you the job. It's too much of a coincidence—Dan moves to British Columbia, and then suddenly something opens up for you." Julie pressed. "You still have time to take a part-time job here in New York—get some teaching experience, publish a few more papers—and then go back out on the market and get the job you really want."

Susan exhaled with exasperation and said, "Julie, I tell you what. Let's trade parents. I'll take yours who slip you money for rent when you're short of cash. You can have my parents who've never given me a dime because they don't have any money to give. The settlement I got from my divorce is almost gone, and I can't support myself in this city on part-time work. Besides, I don't want to start my career as a second-rate adjunct. I want a full-time position right from the start in a department with research labs and grad students. The job at James Douglas is the only chance I have to get what I want right now."

Julie frowned. Susan knew she disliked reminders about her doting parents in their affluent enclave on Long Island. Their financial cushion set Julie apart from most of the graduate students like Susan who struggled to survive on fellowship stipends, student loans, and research assistantships. Susan doubted that Julie fully understood the financial bind restricting her choices.

"I'd feel better about this move if Dan was staying at the Institute. I know what you want, but I'm worried about what will happen when you're alone in British Columbia with Dan as the only familiar face." Susan started to protest, but Julie waved her hand. "Let me finish," Julie said. "Dan's not just leaving the Institute. He's leaving all his extramarital affairs behind, too. When he goes back to his old philandering habits, which I'm sure he will after he settles down at the University of Vancouver, I think he'll try to replace the women he's leaving behind with you."

"Julie, I know Dan sleeps around or, at least, he's involved with Jennifer Evans. Dan's sexual escapades are the constant topics of gossip in the lab. Frankly, I think all the men are jealous, and they get vicarious kicks out of monitoring Dan's activities."

"It's not just Jennifer Evans. I've heard rumors that Dan has had affairs with other faculty at the Institute and with a few grad students advised by his faculty friends at NYU."

Susan laughed. "So Dan likes to sleep with a lot of women—so what? Dan's sex habits are his wife's problem, not mine."

"My point is—Dan's a dishonest guy. He only cares about furthering his career, and he uses people to do that. Sleeping with women he works with is convenient for him and easy to hide from his wife. I just don't want you to become his West Coast Jennifer Evans. That's all."

"Dan has never shown any interest in me."

Julie shook her head and laughed derisively. Susan countered. "It takes two people to start an affair. If neither person is interested, or if only one is interested, there's no sex. I'm certainly not interested in Dan—not sexually, anyway—although you seem to think he is interested in me. Actually, I think Dan treats me more harshly than the other grad students—he gave me hell for months over my dissertation revisions."

"Sue, it's fortunate you didn't choose clinical psychology. Your ability to read people is non-existent. Dan's sexually interested in you, alright. I can tell by his body language when he's around you. The only reason he's not been overt is because you were married until only a few months ago and he's been busy with Jennifer and his other interests. There are only so many hours in a day, even for Dan." Julie chuckled. "As for the treating you harshly part—if I were a Freudian, which I'm not—I'd say he was using the defense mechanism of reaction formation when he's around you—treating you in a way that is directly opposite to his feelings."

"Let me get this straight. You're saying Dan wants to sleep with me but hasn't done anything because of his other interests as you call them.

But, as soon as he is deprived of these other interests, he'll drop his archaic Freudian defenses and hit on me."

Julie nodded. "Yeah, that's what I'm saying."

"Julie, I know you think you have great clinical intuition, but you're wrong this time. If Dan arranged the job at James Douglas for me, and he says he didn't, he did it because he wants help with the textbook, not because he wants to start an affair."

"I'm serious about this," Julie replied. "You're wrapped up in your research, and you tend to ignore the fact that researchers are human too. Your work can only get you so far, and I think you overestimate its power to get you through the tough times. I know you. You're going to be lonely, and you're going to need someone. When that happens, remember you deserve somebody a lot better than Dan Kavline. He may be a brilliant researcher, but otherwise he's a deeply flawed person."

Susan stared at her friend. An acrid taste of apprehension seared the back of her throat. Susan never thought about Dan in this way. Their interactions were always about the work going on in the lab or her dissertation. Susan rejected Julie's Freudian explanation of Dan's stern attitude toward her. She was the only woman in Dan's lab group. She thought his constant criticism was a test to ensure she was worthy to carry the banner as one of his former students when she left the Institute. They never socialized, not even at lab parties. Dan and Jennifer Evans presided over regular Friday gatherings where the small talk revolved around the lab research projects. Occasionally, Susan wondered about Dan's marriage and whether his wife knew about his extramarital sex life, but Dan's life away from the Institute was a mystery Susan had no interest in solving.

Susan glanced around the dimly lit coffee shop. A few customers were arrayed along the sweep of the red Formica counter. They looked like commuters waiting for rush hour to pass before they tackled the subway. She and Julie were the only booth inhabitants in sight. Murphy, her favorite waitress, approached their booth, coffee pot in hand, offering a refill. Susan grinned. "No, just give us the check, Murphy." Murphy nodded, scribbled on her pad, and laid the check on the table. She returned to the counter and started pouring refills—moving expertly down the counter from one cup to the next—filling each one without a splash into the saucer underneath.

A fierce pang of longing flooded over Susan as she watched Murphy. She had already started the transition to the West Coast by constructing a mental catalogue of what she disliked about New York. Everything she would be happy to leave behind—the noise, the street crime, the crowded subways, the high rents for tiny apartments. Her list was long, but this coffee shop was not on that list. It was a familiar refuge not only for her but for many of the psychology graduate students at the Institute. She and Julie had spent hours in this booth by the window overlooking the subway entrance. They had shunned the trendy cafes in the neighborhood for this old-fashioned hangout. Murphy, with her starched bubble gum pink uniform, white apron, and flatfooted, shuffling walk, like the coffee shop, was part of another era. Susan knew she would miss the ancient waitress and the comforting smell of brewing coffee mingled with the odor of the disinfectant used to sterilize the weathered, tiled floor. This coffee shop and Murphy were, for her, New York at its most colorful best.

Susan took a sip of her tepid coffee and watched Julie watching her with a worried expression. Julie was right about one thing. She immersed herself in her research projects and ignored anything that interfered with concentration on her work. She was enthralled by the process of formulating theories and devising clever experiments to test them. These challenges were all-consuming and a comforting and predictable escape, especially as her marriage slowly dissolved. Despite all the gossip and—Julie was right— despite Dan's flaws, Susan regarded him as a valuable mentor and partner in her scientific progress. She was happy to leave the mixture of sex and work to Jennifer Evans—she was concentrating solely on the work.

Julie usually had good instincts about people, and her prediction that Susan would be homesick and lonely was likely true. Susan cautioned herself to remain calm because Julie was not always right. She was wrong about Susan's ability to cope with loneliness. Her work was and would continue to be her salvation and her friend.

T W O

"We are now over the Canadian Rockies and will be arriving in Vancouver in approximately one hour. The local Vancouver time is two PM."

Susan woke with a start when the pilot's announcement broke through her sleep. She leaned back in her seat to relish these precious moments of tranquility. Her immigration papers had arrived without complication, and after weeks of anxious anticipation and hectic farewell preparations, she was on her way to British Columbia. The crumpled mountain landscape passed beneath the plane as she exhaled with relief.

The stewardess appeared offering a round of drinks, and Susan bought a scotch to toast her successful departure. Scotch was the favored drink at the Institute lab parties, and the familiar acrid taste evoked memories of New York. It was ironic what was about to unfold. For years, she had lived with the threat of Paul, her ex, moving to Canada to avoid the draft and service in Vietnam. He had talked about fleeing since the earliest days of their relationship when they were both undergraduate students in Philadelphia, living together in a tiny apartment. Events of the late sixties provoked vehement anti-war protests among their friends, and Paul was not alone in contemplating life as a draft evader. As graduation approached, he spent most of his time investigating schemes to extend his draft-exempt status.

One day, without warning, Paul announced, "I applied, and I've been accepted into a program that puts teachers into schools around New York City. It's a draft-exempt job for at least another two years."

"You don't know anything about teaching. You don't have an education degree," Susan had protested.

"It doesn't matter. It seems the New York City government wants to save some of us from the terrors of being drafted or the alternative of skipping to Canada. You just need a university degree to apply. It's not as if I've got a choice. I'm not going into the army to end up in Vietnam. I don't have a lot of options."

Reluctantly, she let him persuade her that his draft avoidance was their top priority and she followed him to New York. They got married—Susan could not remember why they thought marriage was a good idea. She was accepted into graduate school at the Institute, while Paul taught in an elementary school in Brooklyn. Susan struggled to remember the few happy moments they shared after their move.

Her final encounter with Paul happened on the day she went to their—now his—apartment to collect a box of books and record albums left behind when she moved out.

"When are you leaving for the West Coast?" Paul asked.

"At the end of August. I start teaching in mid-September." Susan hesitated, but curiosity drove her to ask, "How's your social life?"

"Oh, about the same. After word spread that we were divorced, lots of women came around. Some are okay, although others are just weird," Paul answered as he ushered Susan to the door. "My latest is coming over in a few minutes, and I think it'd make us all uncomfortable if she ran into you."

Susan was stunned by his gruff attitude. She resented being swept away as an unwelcome annoyance. She tried to control the anger in her voice. "Okay, but keep in touch. I'd like to hear how you're doing once in a while."

Paul scanned her face with a detached expression. "I don't think that's a good idea. People who've been married and divorced can't be friends." His voice turned bitter. "You have what you want. I'm not standing in the way of your research career anymore. You got your name back as part of the divorce just as you insisted. I wish you well, Susan Barron, no longer Cohen, but I don't think we can be friends."

Shaken, Susan had countered, "Aren't you curious about what life is like in Canada? For a long time, you thought you'd end up there."

Paul chuckled. "Funny how things turn out, isn't it? I spent years trying to get exemptions so that I didn't have to move to Canada to avoid the draft. I'm still here, the war's over, and you're the one moving up north."

Susan's cheeks burned as she remembered Paul's farewell. A rough ending to six years of marriage, she thought bitterly. As the scotch took effect, Susan closed her eyes, took a deep breath, and allowed her thoughts to wander. She laughed as she remembered the gossip about her at the Institute. Surrounded by a gaggle of mostly unattached men, she had relished her freedom from marital fidelity as much as Paul. She enjoyed the company of her male lab mates and had shared sensuously delightful evenings with a few of them. These brief relationships were not the impersonal "zipless fucks" glorified in Susan's current favorite novel, *Fear of Flying*, but companionable interludes in an otherwise intense work environment.

Dan's lab group crackled with the electricity of working on the cutting edge of the emerging cognitive psychology wave. All of them were committed to unraveling the mysteries of the black box of the mind, and they competed to concoct new experiments based on the recent computer modeling of human thought. Their research was unique and exciting—information flowed through the senses into memory in discrete stages that could be examined one at a time. Susan became fixated on her dissertation research—what is processed in one glance. Her obsession swept her away from Paul who had his own obsession with avoiding the draft and Vietnam. Their outside passions eventually crushed their desire to stay together. Susan did not feel guilt, just sadness at the loss of something that had been good—that was once warm, loving, and fun.

"Please fasten your seatbelts and return your seat backs and tray tables to the upright position for our landing at Vancouver International Airport. We will be landing in approximately ten minutes."

The announcement brought Susan back to the present. She obediently buckled her seatbelt and leaned toward the window to examine the city below. The late August sun bathed Vancouver with a luxurious glow. As the plane banked for the final landing approach, the city skyline projected itself against a backdrop of mountains lightly dusted with snow. She saw a peninsula of wooded land jutting out into the bay of Vancouver harbor. A spattering of sleek sailboats with brightly striped spinnakers bobbed in the white caps among weather-beaten freighters anchored and still.

"That's Stanley Park."

Susan turned toward her seatmate, startled to hear his voice after the long hours of silence during the flight. "It looks wonderful." Susan exclaimed, delighted at the view and at the chance to make contact with another person.

Her companion adjusted his seat position and said with a yawn, "Yeah, it's a pretty spot. There's a seawall that goes around the entire park—six miles, I think. It's a great place to walk and enjoy the views of the harbor and mountains."

"Do you live in Vancouver?" Susan asked, hoping to keep the conversation going.

"Yeah," he replied, shuffling the papers on his tray table into a disheveled pile on his lap. He retracted the table to retrieve a briefcase wedged in an awkward position under the seat in front of him. After a struggle, he placed the briefcase on his lap and opened it to shove the stack of papers inside. "Is this your first trip to BC?"

"Yes, it is. I'm coming here to live. I'm moving to Victoria. I have a job there."

Her seatmate examined her face with renewed interest. "So, you're moving to the town of the newly-wed and nearly-dead. What are you going to do there?" His tone was sarcastic.

Bewildered, Susan responded, "What did you say?"

Her companion laughed. "Victoria's called the town of the newly-wed and nearly-dead—meaning that you only go there on your honeymoon or when you retire." He chuckled. "That was the only time I've been to Victoria—on my honeymoon." He paused. "Victoria can be pretentious— masquerading as British. I'd call it phony British, myself. Lots of tearooms and antique shops. Fake Tudor architecture. It's a sleepy little place but a beautiful coastline—great views of the Olympic Mountains in Washington in the States. Having afternoon tea at the famous Empress Hotel is the thing to do if you're interested in that sort of thing. I prefer a beer myself. Fortunately, I found a couple of good pubs." While he slid his briefcase under the seat in front of him, he asked, "What are you going to do in Victoria?"

Susan answered with a whiff of pride in her voice. "I have a faculty position at James Douglas University as an assistant professor."

Her seatmate straightened. He looked at Susan with a bemused smirk. She prepared herself for the inevitable comment about not expecting a woman to be a professor or something along those lines.

"James Douglas has the reputation for hiring faculty who are winding down towards retirement. Victoria has a large retirement community because it sells itself as having the best weather in Canada—probably true—relatively mild winters and not as much rain as we get in Vancouver. The idea is to get a head start on retirement by working at JDU at the tail end of a career and then staying to live in Victoria in retirement."

"How do you know this?" Susan tried not to sound defensive.

"I have an economics degree from the University of Vancouver, and the profs in the department used to joke about it—saying they would retire to JDU and Victoria when they thought they couldn't cut it anymore," he answered. "What department hired you?"

"Psychology."

He smiled and said, "You don't look like you're about to retire, so maybe the psychology department is different. Anyway, it's just gossip, more like academic cattiness if you ask me."

The landing gear descended with a thud. "Good luck in your new job. If you find Victoria too boring, there's always the scenery as a distraction—it is beautiful there." Susan's companion closed his eyes and crossed his arms over his chest, signaling an end to their conversation. Susan sighed—there was more she wanted to know about Victoria and JDU. Disappointed but now more curious, she turned toward the window to watch the plane's gradual descent to the runway.

THREE

Susan spotted Dan pacing in front of one of the baggage claim carousels. He phoned her before she left New York to insist on meeting her plane when she arrived in Vancouver. "What took so long?" Dan shouted above the din of the horde of arriving passengers. "Your plane landed almost two hours ago. Have you been in customs all this time?"

Susan sighed with frustration. "After the immigration officer stamped my papers, there was a controversy about my typewriter—whether or not I was bringing it into Canada for resale seemed to be the issue. I explained to the officer that I'm a professor and I use a typewriter for my work. He wasn't convinced I was telling the truth, so I had to dig around for the job offer from James Douglas and that took extra time."

Dan laughed. "Canada Customs is touchy about bringing goods across the border to sell. It must be a brand that's not sold here."

"It may have been that, but I think it was more that I 'don't look much like a professor,' to quote one of the officers. I think I just didn't convey the right image. They were hard to convince even when I showed them the letter."

"Well, you're here now and a welcome breath of fresh air from back east and the big city." Dan grabbed both the typewriter case and her bulging suitcase. With a dramatic flourish he gestured toward the exit sign.

Susan decided not to tell Dan the delay involved more than customs clearance. She had spent twenty minutes in the restroom trying to rehabilitate herself. The weeks before her departure were too hectic to pay attention to her appearance, although she had managed to splurge on a final haircut at her favorite salon in Greenwich Village. As she leaned over the sink to examine herself in the mirror, she was relieved that the short bob of her straight dark hair framed her face with flattering wisps. Her usually alert brown eyes were dulled with fatigue, and her skin looked paler than usual. She had lost weight, which ordinarily Susan would have considered a good thing, but now her look was more haggard than stylishly slender. Her perfect slim-fit jeans sagged around her waist and hips. There was a coffee stain down the front of her white t-shirt that scrubbing with water made worse. She rummaged through her suitcase for a clean top and hastily applied some color to her lips and cheeks. When she stepped back to assess the effect, she hoped she looked chic in a disheveled, rustic way. As her ex, Paul, would have said, "You do the best with what you've got" and that seemed to be the case today.

Susan walked beside Dan and studied him as they wove their way through the airport crowd. Two months in British Columbia and Dan was transformed or, at least, his appearance was different. His clipped military-style haircut was replaced with a shaggier look—strands of hair fell over his ears and even touched his shirt collar. At the Institute, Dan wore conservative business clothes—white shirt, tie, and dark trousers. Today he sported a plaid cotton shirt tucked haphazardly into the waist of a pair of faded jeans. Dan was slim but flabby with the softness of someone who spent long hours in a library rather than a gym. He was notorious at the Institute for his disdain of activities that promoted physical fitness. Today he looked leaner, taut, although the grey in his hair was flowering into more than a light sprinkle. He looked older. His blue eyes had their usual intensity, but the deep shadows underneath hinted at many sleepless nights.

Susan was not prepared for a changed Dan. She expected him to be the same person she knew at the Institute. After all, it was only two months since he had left. Dan dressed in jeans and a plaid shirt was strange and unsettling. "You're looking very casual," Susan ventured. She was tentative, like testing the water temperature at the beach before taking a plunge. A conversation with Dan about something personal was unknown territory.

Dan smiled. "I guess you've never seen me wear jeans. I turned conservative when I started at the Institute. I was trying to make a good impression in my first faculty job with the powers that be, that sort of thing. Now it doesn't matter. I got tenure and the promotion I wanted when I moved here, so I can wear what I want. U of V is more like the atmosphere I was used to as a graduate student at Stanford—more relaxed. I like the casual approach, and I'm glad to be back out west."

Dan panted under the strain of lugging Susan's overloaded suitcase. "It's a change, but I'm settling in. My work's going okay, too," he puffed. "I've already submitted my first paper for publication under my new U of V affiliation." Susan smiled. Some things do not change. One of them was Dan's insatiable drive to publish. She hoped his publication compulsion would rub off on her—that was why she was here.

Outside the terminal building Dan directed Susan toward a battered station wagon, hoisted her belongings into the back, and beckoned her to get in. The late afternoon sun dimmed suddenly, and a light drizzle of rain spattered the windshield. Dan leaned over the steering wheel and scanned the ominous clouds forming overhead. "The weather changes from sun to rain almost instantaneously around here. You get used to it after a while."

Dan smiled at Susan. "You're staying at our house tonight. Mona can't wait to talk to you about New York. She's really homesick."

Susan stiffened. She was light-headed after the long flight, and the invitation to stay at Dan's house was an unwelcome surprise. "I've talked to the department at JDU. It's arranged for me to stay in a hotel tonight, and then take the bus and ferry to Victoria tomorrow."

"We can change that. The department will be happy to save a little money on your moving costs. Besides, I can't disappoint Mona. She's been planning tonight's dinner for two weeks."

Susan watched the modest stucco bungalows of Vancouver's suburban neighborhoods slip by as they drove into the city. Her dream of a revitalizing night in an impersonal hotel with room service and a good night's sleep, the first in weeks, evaporated. Instead, she faced another unknown—an evening with Dan and his wife and children. Susan was too exhausted to protest. "Thanks for going to all this trouble—dinner and a place to stay, I mean. Are you sure you have enough room?" She stopped and laughed. "Funny, I don't think of people living in houses anymore, just apartments. That's what years of living in New York does to you."

"Yeah, I know what you mean. It's a different way of life out here. We didn't have a lot of choice but to buy a house and two cars. I can just barely afford this stuff on my salary," Dan groaned.

Susan stared at Dan, surprised by his uncharacteristic personal disclosure—something had changed. She shifted to a more comfortable topic. "Dan, what're your children's names?" Susan asked. "Since I'm going to meet them, I want to know what to call them."

Dan looked surprised and hesitated a moment. "Okay, well, Jacob is five and starting kindergarten. Leah is seven and going into second grade, or grade two as they call it here, and Sarah is nine and starting grade four."

"Very neatly spaced," Susan quipped. "Planning is the mark of a good academic."

Dan shot her an irritated look. "Yeah, for a time there, that's all Mona was—pregnant."

"Nice names—very traditional and simple," Susan mumbled, regretting her sarcasm.

"Mona wants the kids to have traditional Jewish names. She's pretty religious." Dan's voice tensed. "Mona's having a hard time adjusting because there's not much of a Jewish community in Vancouver. There's a synagogue, but the ambience, ethnic consciousness—whatever you want to call it—is very different here. Mona misses everything from the Jewish community center in our old neighborhood back in New York to the kosher delis." Dan sniggered, "I had to stop her from calling to ask you to bring some pickles and corned beef."

Dan stopped the car at a traffic light and turned toward Susan. "I couldn't deny Mona the pleasure of spending an evening with someone from New York. She's been unhappy here and is really looking forward to talking with you." Dan grinned. "It'll be okay—I have some good scotch waiting. You look like you could use a drink."

"I thought maybe you'd stopped drinking after the last farewell party at the Institute," Susan laughed. "I remember you were draped over the rim of one of the waste bins in the lab. Two of the post-docs drove you home because everyone thought you were too drunk to walk the five blocks to your apartment."

Dan laughed, too. "Don't remind me. I was hung-over and couldn't write for two days. Don't remind Mona either. She thinks I drink too much, and she's put me on a pretty strict liquor budget using our mortgage payments as an excuse for abstinence. But we have a good bottle of scotch for tonight."

Dan steered the car into the intersection. "I wanted you to stay at our house tonight instead of a hotel because we have to get up early tomorrow morning to catch the ferry to Victoria."

"What do you mean, *we*?" Susan asked.

"I'm driving you to Victoria. One of my old Stanford professors, Jim Kracknoy, is now in the department at JDU. Jim was talking to a colleague in my department and found out I'd come to U of V. He called me last week and invited me to visit. So tomorrow, I'm taking him up on his invitation and driving you to Victoria—kill two birds with one stone."

"Is your family coming, too?" Susan asked.

"No, of course not." Dan shook his head, impatient at the question. "Mona doesn't like visiting my colleagues. She's more the stay-at-home type, and she's got the kids to get ready for school." Dan smiled at Susan. "The ferry ride to Victoria is supposed to be quite scenic, so I hope the rain stops by tomorrow morning."

* * * * * * * * * * * * *

Mona Kavline hugged Susan, greeting her like a starving dog pouncing on a piece of meat. Within minutes she was detailing her nostalgic list of what she had left behind in New York. "I miss just about everything," Mona lamented. "The shopping, the deli food, walking in Washington Square Park—"

Susan eyed Mona with some sympathy. "I can see why you're upset," Susan responded. "Very few cities have the theatre, any film in any language, world-class newspapers like the Times, all the museums and art galleries..."

"Oh, I wasn't talking about any of those things. I always read the Daily News—when I read a newspaper—which isn't often. I'm talking about being able to buy real kosher food. I can't find any knishes in Vancouver. And what passes for bagels—my grandmother would scorn the mushy buns called bagels around here. Wait until you try shopping in the department stores, which is what, I suppose, the Hudson Bay Company and Woodward's are called. You could put both of those stores into Macy's basement."

Dan departed for the kitchen, mumbling about making his special gravy for the roast beef. Mona continued her litany of complaints. "I worry about the kids losing their Jewish identity living here. I want them to learn Hebrew, but now Sarah and Leah are studying *French*. Dan insists they learn French since we're living in a country where it's an official language. French classes are held in the synagogue—can you imagine? It shouldn't surprise me, though. The synagogue here isn't like any I've been used to. Even the synagogue near Stanford had more respect for Jewish traditions than the one here."

Susan squirmed in her chair. Discussions about synagogues and Jewish traditions were out of her element. Maybe Mona thought she was Jewish. The dreadful Leonard Wesselman, the senior professor in the experimental psychology labs at the Institute and Dan's mentor, once confronted her at a lab party to ask if she was Jewish. "No, my husband is Jewish, but I'm not," she replied. Leonard snorted in an attempt at a joke. "I don't know any women academics that aren't Jewish." Susan wondered if Mona thought the same thing.

Looking for a diversion, Susan asked, "Your display case is very interesting. Do the daggers, skulls, and bones belong to you or to Dan? One of you must have an interesting hobby."

The wood frame of the glass-fronted display case in Dan and Mona's living room was elaborately carved with zodiac symbols. The shelves held an array of ornamental daggers, and, what seemed to be a group of human finger bones. Three daggers were neatly arranged on the top shelf, while the bones were tucked into the folds of black satin runners covering the remaining two shelves. A long shawl of red velvet with decorative yellow tassels at either end covered the top of the case. Two human skulls were perched on the red velvet on either side of a large silver goblet.

Mona's grey eyes turned icy, and she fixed Susan with an intense stare. "Those are sacred objects, not a hobby. I use them in my work—freeing unfortunate people from evil curses."

Stunned, Susan stammered, "It's such an unusual piece of furniture. Is it an antique?"

"The case was made for me by a specialist in occult design. Each carved symbol has a specific meaning in the spiritual realm."

Susan noticed Dan standing in the kitchen doorway, a glass of scotch in hand. Relieved, she raised her voice. "We were just discussing the very interesting display you have."

"These sacred objects belong to me," Mona said with pride. "Dan's got nothing to do with them—tell her, Dan, while I set the table for dinner." Mona left the room, her face set in a stern expression.

Dan settled himself onto the shapeless cushions of the chair opposite Susan. "Mona takes her witchcraft pretty seriously."

Susan remembered she had a glass of scotch in hand and sipped her drink. Witchcraft was not something she imagined as part of Dan's home life.

"Mona's a witch. It's an old tradition among the women ancestors in her family. Her grandmother started to instruct Mona in the occult arts when she was a little girl." Dan rose and walked over to the display case and picked up one of the skulls. "I bought these for Mona at a medical supply company before we left New York. It was hard to find human skulls with no imperfections and bleached white like these. Mona needs perfect specimens in some of her rituals. She didn't want to leave New York, so these were sort of a peace offering."

Dan took a large swallow of his drink as he placed the skull back into position on the red shawl. Susan watched him in astonished silence. Suddenly, she heard a chatter of children's voices at the front door. She exhaled with relief. Having children around would end this dreadful conversation.

"Here come the kids." Dan swallowed the last of his drink and placed his empty glass on the battered oak coffee table. He seemed to welcome the distraction as much as Susan. "Come on, I'll introduce you." He grabbed Susan's hand and tugged her upright. They joined Mona and three giggling children in the hallway.

FOUR

Dan and Susan were on the road to the Vancouver Island ferry terminal by seven the next morning. The lethal effects of scotch, jet lag, and a fitful sleep on a lumpy sofa bed pulsated behind Susan's bloodshot eyes. Scotch was the preferred drink at the experimental psychology labs at the Institute because it was Leonard Wesselman's favorite. As the head of the lab he insisted everyone drink his chosen brand. Susan and scotch were not a good mix. She usually avoided it because her scotch hangovers were always as wretched as the one today.

Dan appeared unaffected by the indulgences of last night despite matching her drinks two to one. His eyes were eager as he grinned at her. "Let's start your acculturation to Canada," he announced as he set the car radio to the local CBC station in Vancouver. Susan closed her eyes as they drove. Dan's cheerfulness was not infectious, and her headache blossomed. She welcomed the respite from idle conversation and let the chatter of the radio news fill the void.

Last night had been an ordeal. In all the years Dan supervised Susan's dissertation, they never discussed their lives away from the lab. It was a shock to be a dinner guest where social small talk rather than lab business dominated. She accepted that she was no longer a graduate student—she was faculty—and faculty socialized with each other. Still, last night was too much too soon.

Mona was a surprise—an astonishing beauty with ebony hair falling in a luxurious wave to the middle of her back. She was dressed in mint green slacks and matching jersey with the superb fit of an expensive brand that emphasized her slim figure. Except for the clothes, she looked like a witch—exotic and surreal. Otherwise Mona fit the stereotype of a traditional faculty wife. She complained continuously during dinner. There was no Jewish culture, no kosher food, and no real shopping in Vancouver. She was obsessed with what she had left behind. The social status of being the wife of a university professor was obvious. Her voice dripped with name-dropping glee as she described the weekly faculty club lunches with the wives of deans, vice-presidents, and the university president. She gloated over the president's personal request to take care of Dan Kavline, one of his rising faculty stars. This story was the only reprieve from her never-ending list of Vancouver's shortcomings.

Dan's children resembled their mother, dark hair and pink cheeks with round faces. They were bright and inquisitive, bursting with energy like their father. Dan played word games with them during dinner, challenging them to guess at the meanings of words while he gave them hints. At one point, one of his daughters ran to the den to retrieve the dictionary because she was skeptical of her father's explanation—so much like Dan, Susan thought. When he was nine years old, he would have done the same thing—do not accept what you do not believe. The children were a diversion and a welcome relief from Mona's nonstop complaining. Susan laughed and teased the kids until, after the requisite polite interval, she pleaded that her jet-lagged body needed rest and fled to the den for some welcome solitude.

Dan and Mona appeared to be a well-adjusted couple with a young family, but Susan noticed their aura of separateness. They did not touch—not even a casual passing tap on the shoulder. There was no bickering or quarreling, but Susan sensed their emotional distance. Their companionship was civil but without signs of overt affection. Susan wondered if Mona knew about Dan's affairs. If she did, would she use her witchcraft in an occult fury to interfere? Susan conjured up a number of tantalizing scenarios—lovers struck down with a mysterious illness, Dan suddenly impotent—all the result of Mona's vengeful spell casting. Enigmatic Mona—simultaneously a boring faculty wife craving status and recognition and a beautiful witch moving with the grace of a black cat, a witch's familiar. Physically, Mona was perfect. If Institute gossip was true, it made Dan's many affairs more puzzling. He must not be seeking physical perfection in a lover because he had that in Mona, his wife. There had to be other motivating forces behind his infidelity.

Where did Jennifer Evans fit in? She was attractive but not a member of the club of classic beauties where Mona belonged. Jennifer was Ivy League preppy, cultured, and sophisticated—able to carry on an animated conversation on any topic. Susan admired Jennifer's assurance and her aura of subtle entitlement. Unlike Dan and the other Stanford PhDs on the faculty at the Institute, Jennifer did not seem desperate to climb an academic ladder of fame. Her Harvard background bestowed a prestigious edge in the world of academic psychology, so she did not need to flaunt her accomplishments. Jennifer's appeal for Dan was probably her calm assurance of her own worth—something Dan lacked. Susan studied Dan's profile. This new curiosity about Dan's personal life made her uneasy. Being Dan's student—seeing him only as a researcher and mentor—was simpler and less troubling.

The enormity of the British Columbia ferries fascinated Susan. Cars, vans, cargo trucks, buses, and all varieties of campers and trailers were in line to be swallowed by the vessel's gaping doors. These were not the passenger-only boats that plied the waters around Long Island or ran from Staten Island to Manhattan. As she watched the line of vehicles snake up the ramp into the cavernous ship, she remembered her conversation with the psychology department secretary at JDU. Susan had phoned about travel arrangements to Vancouver Island. Was there enough room on the ferry to bring her luggage with her? The secretary, Mrs. Wong, laughed. "Vancouver Island is as big as England. The BC Ferry system is a large fleet of ships carrying all types of vehicle traffic to and from Vancouver Island every day. I'm sure there's room for your luggage." Dan steered his car up the ramp and onto the ship. Following the directions of the car deck attendant, he inched the station wagon into position. Watching these intricate maneuvers, Susan blushed at how foolish she must have sounded to Mrs. Wong.

"The trip is supposed to be scenic once the ferry starts winding through the channels separating the Gulf Islands, the chain of islands between the BC mainland and Vancouver Island," Dan explained. "Maybe we'll see seals and even some bald eagles."

Susan and Dan climbed the stairs from the car deck to join the line of passengers outside the ship's cafeteria. The massive engines rumbled, and the ship shuddered as the ferry pulled away from the dock and headed toward open water. Susan inhaled the freshness of the briny sea air, and her headache started to wane. She mustered the energy to start a conversation with Dan motivated more by curiosity than any desire to be sociable.

"Mona's very beautiful. Was she a model?"

Dan smirked. "Mona's never worked. Her parents wouldn't allow their daughter to engage in mundane pursuits like that—motherhood is what they want from their little girl." His bitterness was obvious.

Feeling bold Susan asked, "What's it like to live with a witch?"

Dan sniffed. "I was wondering when you'd bring up the witchcraft thing. You thought I was putting you on last night, didn't you?"

Susan hedged, "It's not every day I meet somebody claiming to be a witch. I've seen people interviewed on television around Halloween who say they're witches, but I always thought they were cranks. I never thought I'd meet someone who takes that stuff seriously. What does Mona do with the skulls, bones, and daggers?"

"She uses them in rituals to break curses."

"Let me understand—people who think they're cursed come to her for a cure, like going to the doctor if you're sick."

Dan nodded.

Susan could not contain her cynicism. "Who places these curses anyway?"

"Witches who practice black magic. Mona helps remove evil spells from people who've been cursed by a black witch."

The amused sparkle in Dan's eyes betrayed how much he was enjoying the shock value of these stories. Seeing his delight, Susan wondered if there was any truth to what he was saying. "It's just another form of religion, and that's how I treat it. Being married to a witch is like being married to any religious person who's devoted to the rituals of that religion." Dan shrugged.

"Does Mona tell fortunes and use a crystal ball and all that stuff?"

"She's trained in fortune telling. She uses mostly Tarot cards. She's got a pretty good hit rate at predicting events. I once took her for testing at the parapsychology labs at Columbia, and she was about 85% accurate in predicting the contents of the cards they use to study pre-cognition."

"So Mona tells fortunes and removes curses and spells. Does she charge for her services?"

"No, she's more like a member of the clergy in a religion than like a fortune teller or a medium leading séances where people pay."

"Are there many believers?" Susan asked.

"There seem to be quite a few witches in the Vancouver area. I think it's the only thing about Vancouver Mona likes."

"She enjoys the faculty wives club at U of V. She's very proud of you."

Dan frowned. He answered more to himself than to Susan. "She gets that from her parents. It's prestigious to have a son-in-law and a husband who's a university professor—it impresses friends to have an intellectual in the family. The only thing they're not impressed with is the salary. That's why they're always sending her money. The outfit she had on last night cost about two weeks of my salary. I could never afford anything like that, but her parents want her to look the part of whatever role they think she's playing so the checks come every month and she spends the money on herself and the kids."

Susan turned away, once again embarrassed by Dan's frankness. She did not want to know details about his marriage but suspected, at the same time, that Dan was starting to confide in her as a colleague. Susan saw this as a step toward being accepted as an equal with faculty rank, this sharing of personal confidences, and she was pleased.

They were finally at the door to the cafeteria. Dan placed a tray on the counter and siphoned coffee from the urn into two empty cups. "Let's get a quick bite, and then go out on deck for the trip through the Gulf Islands. I brought my binoculars." Dan patted the brown case hanging over his right shoulder. "I'm hoping to see some seals."

Thirty minutes later Dan and Susan were on the ferry's upper deck perched on the lid of a large bunker packed with life jackets. Dan scanned the water's edge on either side of the ship with his binoculars, while Susan scrutinized the rocky shoreline. The large vessel churned its way through the narrow waterway between two islands. The shore was so close she imagined reaching out to touch the pine trees lining the coasts on either side of the slender channel.

Dan began to fidget. "I can't find anything too interesting—just a lot of seagulls." He placed the binoculars inside their case and slid across the bunker toward Susan. Uneasy, Susan shifted sideways and turned to face Dan, making sure there was distance between them.

Dan studied her face. "I'm glad you're here, Sue. I have the outline of the book and the first draft of the introductory chapter in the car. Over the next couple of weeks, we should divvy up the writing duties. I have some ideas for experiments we can start, too. I want my research up and running as soon as possible. The paper I wrote this summer used old data, but I need to start new experiments. I'm applying for government grants, but I probably won't see any money until next spring. Has the department at JDU said anything about research space for you yet?"

Susan relaxed. This was a safer conversation. "The chairman of the department said something about lots of available research space. He hinted that several department members have given up on the publishing game, as he put it, so their lab space is available if I want it."

"Grab as much departmental territory as you can, Sue. The name of the academic game is empire building." Dan shifted his gaze to the passing shoreline. "Where are you planning to stay once we get to Victoria?"

"The department arranged a room for me in a student dormitory. I'll stay there until I find an apartment to rent."

"I've booked a room at the Empress for two nights. The Empress Hotel is a famous landmark, and everyone says you have to stay there when you visit Victoria." Dan turned and leaned toward Susan and dropped his voice to a whisper, "You can stay there with me if you want."

Startled, Susan flushed. "What about Jennifer Evans?" she blurted, instantly humiliated by her juvenile reaction. The question should have been, if there was a question, *What about Mona?*

"What *about* Jennifer Evans?" Dan bristled.

Susan stammered, her voice trembling. "I just thought—well, everyone at the Institute assumed you're with Jennifer when you're not with your wife." She coughed to relieve the tension in her throat.

Dan stared at her with his familiar demonic look. "Listen, Sue, we'll be working together on the book and on other research projects. We'll probably spend weekends together in Victoria working. The whole work thing would be easier—more complete—if we had other things going on, too." Dan sounded like he was lecturing a small child who had forgotten to say thank you.

Susan was determined not to humiliate herself further. She forced herself to face Dan squarely. Had he used the same line with Jennifer Evans? "I don't mind coming to Vancouver to work. There must be rooms on campus where I can stay, or I'll stay at your house. Your kids are fun. I don't mind kids."

Dan glared at Susan. "Yeah, I guess you could do that," he said finally, his voice flat. He pushed himself off the bunker, turned, and walked toward the railing. Susan studied the defiant tilt of his head before rising to stand beside him, although at a safe distance. Seagulls squawked over head as she took a deep breath to inhale the scent of the sea. The ship cut its speed, and she saw the outline of the ferry terminal ahead. "I think I'm going to like living surrounded by the sea. It will be fresh and clean, not shrouded in smog like big cities," Susan murmured. Dan did not respond. His head was turned toward the shoreline ahead.

The ship's public address system announced the imminent arrival at Swartz Bay on Vancouver Island. Without speaking, Dan left the railing to join the crowd descending the stairs to the car deck. Susan sighed, took one last deep breath, and followed Dan. When she reached the car, Dan was already seated behind the wheel reading a research article he had propped against the steering wheel. Julie's warning about becoming Dan's West Coast Jennifer Evans pounded in Susan's head, drowning out the roar of the giant engines reversing their thrust as the ferry docked. Susan slid into the passenger seat. She bit her lip to stifle a groan. Her headache was back with a vengeance.

FIVE

Dan's stony silence was unnerving. Susan, determined not to be intimidated, decided to read the brochure sent by the JDU psychology department. The last few weeks were frenetic, and she needed to refresh her memory about the details of her new university home. She found the pamphlet in her purse and started to scan the pages. Dan glanced at the booklet in her hands and demanded, "Read some of the campus description to me. I don't know much about JDU, so give me an overview." Relieved to be communicating with Dan again, no matter how awkward, Susan cleared her throat and began to read.

"The James Douglas University campus is situated on the shores of the Strait of Juan de Fuca, a body of water between Vancouver Island and the state of Washington in the United States of America. The central focus of the university is an imposing Victorian mansion, called The Castle, which houses the president's office along with other administrative centers. The two-hundred-acre campus is the former country estate of the McEwan family who amassed great wealth in the logging industry on Vancouver Island and the Queen Charlotte Islands. The estate grounds and buildings were donated to the Province of British Columbia for educational purposes in 1920. During World War II the campus was used as a pilot training camp for the Canadian Air Force. Many of the World War II military barracks remain standing and are used as offices and laboratories. The year 1964 marked the beginning of the campus expansion into its current form.

"There's the sign for the JDU campus—make the next left turn," Susan directed, relieved that the tense trip from the ferry was about to end. Dan swung his car through the intersection and headed toward the campus main gate.

It was easy to spot The Castle, a massive Victorian architectural splendor complete with turrets, elaborate filigree moldings, and two handsome statues of reclining lions guarding the entrance. More impressive was the wide expanse of lawn bordering the mansion, sloping down in a luxurious green sweep to a sandy beach at the water's edge. Benches facing the water were clustered across the lawn. A few sunbathers lazed on the beach. One was napping with a stack of books under his head. A stone path led from the road to a broad veranda in front of the main entrance to the building.

Dan stopped the car beside a kiosk with a campus map. He sprang out of the car and sprinted up the path toward the veranda steps, while Susan stayed behind to study the map. Locating the *You Are Here* arrow, she traced the main road to the Angus Building, home of the psychology department. She was studying the campus layout when Dan returned.

"Great view," Dan exclaimed. "Where's the psychology department?"

"It looks like we follow the main road to the top of the hill." Susan gestured toward the steep rise in front of them.

As they climbed back into the station wagon, Susan remarked, "It's odd that the administrative building is at the extreme edge of campus. Most campus administrators want to be in the center of things. I guess the JDU president opted for an elegant house and this magnificent view." The sight of the gentle waves sparkling in the sun lapping at the shoreline lifted Susan's flagging spirits. She was entranced by the brightly colored spinnakers billowing in the wind as scattered sailboats sped across the bay.

"Maybe he wanted to be inaccessible. JDU had a pretty volatile student body up to about three years ago with lots of protest demonstrations. The previous president resigned in disgrace when the student newspaper discovered he had fake academic credentials. The students were relentless in publishing stories about the president's phony background and his purchased degree. Maybe the new president thought he'd be better off away from the main part of campus—out of the line of fire and harder to find."

"I didn't know about any protests. How did you find out?" Susan asked.

"Jim Kracknoy told me during our phone call. He said he wanted to entice me to visit by sharing a few colorful local stories," Dan answered with a laugh. "Let's head to the psychology department so I can find him and go for lunch. I'm starved."

Dan accelerated, and the station wagon lurched up the steep grade. The main part of the university campus contained a cluster of academic buildings scattered around a flat central quad. The individual buildings were separated by either small wooded areas or expanses of well-groomed lawn. Neat rows of red-roofed barrack buildings, remnants of the World War II training camp, sat beside the university sports stadium.

They found the Angus Building, and Dan parked the car near an entrance. "There's not much action here today." Dan's eyes roamed over the sparsely populated parking lot. "August is a quiet time in BC universities because it's the traditional time to holiday as they call it here," Dan continued. "A lot of my colleagues have sailboats, and they spend most of August on the water. Looks like the same goes for your colleagues. There are more sailboats on the water this morning than there are cars in this lot."

Dan tugged Susan's overstuffed suitcase and typewriter case over the tailgate of his station wagon and dragged them into the darkened hallway of the Angus Building. Almost immediately, they collided with a slim, athletically built man with steel gray hair.

"Jim, it's good to see you again after all this time!" Dan exclaimed.

"Dan, my boy, good to see you, too." Jim Kracknoy grasped Dan's hand with both of his. "How long has it been since Stanford—seven, eight years, maybe more, I reckon?"

Dan turned, grasped Susan's elbow, and pushed her forward. "Jim, this is Susan Barron."

"Susan, of course, pleased to meet you." Jim gripped Susan's outstretched hand, pumping it up and down with vigor. "We're pleased to have you join us—very impressed with your vita and, of course, your academic lineage. Dan as an academic father is hard to beat."

As a graduate student, Susan learned to accept the tendency of psychologists to consider themselves descendants of an academic family. The transmission of research expertise through dissertation advisors was respected with a reverence usually reserved for the family trees of European royalty. Psychologists educated at Stanford were particularly fond of tracing academic lineage as a sign of professional prestige. Calling Dan her academic father was not surprising, but the tension between them this morning made it an awkward comment. "I'm really excited to be here," she answered with genuine enthusiasm.

"Well, we feel the same. When Dan wrote asking about the position we'd advertised, I was eager to get your application. We decided, because of your strong background, and my knowing Dan as I do, we'd hire you sight unseen. I must say, we got a much prettier package than we expected based on your academic credentials." Jim sputtered, "I mean, often women applicants with graduate student records like yours are not—" Jim blushed. "Good gosh, what *am* I saying? My daughter would kill me if she heard me talking like this. I do ramble on about nothing—sorry, just don't pay any attention to my random blithering."

Recovering his composure, Jim cleared his throat. "Well, to business—Mrs. Wong, our department secretary, is expecting you. Just go on up to the department office on the second floor. I'll take Dan to lunch so the two of us can catch up. My wife reminds me constantly that gossip about the Stanford psychology department is deadly boring for anyone who wasn't there, so I'll spare you the experience. Let's meet in my office, here," he pointed toward an open door, "around three o'clock—how's that?"

Susan nodded, relieved to be left out of the lunch invitation. She was overwhelmed with fatigue, and her head was pounding from the shock of

Dan's offer to share a hotel room. Now she had a second piece of unexpected news to digest. Dan lied to her. He *had* arranged her faculty position at JDU. There was no campus interview because she was recommended by a Stanford graduate to his former Stanford professor. Her nagging questions about the hiring peculiarity were answered. Dan and Jim had made an arrangement.

"Hold on here, Dan, I'll tell Mrs. Wong where to reach me if she needs to. I'm acting chairman while Giles, our chairman, is off sailing in some race." Jim ran up the stairs leaving Susan and Dan alone in the darkened hallway.

Susan picked up her typewriter case. "Dan, didn't you tell me back in New York that my job offer from JDU was a coincidence you had nothing to do with?"

"Come on, Sue, you must've known someone was pulling strings when you got an academic appointment without an on-campus interview." His voice was conciliatory, and he reached out to touch her shoulder, but she stepped back to avoid his hand. "What does it matter, anyway?" His tone turned curt. "You got a good job. Everyone needs some help these days given the tight job market. Leonard was my dissertation advisor and he got me my first job at the Institute. I came with him to help him set up the labs. It's not unusual—don't look so grumpy about it."

They heard Jim clatter down the stairwell back to the first floor. Dan hissed under his breath, "You have your degree now. It's time you learned how the profession works. No one will care how or where you got your first faculty job as long as you publish and get your name out there. That's why you're here, isn't it? Besides, it wasn't like you had a lot of choices." Too angry to respond, Susan turned and ran up the stairs to the second floor, leaving her suitcase, Dan, and Jim in the hallway outside of Jim's office.

She found the psychology department office and introduced herself to a tiny Asian woman sitting behind a massive desk stacked with papers. Mrs. Wong twittered like a bird, "Dr. Barron, I've been waiting for you. Your office is ready, so follow me and bring your things." She waved at Susan's typewriter case as she left her office and started briskly down the long corridor.

Mrs. Wong sped through the hallway at a remarkable rate for such a tiny person. Susan scurried to keep up with her. The two of them passed a sequence of closed office doorways before Mrs. Wong stopped abruptly at one of them. She unlocked the door and gestured inside, "Well, here you are."

Susan peered around the corner of the door jamb. The office furnishings were a passable imitation of oak. The room was luxurious compared to the bland offices at the Institute filled with scuffed and dented metal furniture. Susan walked over to the large window covering one wall to admire the stretch of well-kept lawn below. "This is very nice," Susan said as she turned away from the window and accepted the door key from Mrs. Wong's outstretched hand.

"I left a copy of the James Douglas University Faculty Handbook in your mailbox in the department office. And I booked your room. The student residences are run like a hotel during the summer. Your room is guaranteed for only one week because classes begin in two weeks and students start returning the week before classes begin. You may have to give your room to the student who has booked it for the term, or you may be able to stay longer, no one knows."

"Looks like I better rent an apartment as soon as possible. Do you think I'll have a hard time finding one?" Susan asked.

Mrs. Wong looked puzzled. "I really can't say. I don't know much about renting suites—or apartments as you people from the States call them. The department doesn't help new faculty find housing. You can contact the university housing office. They may be able to help you." Mrs. Wong spun around and raced back down the corridor.

"Thanks, I'll do that." Susan leaned against the door jamb watching Mrs. Wong's tiny form retreat toward the department office. She put her typewriter case on the desk and closed the door. She sank into the welcoming arms of the upholstered desk chair and looked up at the cloudless sky outside her office window. Overcome by weariness and anger, she dropped her head onto her folded arms and fell asleep at her desk.

Susan woke with a start and glanced at her watch—it was three-thirty. Through a sleepy haze she remembered the plans to join Dan and Jim at three o'clock. Susan struggled to clear her mind as she ran down the stairs to Jim's office on the first floor. She followed the laughter coming from the only open office door in sight along the darkened and deserted hallway.

"Susan, come in," Jim beckoned when Susan appeared at the door. Jim's office was large, much larger than hers, with three windows facing a broad lawn rimmed by tall pine trees. The furniture was the university standard issue, but Jim had transformed his office into a homey space. A colorful Mexican throw rug lay in front of his desk, and a chestnut leather loveseat stood against one wall. Dan sat slouched on the loveseat. An attractive young woman with a blond ponytail was perched beside him. Her tanned legs below her white shorts were muscular but shapely. Dan was eyeing them with obvious pleasure.

"Susan, this is my daughter, Laura. She's working in the department as a research assistant this summer while she takes a break from her graduate studies at Stanford." Jim grinned at Laura with affectionate pride. Susan smiled despite feeling awkward and self-conscious. Her faded jeans and wrinkled t-shirt looked frumpy and unkempt in comparison to Laura's casual elegance.

Laura smiled at Susan. "Hi, Susan, Dan's been telling us about the book project the two of you have going. My advisor at Stanford thinks one shouldn't hurry to publish integrative works like books early in one's career. He thinks you need a bit of seasoned experience and theoretical sophistication before attempting a book." Laura's smile was smug as she leaned toward Dan and tapped her fingers on his knee. "Of course, you'll have Dan to guide you through the whole process. What could be better?"

Susan stared at Laura and fumed at her snide taunt. She wanted Dan to defend their project, but he appeared oblivious to Laura's words. His arm was stretched across the back of the loveseat. His fingers brushed Laura's shoulder as he eyed her with unabashed delight. Obviously, Dan had had a few drinks with lunch. Susan watched with distaste as he leered at Laura.

Jim broke the silence. "Susan, Dan's invited Laura and me for drinks at the Empress. Come with us, why don't you? I feel guilty dragging Dan off to lunch like I did, so please, join us." Jim began stuffing his briefcase with the stack of papers piled on his desk.

"Don't feel guilty about lunch. I have a good case of jet lag and I haven't been hungry. Besides, I must check into the student dorms. Once I get my room, I think I'll take a nap."

Jim looked sympathetic. "Laura and I can drive you to the residence hall on our way downtown." He jerked his bulging briefcase from the top of his desk and called over his shoulder as he ushered Susan out of his office. "Dan, Laura, meet us outside in the parking lot in a few minutes."

Susan leaned her head around the door jamb to say good-bye to Dan, but he was too involved to notice her. He was relaxed on the loveseat, and one of Laura's sandaled feet was rubbing his calf. "Maybe we can dump Dad in a few hours and go dancing. The Empress has a great disco." Susan heard Laura's flirtatious offer and Dan's answer.

"Perfect," he replied.

SIX

A second sleepless night, this time in a desolate dormitory cubicle, and Susan was on the verge of a tearful collapse. She fled the gloomy room as soon as the cafeteria opened its doors. With coffee in hand Susan surveyed her office—forlorn and uninviting at this early hour. She slumped into her desk chair and closed her eyes. One day in British Columbia and her fantasies lay in shambles. She did not know which was worse. Was it Dan's lie about his connection to the JDU psychology department and his bargain with Jim Kracknoy or his blatant attempt to get her into bed? Julie had warned her about both. Susan accepted Julie's assessment of Dan's sexual exploits. She even grudgingly accepted Julie's suspicion Dan was sexually attracted to her. She thought she could handle any unwanted sexual dynamic between them—and she still did.

The fact she did not get the JDU job on her own merits was a more potent blow. The months of job applications and endless rejection letters eroded her self-esteem in a profound way. She did not realize until now how desperately she craved to be accepted in her own right as an academic. She could not turn back because her East Coast bridges were burned. She felt trapped and out of options. Julie was right. What would happen now that she was here, alone, with no one to turn to?

Susan's troubled musings were interrupted by a sound in the hallway of someone unlocking an office door. She jerked upright. She would be walking the streets of Victoria if she did not find an apartment to rent. She spread the pages of the local newspaper spirited from the cafeteria across the empty expanse of her desk. She shuffled through the classified listings searching for an *Apartments for Rent* column. What she found was a small section marked *Suites to Let*. Remembering Mrs. Wong reference to suites rather than apartments, she scanned the meager listings.

"Knock, knock."

Susan looked up to find a scrawny male face peering at her from behind the door jamb. A tall, skeletal man attached to the gaunt head swung into full view in the doorway.

"Well, well, so here you are. I'm Doctor Giles Plimley-Jones, department chairman. We've talked on the phone, but we've never met."

The unexpected appearance of the department chairman unnerved Susan. "Jim Kracknoy told me yesterday that you were away sailing, so I didn't think I'd meet you until next week," she blurted.

Giles Plimley-Jones was tall, over six feet, with thinning, unruly hair sticking out in multiple directions from the top of his head. His erratic hairdo and bony face reminded Susan of a scarecrow. His trouser belt sagged below his waist, and his faded windbreaker hung from his thin shoulders in an ill-fitting droop. Giles was somewhere around sixty years old, Susan guessed. He looked like the crumpled stereotype of a university professor complete with a slight British accent.

"Jim told you *that*, did he?" Giles mocked. He sounded displeased at the thought of a discussion of his activities in his absence. "I'm only here for a few minutes to pick up my mail. That's why I came so early. I want to avoid everyone, especially Mrs. Wong. She's a bloody nuisance—always asking me to solve some departmental problem. If I can successfully avoid Mrs. Wong, I'll be sailing this afternoon." Giles pointed to the insignia on his windbreaker. "I'm a member of the Royal Victoria Yacht Club and we have a regatta today."

Susan's eyes widened. She had never met anyone who belonged to a yacht club.

"Well, I trust you're settling in. If you need anything for your office, just ask Mrs. Wong. She takes care of everything around here." Giles turned to leave.

"If you've got a couple of minutes, could I ask you a few questions about Victoria?" Susan asked.

Giles looked impatient and then, with an exaggerated sigh, replied, "I guess I should show some pretense of hospitality to a newcomer." He settled his lanky frame into Susan's office chair. "What do you want to know?"

Susan picked up the classified section of the newspaper. "I need to rent an apartment—suite, I guess they're called here—but I don't know the areas of the city and what each one is like. There are ads for places in James Bay, Esquimalt—" Susan shrugged looking for help.

Giles interrupted her. "You don't want to live in James Bay. That's downtown, and only draft dodger hippies live there. Esquimalt is a slum near the navy base. You don't want to live there either." Impatient, Giles added, "Quite honestly, I don't know much about renting suites in Victoria. Talk to some of the graduate students. They rent suites and houses all over the city and they'll give you better advice than any you'd get from me."

Giles started to rise from the chair, but Susan interjected. "What about the public transportation in Victoria? Are there buses or taxis? I'm staying in one of the student dormitories temporarily and I won't have my car for a while."

Giles looked at Susan with derision. "My dear, Susan, I don't ride the bus and I don't use taxis. Since you're staying in the student residences, ask the students about bus service. They must ride the bus."

"Okay, thanks—" Susan watched dejected as Giles rose to leave.

"Well, jolly good then—I see you have things well in hand. I'll see you next week—ta." Giles waved a weak good-bye and lurched out of her office but then reappeared. "Before I forget, since you're from the States, what do you think of Nixon's resignation and Ford's pardon?" Before Susan could respond, Giles continued. "There's a tad of interest in south-of-the-border politics around here. We've got a few draft dodgers at JDU, even a couple in the psychology department." Giles smirked. "Nice chaps for the most part, although a bit on the hippie side if you ask me. Well, I'm off for good now, so carry on." Giles disappeared for the second time.

Susan stared at the empty space Giles had occupied. She remembered from her phone conversations with Giles that he liked random chatter and he tended to ask questions without waiting for answers. Susan sighed and turned back to the newspaper and her study of the classified ads. Her interest in the political drama of the past few months was waning. She lived in another country now and was relieved to have an excuse to forget the presidential intrigues that mesmerized her when she lived in the States. Her central focus was on the intense uncertainty facing her. South-of-the-border politics, as Giles put it, must take second place to her efforts to sort out her new life.

Susan was startled when her office phone blared through the silence. It must be Dan on the other end of the line. No one else knew she was there.

"Hi, Sue, this is Dan. Glad to see you're getting an early start. How're things going?" Before she could answer his question, Dan continued. "I'm going to spend the day sightseeing in Victoria. I'm told the provincial museum has great native artifacts, and Laura says I can't miss having afternoon tea here at the Empress, a Victoria tradition. The Empress is a grand old spot. I think it's the Victoria equivalent to the Plaza in New York."

"I thought we were going to discuss the division of duties on the book today," Susan snapped.

"Yeah, I thought so, too, but it doesn't look like I'll get to Victoria again anytime soon, so I thought I'd let Laura show me around. We can talk on the phone next week."

"Well, enjoy Victoria and tell Laura I wish her well in her research when she gets back to Stanford." Susan was annoyed at Dan's casual change of plans.

"Will do," Dan answered. He sounded so cheerful it was obvious Laura was Dan's overnight companion at the Empress. "Talk to you soon."

SEVEN

The memo in her department mailbox was firm. A required orientation for new faculty led by the department chairman was scheduled for the next morning in the department library. The message was unambiguous—the meeting was not optional. Susan entered the library at ten o'clock as directed and found two men sitting on opposite sides of a huge oval conference table that dominated the room. Glass-fronted bookshelves secured by intricate locks lined the library walls. One man was idly inspecting the bookcases containing shelves of student theses in elaborate bindings. The other man was writing in a journal. The room was silent except for the soft hum of the ventilator fan.

Susan took a seat near the door. "Hi, I'm Susan Barron." Her greeting reverberated through the silence, making her voice sound more eager than she intended.

"Nice to meet you, Susan, I'm Lucas Selkirk." The man sitting nearest to Susan extended his hand in greeting.

They both looked across the table toward the second man who continued writing.

Susan turned to Lucas. "What's your area?"

"Neuropsychology—what about you?"

"My degree is in experimental psychology. I study human memory," Susan responded.

The man across the table raised his head. He looked pugnacious, but he introduced himself anyway. "I'm Jack Bernoski. I'm a developmental psychologist. Sounds like the two of you are from the States."

"Yeah, I'm from North Carolina by way of Boston where I did a post-doc," Lucas confirmed.

"I got my degree in June from the Institute for Research in the Social Sciences in New York City." Susan smiled at Jack.

"I'm from Nova Scotia. I got my degree a few years ago from Memorial University in Newfoundland. Since you're both from the States, I don't suppose you've ever heard of Memorial," Jack said.

"I've heard of Newfoundland," Susan offered, trying to be friendly. Jack shot her a withering look. "Well, good for you. Most people from the States don't know where Canada is let alone Newfoundland." He tapped his pen on the table looking irritated, then returned to writing in his journal. Susan was about to protest but suddenly remembered a conversation with another student at the Institute. She had mentioned her faculty position in British Columbia and his response was, "I thought you were going to Canada not South America." At the time Susan attributed his confusion to the geocentrism of most Manhattanites whose knowledge of the continent did not extend beyond New Jersey. She had to acknowledge that Jack had a point.

A tense silence fell over the room. Lucas continued his inspection of the student theses in the bookcases, and Susan studied her two colleagues to pass the time. Lucas was tall and slim. His shaggy black hair curled over his ears and covered the back of his neck. His loose-fitting caftan shirt had an embroidered border around the neckline and wrist cuffs. He wore faded jeans and tattered sandals. Jack, by contrast, was short, stocky, and balding. He was dressed in a navy blazer, grey slacks, and a white shirt with a conservative but elegant silk tie. Lucas looked like he was ready to hit the beach, while Jack could pass easily for a junior executive.

Jack seemed oblivious to their presence, so Susan smiled awkwardly at Lucas and wondered if he was analyzing her in the same way. She had tried to achieve a professional look for today's meeting. She was not as formal as Jack nor as casual as Lucas but somewhere in between in her beige slacks and striped knit top. Susan thought of herself as standard issue when it came to looks—average height, average weight, not too pretty, and not too plain. Her upturned nose would always be oddly shaped, and her dark brown hair would always be too fine and too straight. She hoped her splurge on a farewell-to-New-York haircut that framed her face in flattering pixie-like strands looked sophisticated. Her best feature, her large brown eyes, were alert again now that jet lag had disappeared.

Giles Plimley-Jones burst into the room looking harried and distracted, slamming the library door behind him. He grabbed a chair facing the three of them and sunk into it with a loud groan. "Bloody meetings—that's all I do is go to bloody meetings." Despite his tweed jacket and brown slacks, Giles looked unkempt. The neck of his white shirt was too large, and his tie puckered the collar against his scrawny neck. There was a round yellow badge fastened to his jacket lapel. The bold print read

Big Cheese

Psychology Department Chairman

Giles noticed Susan inspecting the button. "I wear this at registration," he grunted, tapping the embossed surface with his index finger. "It helps the students know who the boss is in case they have any questions or complaints." Giles cleared his throat and slapped his right hand on the tabletop with a resounding crash. "Well, let's get started. It's my habit to meet with new faculty to discuss our department expectations regarding teaching, research, contract renewal, and the granting of tenure. I'll launch into my spiel, and if any of you have questions just interrupt me." Giles peered at the three of them as they nodded.

"I'm assuming you introduced yourselves to each other while you were waiting for me, so I don't have to bother with introductions—right?" Again, Susan, Lucas, and Jack nodded.

"Jolly good—" Giles paused for dramatic effect, leaned back in his chair, raised his eyes to scan the ceiling, and rested his fingers on his chest forming a pyramid. "I'll talk about research first. The department expects new faculty members to publish research papers. Your contract renewal and eventually your tenure will be in jeopardy if you don't publish."

Jack interrupted, "How many papers do we have to publish each year?"

"That's a good question but one for which I have no answer." Giles gave a hawkish laugh, relishing the ambiguity. "The department has granted tenure to faculty with only one or two publications in very good journals. In general, we like to see more than one or two publications at tenure time. We're hiring people like you, who have more publications than I had when I was promoted to professor, so we expect you to do more than old-timers like me." Giles eyes rose again to examine the ceiling. "Times change as do expectations. I often think, if I were to apply for a job in this department today, I wouldn't be hired because my publication record wouldn't be good enough. Very odd how things evolve," he spoke more to himself than to the others in the room.

For a few seconds, Giles seemed lost on a personal mental journey. Then, as if being pulled back by the jerk of an invisible string, he raised his voice and continued, "Personally, I think research and publishing are crap and I don't do much of either. I don't have much extra time after teaching now that I'm chairman. Some tenured faculty in the department conduct research, and others don't. We have one chap who gave his research grant back to the government because he decided he didn't want to be in the lab anymore."

Susan, Lucas, and Jack looked at each other. Jack appeared anxious, and beads of sweat formed on his forehead. Lucas began to massage the back of his neck, looking apprehensive. Susan's anxiety spiked.

Giles sat upright in his chair and glared at each of them in turn. "I should warn you that the new dean and the new president are hell bent to see James Douglas better its research profile among Canadian universities.

So, my message to you is *you better publish.*" Giles thumped the table to emphasize his point.

Susan ventured a question. "Since research and publishing are important, is there financial support for new faculty to start up their research?"

"Ah, that's a question I can answer." Giles regarded Susan with gratitude. "The president has a research fund for new faculty. Ask Mrs. Wong about how you apply for this money. I can't remember, but she'll know. The president and the dean have started all sorts of new procedures and policies. It's too much of a bloody nuisance to keep track of them all. That's why I have Mrs. Wong."

Giles glared at Lucas. "Any other questions—particularly ones I can answer?" Lucas waved his hand no, so Giles continued. "Well, now, let's see, I've talked about publishing—what's left? Oh, yes, teaching—" Giles took a deep breath and plunged into another prepared speech. "We expect all faculty members to be able to teach introductory psychology. That's why we assign all of you to this course. We don't have a set procedure for evaluating teaching. Some faculty members distribute a questionnaire to students at the end of the term and the students rate the course and instructor. This questionnaire is controversial, so some faculty members use it while others refuse to have anything to do with it. At the dean's insistence, we've started to evaluate the teaching of untenured faculty by using classroom visits from senior faculty who then write a report based on their observations."

Jack pulled out a handkerchief and mopped the sweat from his brow. He cleared his throat and asked, "Can we choose the faculty members who visit our classes to evaluate our teaching?"

"Actually, no," Giles responded. "We have a committee of faculty members, called the Executive Committee. Members of this committee make all the decisions regarding faculty reappointment, tenure, and promotion. I'm a member of the Executive Committee as department chairman—so is Jim Kracknoy as assistant chairman. There are three other faculty members elected by the department. One or two of these committee members will do the classroom visits. I usually don't bother with new faculty teaching evaluation because I'm too busy with other things." Giles sniggered. "As a general rule, if students aren't in my office complaining about your teaching, then you can assume you're okay. Otherwise, you'll hear from me."

Giles scanned the three faces before him, then banged the tabletop again with his open palm. "Well, that's all I have to say. If you have any other questions, look at the JDU Faculty Handbook, particularly the section called the Tenure Document. It's bloody boring reading but probably a good thing to do if you want to get tenure here. The dean is very proud of the Tenure Document—he chaired the committee that wrote it. If you ever run into him, it may be politic to have read it, in case he gives you a little quiz." Giles chuckled, amused at his own joke.

"Well, that's all I have to say. You can meet with me if you need something but try not to make it too often." Finished, Giles pushed back his chair and stood. Without a further word or glance in their direction, he bolted out of the library and crossed the hallway to his office, slamming the door behind him. Jack scrambled out of his chair and departed, leaving Susan and Lucas alone in the empty room.

"I guess this meeting's over," Lucas muttered. Susan and Lucas studied each other in puzzled silence until Lucas started to laugh. "Well, let me see if I can sum this up," he said, grinning. "In order to get tenure, we have to publish research papers although we don't know how many we have to publish—and we have to make sure that students don't complain to Giles about our teaching. Sound about right to you?"

Susan rose to her feet. "You forgot the part about research and publishing being crap, but we're expected to do it anyway. Other than that, I think you've got the gist of the meeting."

Lucas and Susan left the library. "I admire your sense of humor about this meeting, Lucas. I must admit I feel discouraged. It's hard to know what to make of Giles. He's not exactly what I expected a department chairman to be like."

"What did you expect?" Lucas asked as he stopped in front of his office door and fumbled in the pocket of his jeans for the key.

"I don't know—more professionalism, maybe, more collegial support and wisdom. Certainly not someone wearing a campaign button advertising he's chairman. He seems sort of pathetic." Susan sighed.

Lucas grinned and opened his office door. "Welcome to academe, Susan. Get used to the pathetically unexpected."

Lucas's office was identical to Susan's except the shelves of his bookcase were overflowing with books and journals. Stacks of papers and file folders covered his desk.

"I'm envious. Your office looks lived in—mine is completely bare except for the JDU Faculty Handbook sitting alone on a shelf of my empty bookcase."

Lucas teased, "If all you have in your office is the Faculty Handbook, now's your chance to read the infamous Tenure Document so you can impress the dean."

EIGHT

The tomblike hallways of the Angus Building came to life when the faculty returned for the fall term. Susan rushed into the department library and collapsed in an empty chair. The first department meeting of the year would start in a few minutes. Most of the faculty was male, and from what Susan could see they formed distinct clusters. The younger men sported scruffy haircuts, some long, some short, but none looked like their hair was touched by a barber. A few had beards. The requisite wire-rimmed eyeglasses favored by young academics were present either alone or in combination with the beard. A subset of this group favored an outdoors look, plaid flannel shirts, faded jeans, and hiking boots, while others wore t-shirts, shorts, and sandals. Most of the older men were dressed in casual shirts with golf or sailing club logos on the breast pocket.

There were three women in the room other than Susan. The roster on the wall outside the department office listed three women faculty, so one of these women was a student, Susan guessed. Across the table she noticed a couple engaged in animated conversation. The man's hand was placed casually over the woman's wrist. The department faculty roster listed two individuals with the same last name—these two must be married. The man looked several decades older than his wife. He and Jack Bernoski were the only men in the room wearing a jacket and a tie.

Susan smiled at Jack and Lucas. Lucas returned her smile, but Jack, looking grim, shifted his eyes to his open journal on the table and began writing. A chair near the entrance to the library sat empty, and as the latecomers entered, they avoided it. Jim Kracknoy, the only other person in the room Susan recognized, was seated next to the empty chair. When she caught Jim's eye, he gave her a brief wave hello.

"Hello, I'm Bill Forsythe," said a grey-haired man as he slid into the chair next to Susan. "Welcome to JDU."

Susan smiled, grateful that someone had finally noticed she was a newcomer. "I'm Susan Barron," she hesitated then continued, "You're one of the neuropsychology faculty, aren't you?"

Bill chuckled. "I guess you could call me part of the neuropsychology group. I'll be retiring in the spring, so I only teach one graduate course now. After thirty-five years of teaching, I'm looking forward to finally having time to finish the book I've been working on for the last ten years."

"You've taught for thirty-five years—that's remarkable. I haven't started my classes yet and I'm finding the course prep work exhausting already." Susan laughed, trying to hide her truthful admission as a joke.

"You have to get used to teaching, but it gets easier over time and, if and when you have some good students, you'll start to enjoy it."

"I hope so," Susan answered, appreciating the encouragement.

The clamor of voices grew louder as more faculty members seated themselves at the table. Giles Plimley-Jones, dressed in his faded yacht club windbreaker, shuffled into the room and closed the door behind him. It must be another regatta day, Susan mused. Giles took his place in the one remaining empty chair and raised his head to face the room. The assembled faculty ignored him, showing no sign a meeting was about to begin. If anything, the din of conversation climbed to higher noise levels. Suddenly, a booming explosion pierced the room. A deadly hush fell over the group as everyone turned to stare at Giles in stunned silence. He was standing in front of his chair with his right hand raised above his head. He held a smoking pistol pointed toward the ceiling.

"I knew this starter gun would come in handy one day," Giles announced with a smirk as he sat down, placing the firearm on the table in front of him. "Now that I've got your attention, are we ready to begin the meeting?" The faculty members shuffled in their chairs. The expressions around the table were mixed; some showed amusement, while others reeked with disgust.

"We'll be lucky if someone doesn't call the campus police to report a gun shot," Jim Kracknoy snapped. "You better get on with the meeting, Giles."

"Okay, let's start. We don't have agendas for these meetings, but I guess the first order of business is to tell everyone that we have three new faculty members." Giles waved in multiple directions at Lucas, Jack, and Susan. "I don't want to take time to do introductions today. Those of you who've been around for a while can introduce yourselves to the new people when the urge hits you. I'll introduce our new graduate student representative. Where are you?" Giles peered around the room in aggravation unable to locate the student.

"I'm here, Doctor Plimley-Jones. I'm Wanda Martin." A dark-haired young woman raised her hand and smiled.

"Jolly good," Giles exclaimed. "Now, let's get on with things. It's three-thirty on Friday afternoon, and this meeting has already cut into my weekend drinking time." Giles looked like he expected a reaction to this remark, and a few faculty members complied with nervous twitters. "We have some undergraduate curriculum business to take care of with a bloody deadline coming up, so I'm turning the meeting over to Jim so he can do his assistant chairman rigmarole."

With an accommodating nod of his head toward Giles, Jim Kracknoy opened a large folder and began to recite a list of proposed department course revisions. He droned through the list, calling for votes on each item. Bored with the mundane start-of-the-term department business, Susan's thoughts drifted to her recent trip to Seattle. She was delighted to find her car and its contents undamaged after its cross-country train ride. She was grateful there was no interference from Canada Customs when she drove the car across the border. The Customs official considered all her belongings to be legitimate because she was entering Canada as a landed immigrant, her official government designation. Two days ago, she had moved into the suite she had rented, happy to escape both the cell-like cubicle and the non-stop partying of the student residence hall. Practical things were falling into place, and she liked that—it made her feel more at home.

Giles's strident tone replaced Jim Kracknoy's soft drone. "Does anyone have any other business to bring up?" His attitude conveyed a strong desire for a "no" answer, and he got his wish. "Good, then the meeting is adjourned to the bar in the faculty club if anyone wants to join me for a drink." A few of the men in the room accepted this surly invitation and patted Giles on the shoulder with a "see you at the club," as they left the library.

Susan expected she would be surrounded by department colleagues eager to meet her after the meeting. This hope was trampled by their rush to leave the library. Only one or two gave her a cursory sideways glance as they hurried out the door. Lucas and she trailed behind the crowd. As they walked down the hallway, Lucas remarked, "You look exhausted."

"Yeah, these first weeks in Victoria and at JDU have been tiring. I'm feeling overwhelmed, and I'm still trying to make sense of a few things."

"Come over to my place for dinner tomorrow night—unless you have other plans?" Lucas stopped at the door of his office.

"Are you kidding? I don't know anyone here—how can I have other plans? I'd be happy to come to dinner. I've just been eating crackers and cheese and drinking cheap wine for the past few days."

Lucas unlocked his office door and grabbed a pen and a scrap of paper from the debris piled on his desk. He scribbled the directions to his suite and handed the paper to Susan. "I asked Jack to dinner, too. I thought the three of us could form a support group of sorts to get us through our first year here." Lucas laughed. "As you can tell from the department meeting, we can't expect much help from anyone else and especially not from Giles.

Jack turned me down, though. He said he and his wife go out on Saturday nights, but I got the feeling he wasn't interested in becoming too friendly."

Susan nodded. "He was pretty stand-offish at the meeting we had with Giles. He doesn't seem to like people from the States."

Lucas shrugged. "Who knows? Anyway, it'll just be the two of us. So, see you around seven."

Susan walked back to her office, opened the door, and stared at the phone. She had not spoken to Dan since his call from the Empress two weeks ago. She was tempted to phone him but was reluctant to make the first move to communicate. She reassured herself. Dan was busy with the start of the term. His silence about the book was not a torture tactic. He was as busy with course preparation as she was and had forgotten to call. No need to interpret the silence as anything other than an oversight.

So much had happened so fast. The abrupt change from graduate student to assistant professor was both jarring and isolating. The changes left her feeling defeated, not in control, and there was nobody to turn to for help with her confusion. There was no Julie surrogate on the immediate horizon of her new life. Lucas seemed the most likely possibility, but he was still an unknown. Jack obviously had determined that she and Lucas were rivals in an imagined competition, so he was keeping his distance. Her department colleagues showed no interest in even the most meager social amenities. The best Giles could offer, when he was not acting crazy, was sarcastic hostility. Collegial camaraderie was missing here. At least, that was her first impression. Even more disheartening, Dan had changed. He was making demands and revealing aspects of his life Susan preferred not to see.

She hoped her mood would improve now that she had her own place filled with oddities of furniture extracted from the recesses of the basement storeroom of the large house. Susan's suite occupied the top floor of a massive stone mansion. When she called to inquire about the rental, the owner told her the suite was available because it was difficult to rent. The house did not have an elevator and there were many steps from the street level to the front door. The owner cautioned that the unit was suitable only for someone who was healthy and did not mind climbing stairs. When Susan saw it, she rented it immediately. The owner was right about the climb. She counted sixty-seven steps from the street level to the door of her third-floor suite.

Susan sighed and gathered her things to leave. She would celebrate her one triumph so far, her new suite. It was shabby but comfortable with a remarkable view of downtown Victoria. Watching the distant city lights at night from her lofty vantage point calmed her and helped put the turmoil of newness in perspective. A solitary toast to the cityscape of Victoria was her only option for a start to the weekend.

NINE

Susan found the house where Lucas lived, a modest split-level on a tree-lined street. She grabbed a bottle of Chianti from the back seat of her car and walked down the driveway, looking for the basement suite Lucas described in his scribbled directions. Susan rounded the rear corner of the house and found Lucas sitting on a lawn chair in the center of a small cement patio. Eyes closed, he seemed to be meditating. For a few seconds, Susan stood and admired him. His dark hair tumbled across his tanned forehead, over his ears and down to his neck. His shirt hung loose, partially unbuttoned over his bare chest. Susan was tempted to reach out and stroke his face. His serenity was erotic. She imagined being circled in his arms, pressed against the flesh of his chest that peeked provocatively from beneath the folds of his shirt.

"Hi, Lucas," Susan whispered.

Lucas opened his eyes and smiled. "Susan, glad you found me."

Susan handed him the bottle of wine.

"Thanks, Susan, that's thoughtful—bringing wine." Lucas drawled. She had not noticed his slight Southern accent before. A wave of sexual longing caught her off guard. Forget Lucas's sensuality, she scolded—he's your colleague and that is where it ends.

Lucas uncoiled himself from his chair. "Let's go inside and drink some of this wine."

Inside, Lucas rummaged through drawers looking for a corkscrew, while Susan surveyed the room. A small table with two chairs sat in front of the kitchen appliances that lined one wall. A bed, covered with a rough-hewn striped cloth, sat against the wall opposite the kitchen. The bed doubled as a sofa and was covered with ethnic cushions—Mexican, Indian, and Chinese. An area rug of radiant red and yellow geometrics covered the bland wall-to-wall carpeting. Lamps of assorted vintages, a small wooden desk, and a brick and plank bookshelf completed the room. She watched Lucas struggle to open the bottle of wine. There are those who are elegant even when performing mundane tasks, and Lucas was one of them.

"This is like a New York apartment, small and cozy," Susan said, accepting a glass of wine.

Lucas looked around his suite. "It's small—I don't know about the cozy part." He grabbed one of the kitchen chairs for himself and motioned for Susan to sit on the bed turned sofa. "This neighborhood's too suburban for me. I'd rather live closer to downtown. Bill Forsythe found this suite for me, so I don't want to offend him by moving out too soon but I plan to find another place."

"Make sure you stay away from James Bay. Giles told me that's where all the hippies live. Hippies seem to be a group Giles doesn't like."

Lucas laughed. "I don't think I'll be guided too much by Giles's opinion, but thanks for the advice."

Lucas sipped his wine. "Bill's a good sort—too bad he's retiring. I'm his replacement. Bill leaves in the spring and Tom Carlisle is building his private practice, so Otto Hartmann and I will handle the graduate students. The neuropsychology program is the JDU department's claim to fame, mostly because of Otto and his work on speech disorders. There are lots of grad students to deal with. Tom took me out for drinks one night and filled me in on the program history."

"It sounds like the neuropsychology group is pretty close." Susan was envious. She wanted to be part of a congenial group of colleagues.

Lucas laughed again. "I've only been here a few weeks longer than you, Susan, but I wouldn't use the word *close* to describe the JDU psychology faculty. Tom bought me a few beers because he wants me to take over the supervision of his grad students. I think the neuropsychology faculty stays cordial because of grad student dissertation committees—friendship doesn't have much to do with it." Lucas explained, "I was hired to work in Otto's tradition, but I want to tackle issues larger than speech disorders. I'm interested in the mind-body problem and how left hemisphere functions may be our key to understanding the mind. I don't know how Otto will take my change in research direction, but what happens, happens, I guess."

"At least you have some people to talk to. Except for you, I haven't found that yet," Susan complained.

Lucas smiled and said, "The grad students will soon start lining up outside your door. They're angry with the faculty for not giving them more attention and research direction. They're looking for some new research blood."

A pot lid rattled on the stove. "Looks like the rice's ready—take a seat." Lucas motioned toward the tiny table set for two. Returning from the stove, he placed two plates of steaming rice topped with an assortment of vegetables on the table. A few strips of chicken lay across the vegetables. Lucas gestured toward a bottle of soy sauce on the table. "This is my version of an Asian stir fry. Hope you like the bean sprouts and bamboo shoots."

"It looks delicious," Susan crooned as she savored the aroma of the dish. "I haven't eaten food like this since I left New York. Thanks for going to all this trouble."

Lucas grinned and took a few hearty bites with a sip of wine. "So, what about you—how and why did you end up at JDU?" he asked between mouthfuls.

Susan described Dan, his move to the University of Vancouver, and the offer of co-authorship on a textbook. She carefully omitted the details of her unsuccessful job search. "My dissertation examined how much information we can take in and remember during the first seconds of perception. Dan's research is more about memory for events. That's why he thought I'd be a good co-author for a textbook on cognitive psychology. I can cover the early stages of information processing he isn't interested in writing about." Susan wondered if she was telling Lucas the truth as she and Dan had not yet discussed the book and its chapters.

"Most new PhDs would be intimidated by the thought of writing a textbook," Lucas said.

"Dan thinks it'll be good for my career—nothing like a successful textbook to get your name out there in the field—to help get a job—that's what he likes to tell me. There're only a few textbooks in cognitive psychology right now so ours has a good chance of selling well."

Lucas looked puzzled. "You already have a job. Why do you think you need to write a textbook to get a job?"

Caught off guard, Susan hesitated, and Lucas started to chuckle. "I get it—what you mean is that your name on a textbook will help you get the job you *really* want. Obviously, it's not here." Still laughing, Lucas pushed his chair back from the table, crossed his long legs, and sipped from his wine glass. "So, you're ambitious for fame in your career and a faculty position at a big-name university." He eyed Susan with amusement.

Susan cleared her throat, realizing she may have revealed too much. She regretted her unintentional slip that the JDU department was not where she planned to stay. "Dan craves fame. He wants to author a classic textbook that'll go on for years—to be known as a cognitive psychology equivalent to B.F. Skinner." Susan shrugged. "As for me, I guess I'm ambitious to do good research and to publish papers in good journals, but I never thought much about becoming famous."

Lucas looked thoughtful. "Writing a book is hard work, especially if you haven't done it before. I know because I watched my ex-wife struggle with it. Like you, she wanted a tenure track position in a prestigious department, so she got involved in a book project."

"You were married? So was I." Susan seized the chance to switch topics.

Lucas twisted the stem of his wine glass between his fingers as he watched the ruby liquid rise and fall. "Yeah, I was married," he said slowly. "Sandy was a couple of years ahead of me in grad school. I took a post-doc in Boston because she already had a faculty position in a medical school there. We drifted apart when my desire to become a rising star in academe began to fade. Sandy found my change of heart—the dampening of my ambitions—hard to take, so we separated and then divorced."

"My marriage ended because of graduate school. My ex, Paul, didn't understand my intensity. When I started working in Dan's lab, I got caught up in the mystery of the first seconds of conscious experience. How do we process sensory information so quickly? What gets through to memory and what is lost? Paul accused me of being obsessed with esoteric issues that no one cared about. I guess he felt abandoned when I spent most of my time on research and studying for my comprehensive exams. He started seeing other women. I found out about his affairs when he came home one day with a nasty bruise on his cheek. The angry husband of his latest lover punched him in the face to drive home the point about staying away from his wife. He had to come clean about his affairs after that."

Susan remembered Paul's shame and outrage when he admitted his extramarital activities. At the time, she had felt sorry for him, especially for his embarrassment at explaining his battered face. "During our marriage, Paul obsessed over the idea that he might have to escape to Canada to avoid being drafted. It's ironic—the Vietnam War is over, Paul is still in New York, and I'm the one in Canada."

Lucas chuckled. "He thought he'd have to defect to Canada? My friends called in front of the draft board either told the truth or lied about being gay. A few figured out a way to fake asthma. Either way that seemed to be enough to get them out of the draft."

Lucas eyed Susan over the rim of his wine glass. "JDU may not be the greatest psychology department, but I like that it's off the beaten track. I want to explore my life and not be wedded only to research, publishing, and getting tenure. I had to get out of the East Coast rat race. My years as a post-doc were a constant competition among those of us in the lab. Who was publishing and how prestigious were the journals? Who was getting funding and how much? It was an endless round of comparing who was on top and who was falling behind. The environment is more relaxed here. I'll have time to think about the brain, consciousness, and the mind, and not just race from one publication to the next."

Susan took a gulp of wine as she listened to Lucas. His post-doc story sounded like Dan's lab at the Institute. She came to JDU to build a research reputation and hoped Lucas was wrong about the department. She did not want to depend only on Dan for research inspiration and encouragement. But it would also be difficult to go it alone. Listening to Lucas she began to realize this faculty thing was not going to be as easy as she had expected.

Lucas reached for the wine bottle and refilled his glass. "I would like to solve the mind-body problem following in the footsteps of Descartes," he said with a grin.

Susan laughed. "Descartes' theory failed. He thought mind and brain connected through the pineal gland. I assume you want to form a valid mind-body theory. If that's your ambition and you're successful, it would make *you* famous."

Lucas leaned over and tapped his wine glass against Susan's. "I came to JDU to escape the competitive Ivy League establishment, and you came as a steppingstone to going back. Here's to our first year and our ambitions—let's see how it turns out."

T E N

Susan lingered at the doorway while three hundred students walked around her like waves flowing past the bow of a ship. A few gave her curious stares as they jostled to lay claim to a preferred seat in the large lecture hall. She wondered if she looked as terrified as she felt. A long, sloping staircase led from the rear of the auditorium to the podium in front of the class. When most of the students were seated, she started her descent. Luckily, she did not stumble as hundreds of pairs of eyes followed her progress to the front of the hall. Struggling to control her terror, she wrote her name on the chalkboard and turned toward the wall of faces rising before her. The room grew silent. The long-anticipated fall term was about to begin.

"Welcome to Psychology 100, Introduction to Psychology. I'm Doctor Barron, and this is my first year of teaching at James Douglas." She started well, speaking with confidence to hide the truth that it was her first year of teaching anywhere. "I'm happy to be here in the Pacific Northwest and I hope—"

There was a loud moan and a faceless male voice boomed from the back of the hall. "This is Canada, and this is the Pacific *Southwest!*" An uneasy twitter spread over the class while the students waited for her reaction. Susan's cheeks burned. "Thanks for the reminder," she croaked, her voice trembling. Being the butt of student ridicule in the first five minutes of the class was not the brilliant beginning to the term she had imagined. She cleared her throat and shuffled through her notes desperate to find a starting point. The question *What is psychology?* leapt from the page. Relieved, she launched into her answer to this familiar question, but it was too late to repair her shattered confidence. The forty-five-minute class seemed endless as Susan limped through her meticulously prepared opening notes. She had fantasized a sparkling first lecture. Instead, her voice was quivering and hesitant. Her greatest fear was confirmed. She was not inspirational; she was boring.

Humiliated and frustrated, Susan rushed across campus to the sanctuary of her office. She ached for reassurance that her first lecture was not the disaster she feared it to be. In New York she would have turned to Julie. But her pride would not let her call Julie for help after only a few weeks in British Columbia. She thought of Lucas. Their parting was friendly. He had even brushed her cheek with a chaste swipe of his lips when she left his suite after dinner. But his amused mockery of her career ambitions nagged at her. It was too soon to think of Lucas as a friend. Exhausted, Susan sat at her desk, massaging her temples to calm her distress. The reality of her isolation slapped her in the face.

She started at the shrill ring of her office phone. "Hi, Sue, how're things going? Did you have your first class yet?" Dan's cheerfulness increased her despair. He could not give the moral support she craved, and she would not ask for it. "I'm doing okay—things are falling into place," Susan lied.

"I'm calling with the latest news about the book. Two colleagues back in New York have signed a contract to write a textbook like ours. The publisher wants to move up the chapter deadlines so that our book hits the market first. I need you to come to Vancouver this weekend so we can set up an accelerated writing schedule. You said you would be willing to do that, didn't you?" The sarcasm in Dan's voice rekindled the memory of the embarrassing scene on the ferry a few weeks ago.

"Yes, I said that," Susan agreed with a sigh. Her promise made from self-defense to deflect Dan's advances trapped her. "I'm very busy, but I guess I can take the ferry to Vancouver on Saturday."

"Good, we need to move fast now that we have competition. I'll call again at the end of the week with directions to my office." A brisk click and Dan was off the line.

Almost simultaneously, she heard a light rap on her office door. Swinging it open, she found a slim, sandy-haired man with a wry grin on his face. "Hi, Doctor Barron, do you have a few minutes to talk?" Surprised, Susan ushered him into her office, then sat behind the protective barrier of her desk. He looked like a student and today she needed protection from students.

"I'm Bob Van Holland. I'm your teaching assistant for the Intro Psych course." He paused, sensing her confusion. "I'm a neuropsychology grad student—working on my dissertation with Otto Hartmann," he explained.

"No one told me I had a teaching assistant," Susan countered.

Bob gave a sarcastic snort. "That's not surprising. Information sharing is not a strong suit in this department."

"What does a teaching assistant do around here?" Susan asked.

"The usual stuff—grading, office hours—I don't mind giving a lecture or two as long as it doesn't interfere with data collection for my dissertation. The TA thing is sixty hours for the term." A smirk spread across Bob's face. "It never takes that much time, though. Most of the students in the Intro classes don't give a sh—" Bob coughed and corrected himself. "I mean, the course has a reputation as an easy elective so the students don't demand much."

"I had a terrible first Intro class." Susan groaned. "I can use all the help I can get."

Bob regarded her with suspicion. Susan wondered if her outburst was trampling on forbidden ground, violating department norms of graduate student–faculty relationships. To her surprise, she did not care. She was only a few months beyond being a graduate student herself, and Bob seemed more likely to be on her side than any other person within easy reach.

"What happened?" Bob asked. He sounded curious rather than concerned.

Susan described the incident and how it had shattered her equilibrium for the rest of the class. "Of course, I've taught before," Susan said, embellishing her very limited classroom experience. "But the size of this class is daunting. When the chairman told me I would be teaching Intro, I had no idea the class would be so large." Susan groaned again.

Bob pursed his lips. "There are a few anti-American students around. They think the universities in BC are too much like those in the States and there are too many professors from the States. They don't like that. Sounds like you ran into one of those students. They're a minority here so I wouldn't worry about it." Susan was only partially reassured. There may be only a few students at JDU who hated the States, but unfortunately one of them was lurking in her class.

"I could come to the next class and introduce myself as your TA and a bona fide Canadian from Alberta if you want." Susan took his comment as more of a joke than a sincere offer of help. Bob just told her he was expecting an easy TA assignment and not a rescue mission for a hapless new professor. Susan declined. "Thanks, but I'll deal with this on my own."

Bob cleared his throat. "I see you're scheduled to teach the grad proseminar section in cognitive psychology."

"Yes, the first class is tomorrow. I never heard of a proseminar before, but I was told it's a class to expose first-year grad students to areas of psychology they missed as undergraduates. I was surprised by the idea of remedial work for grad students, but it's only six weeks so it should be okay—don't you think?" Susan watched a furrow deepen on Bob's forehead.

"The grad students hate the proseminar. They don't think they need any remedial work, as you put it, because, after all, they're in grad school." Bob looked uneasy, like a spy betraying a secret code to the enemy. He lowered his voice to a conspiratorial whisper. "You may get a lot of resistance from the grad students in the proseminar. The new profs are assigned the course because the tenured profs don't want to handle the student hostility."

Susan's stomach clenched. "Is it that bad?"

"It can be," Bob replied. "Most of the new profs survive but not without scars." He shrugged. "I think the grad student–faculty relationships in this department are a delicate truce—hostilities can break out at any time." Bob rose and started toward the door. "If you need me for anything, leave a note in my mailbox. Otherwise, I'll see you around the time of the first exam. Good luck with the Intro class. Remember, the anti-American students are a minority."

* * * * * * * * * * * * * *

Susan stood at her office window admiring the lawn outside. It shimmered like a brilliant green carpet under the September sun. She heard the slam of doors and a jumble of voices as the Friday afternoon regulars at the faculty club left the department for their pre-weekend round of drinks. Exhausted, she tried to recall any positive moments from the first week of classes to elevate her mood.

The highlight was her cognitive psychology class filled with ten eager psychology majors. By chance, she met Giles in the hallway on her way to the first class. When he discovered her destination, he scowled. "We can't afford to let low enrollment courses like cognitive psychology continue for much longer. I'm sure a bright spark like you will have the students knocking on your door and enrolling in your classes in no time flat. Your good looks should have the male students standing in line, at least." Giles glared at Susan with a look of malevolent sarcasm familiar to her from her encounters with Leonard Wesselman, the lab senior professor at the Institute. It was a look perfected by older male academics to indicate, at best, discomfort and, at worst, disdain for the presence of young women colleagues in their formerly completely male domain. It was a look that challenged her to either blush at the compliment, which was the traditional feminine reaction, or to reveal her feminist leanings with a witty but biting retort—something like "I think I have more to offer psychology students than my looks." Based on her experience with similar situations as a female in an all-male lab group, she opted for a withering look and a curt response of "I'm late for class." She left Giles standing in the middle of the hallway as she hurried toward her classroom. Despite Giles, Susan was determined to retain her enthusiasm for teaching cognitive psychology. To her relief, the students responded well to her outline of topics and assignments and the term appeared to be off to a promising start.

Her buoyant mood disappeared after the graduate proseminar convened later in the day. She scanned the six faces scattered around the seminar table, while six pairs of sullen eyes inspected her. Several of the students, judging by the graying hair and weathered skin, were middle-aged. "This seminar is a condensed version of my undergraduate cognitive psychology course," she announced as she distributed a handout outlining the six-week sequence of topics. Protests arose. They were graduate students and expected something more rigorous. Happy to accommodate, Susan launched into her prepared lecture and diagramed a flowchart of connected boxes on the chalkboard.

"This is the way cognitive psychologists have modeled the stages of human information processing from perception to long-term memory. Each stage is studied separately, and our discussion will progress from the early to the late stages over the next six weeks," Susan intoned.

An older male student interrupted. "I think it's ridiculous to conceive of the human mind like this. I agree with William James. We have a stream of consciousness—we don't have discrete boxes in our head that connect to each other with arrows. We're not computers."

"You're right," Susan responded. "Contemporary cognitive psychologists use a computer analogy and these flowcharts to model the stages of cognition. But there are other ways to think about the mind and James's way is certainly legitimate. I thought I'd start out with the current approach and, once you've mastered that, we can make comparisons and debate other points of view." The promise of future debates did not have a calming effect. Disgruntled, other students joined in denouncing computer models of the mind, arguing that cognitive psychology was headed in the wrong direction and away from its roots. Finally, Susan sunk into her chair and said, "Here's a list of assigned readings for the class next week. Let's call it quits for today."

The term just started, and she moaned, mulling over the future facing her. Her most extreme trial by far was the large Intro Psychology class. She must control her stress if she was going to survive the class. There had been no more sarcastic explosions from the throng of Intro Psych students, but the threat was always there. It was a subtle presence eroding her tenuous confidence and causing her insides to cramp as she approached the lecture hall. Her inner turmoil was now a conditioned response. Already, she had adopted the habit of ducking into the nearest restroom for relief before the class started. After only a few class sessions, the lecture hall had become a conditioned stimulus and her stomach cramps a conditioned response. Susan's idea of teaching as a simple extension of the student life she loved was destroyed. After one week she realized that teaching would consume, not only minutes and hours, but days of her time. She was terrified by the obvious certainty there would be no time left for writing and research.

Susan collapsed into her office chair, craving a drink. She laughed. How would her male colleagues respond if she joined them at the faculty club? Other than a few grunts of greeting in the faculty mailroom, Susan had never spoken to any of the drinking group other than Giles. What do they talk about every Friday afternoon? Susan was confident they did not debate the latest hot research topic. The few scholars in the department were not part of the faculty club regulars. Judging by the crests and emblems on their clothes, these male colleagues were likely discussing either golf or sailing. She fantasized a strained hour of small talk with this group of middle-aged male colleagues as they struggled to find a common ground for conversation with her. She was sure they would be unable to refrain from snide references to her femaleness, something like, "What is a nice girl like you doing in cognitive psychology?" She heard variations on this theme often enough to want to avoid further exposure to a question not asked of a man in her situation.

Susan gathered her jacket and briefcase stuffed with weekend work and headed toward the parking lot. Her drinking companion for tonight was the bottle of wine sitting on her kitchen counter at home. The wine would not ask irritating questions.

ELEVEN

A picnic lunch on The Castle veranda was an unexpected treat on this warm October day. The shoreline and the mountains beyond were exceptionally clear and beautiful. The mountain range appeared to be within easy reach, even though Susan knew the waters of the Strait of Juan de Fuca stretched between where she sat on Vancouver Island and the Olympic Peninsula of Washington. She had learned that much about the local geography during her first weeks in Victoria. Susan inhaled, enjoying the clean, briny odor of salt and seaweed. The gentle slap of waves against the sandy beach was tranquil and soothing. For a few minutes, at least, she was at peace.

Today was the start of a long weekend. Susan was elated to discover that the Thanksgiving holiday in Canada was celebrated on the second Monday of October. As a celebration of the harvest season, the Canadian choice of date made more sense than the late November Thursday in the States. Susan bit into her tuna sandwich and eavesdropped on the chatter of students sitting on a nearby bench. She heard snatches of holiday plans—group Thanksgiving dinners and excursions to local pubs. Sounded like fun, although holiday festivities were not part of her weekend plans. The next three days would be dedicated to writing. A month had passed, and her chapter outline lay neglected on her desk. It was time to tackle the writing that hung over her head like an ever-present, dense cloud.

Teaching was a painful and emotionally wearing ordeal. She endured the lectures to her large Intro Psychology class, but the calm she sought remained elusive. Tension gripped her stomach as she walked down the steps to the podium, so she began each class in a state of contained panic. Thankfully, the students appeared unaware of her inner turmoil. Susan attributed their benign attitude to the general indifference toward the course as described by Bob, her TA.

The six-week proseminar was near an end and she had survived the experience—just barely, but she survived. The belligerent debates and challenges continued during each class. One male student liked to display his self-proclaimed superior knowledge of cognitive psychology. He said he had several courses on the topic as an undergraduate, leaving Susan to wonder why he was enrolled in the remedial class. Susan listened patiently to his frequent ill-informed theoretical challenges. It was obvious he was lying about his background. She wondered who he was trying to impress, the other students or her. Either way, she endured and sometimes even triumphed over his relentless academic assaults. She was happy to turn the group over to Jack Bernoski who was scheduled to teach the next segment of the class. She wanted to warn Jack about the class atmosphere, but his general unfriendliness during their brief encounters in the department hallways made her reluctant to approach him. He would have to discover the graduate student disdain without any prior alerts from her.

One afternoon she saw Lucas alone in his office—a rare occasion as he was often occupied with graduate student consultations. She knocked on the open door and, without invitation, plopped into the chair beside his desk with a frustrated groan. Lucas was reassuring as she complained about the proseminar exchanges. "Students always try to show you up, especially when you're new. It happens to all of us. I admit male students may be more aggressive toward a female professor teaching the class. You'll get used to handling these situations once you've taught awhile."

Susan relaxed. "Is that the wisdom you gained from your post-doc years?" she teased.

Lucas leaned back in his chair, his expression thoughtful. "Yeah, partially—I didn't have to teach but I wanted to expand my experience, so I took on some tough night class assignments in Boston. The students were older, vocal, and relentless in their demands so I'm a veteran of trial-by-fire teaching." Lucas joked, "You'll know you're getting old when students no longer think you're too young and too green to know what you're talking about." He added, "From what I'm told, the proseminar is a particularly difficult class to teach. The grad students resent being identified as having gaps in their psychology background. Many of them were undergraduates in the department," Lucas laughed, "so what does that tell you about the quality of the undergraduate major here?"

Susan shrugged. She had not thought about the graduate students' backgrounds or about the department's academic rigor. "Do they want a refund on their undergrad tuition seeing as it was inadequate preparation for grad school?" Susan's tone was facetious.

Lucas responded with a chuckle and a warning. "Don't suggest that, or there may be a revolt. The grad students are already edgy about perceived faculty indifference to their progress." Lucas smiled at Susan. "There's hope on the horizon because of a department movement to revise the undergraduate major—make it more demanding with broader coverage of all the areas of psychology. If that happens, the proseminar goes away, making both the grad students and the faculty happy."

"I hope that happens soon. I don't know how many more of these tug-of-war proseminar sessions I can handle." Susan bit her lip as she watched Lucas bend over his desk and pick up a pen. She appreciated his big grin of encouragement.

Susan checked her watch—almost three o'clock. There was no department meeting this Friday afternoon because the faculty had fled for the holiday weekend. Everyone had plans for a festive get-together—only she had plans to work. Susan gathered up the detritus of her picnic lunch and walked up the hill to the psychology department. The tomblike silence of the empty building reverberated around her. It was strange how stillness could boom like a clap of thunder. Susan shuffled through the vacant hallway.

Every closed faculty office door taunted her loneliness as the click of her key echoed down the deserted corridor. She needed two things—to overcome her holiday weekend apathy and, most importantly, to work on the book. She surveyed the research materials scattered across her desk. They were a reminder of her meeting a few weeks ago with Dan in Vancouver.

She had arrived at Dan's campus office around noon on a Saturday as agreed.

"You're looking none the worse for wear after your first days as a professor. How're things going?" Dan eyed her, sounding grumpy.

She ignored his question and gestured around his office instead. "Your office is about the same size as mine. I thought you'd have a big office like the senior faculty at JDU."

Dan leaned back in his chair with an exasperated sigh. "I'm disappointed with my office. I can't even fit a sofa." Dan gestured toward a tiny upholstered two-seater, and Susan sat down. Given its dimensions, it was unlikely that this loveseat would become as notorious as the sofa in Dan's office at the Institute. Susan stifled a giggle.

"You're never told the truth when you're interviewed, especially if the department really wants you. No one told me the department has a space problem and psychology faculty have offices all over campus. Everyone talked about a new building for the department. When I got here, I found out the new building is probably ten years away, if it happens at all. I was promised four to five lab rooms, but I have only two rooms in the basement of the building and they are crammed with boxes of lab equipment I can't unpack because there's no space." Dan swiveled in his chair with impatience. "I've had one of my ideas stolen. I discussed a theory I was developing with George Millson when he visited my lab at the Institute last year. I just opened the latest issue of the *Journal of Experimental Psychology* and he's published a set of experiments based on my theory with no mention of my contribution. I guess he thought I wouldn't notice his theft since I'm not in New York anymore." Dan looked bereft.

"It's hard to believe a big name like Millson would do something like that without giving you credit or a co-authorship," Susan murmured.

"That's exactly the point—he's a big name while I'm relatively new in the field, so who's going to believe it was my idea first?" Dan sputtered. "It's even more important now to get the book out—really establish my name so this sort of piracy won't happen to me again." Watching Dan's fury, Susan sent a mental thank you note to George Millson for focusing Dan's attention on the book. The sexual advance on the ferry would not be repeated this day.

* * * * * * * * * * * * *

Susan leaned against her kitchen window, sipping her brandy and watching the sky darken. Victoria spread beneath her with the glittering splendor of city lights. The British Columbia Parliament complex was visible in the distance. The building was adorned with light bulbs outlining the shadowy contours of the structure. She liked the gaudy effect, even though long-time residents mocked it as being an ostentatious display of pseudo-Victorian grandeur. The windows of her suite, balanced above the treetops, gave her a view of the city shared only by birds in flight.

The brandy and the serenity of the incandescent city eased her isolation. Susan thought about calling Julie, but she knew if she did, Julie would hear the loneliness in her voice. A series of probing questions to assess depression would be the result if she spoke to her friend tonight. She must get used to spending holiday weekends alone. She could not go whining to Julie every time the sharp pangs of homesickness gripped her. Susan sighed and refilled her glass. She jerked with surprise, spilling brandy on the kitchen counter, when she heard a sharp rap on the front door of her suite. Opening it, she found a woman standing on the landing in the outside hallway.

"Hi, nice to see you again." The woman shoved her open hand toward Susan. Susan, mellowed by brandy and startled by the appearance of an unexpected visitor, stood silent in the open doorway. The woman withdrew her hand and explained, "I'm Wanda Martin. I'm a psychology grad student at JDU and the grad student representative at the faculty meetings. I've seen you a couple of times at department meetings, but maybe you don't remember me."

"Oh, of course, I didn't recognize you at first—it must be the different context—I mean, I didn't expect to see you here." Susan was confused. "Is there some reason why you've stopped by?" she asked, wondering how Wanda knew her home address.

"Oh, I haven't stopped by—I live downstairs on the second floor. I haven't had time until today to come up and welcome you to the building." Wanda smiled.

Susan motioned Wanda through the door, grateful for the unexpected reprieve from her aching loneliness. "I was having a glass of brandy. Want one?"

"Sure, why not?"

Susan entered the kitchen, poured brandy into a small juice glass, and handed it to Wanda. Wanda left the kitchen, sipping her brandy. She wandered into the living room and inspected the tattered carpet and faded wallpaper with a jaundiced eye. The windows of her suite offered great views in all directions, but Susan was acutely aware of its shabby appearance. Wanda's obvious contempt for the décor was evident in the disdainful expression barely hidden behind the glass pressed against her lips.

"My suite has been refurbished." Wanda twirled around in the center of the living room with a superior air. "Of course, I insisted on a number of modifications before I moved in—I wasn't going to live in squalor. Some day you should come downstairs and look at my suite. You can do a lot with some paint and good taste."

Susan bristled but stifled a sarcastic retort. "I didn't bring much with me from New York because I didn't have much to bring. I'm grateful the owner let me use some of the furniture stored downstairs."

"Your suite has a great view of downtown Victoria. You're lucky." Wanda walked to a window to admire the view.

"Yeah, the view is fantastic," Susan agreed. "It's the reason I rented the suite. As for the rest...." Susan shrugged. "I spend most of my time on campus, and when I'm here I spend most of my time sitting at a window transfixed by the view. That's what I was doing when you knocked on the door."

Wanda seated herself on the edge of Susan's sagging sofa. "Speaking of campus," Wanda began. "I wanted to talk to you about something related to the department."

Susan sat down on the opposite end of the sofa and waited. "I'm more mature than most of the graduate students in the department. I already have a master's degree in neuropsychology. I was teaching at a college back east when I decided to get a PhD, so I came here to study with Otto Hartmann."

Susan interrupted, "If you want me to be on your dissertation committee, you could've come to see me in my office."

Wanda reacted with irritation. "No, it's nothing like that. My committee is already set up. This is a little hard to say...." Wanda stood up and moved to one of the two chairs in the room so she could face Susan. "We're both members of the same department, and you may run into people from the department who come to visit me—in the hallway or stairwell as they come in and out of the building."

Susan was puzzled. She had no idea where this conversation was headed. "Okay, so what?" she replied.

"I hope both of us are discreet enough to realize that, although we live in the same building and work in the same department, we're entitled to our private lives—whatever goes on in our homes isn't a topic for department gossip."

Susan studied Wanda and wondered what was going on in Wanda's suite that would generate department gossip. Her mind danced over a few tantalizing possibilities—seances, sex parties, maybe satanic worship.

"Wanda, I don't know a lot of people in the psychology department yet. If I met someone in the hallway here, I might not know they were in the department. As far as telling people about what goes on in the building, I don't think anyone knows I live here. I would have to tell someone that I live in the same building as you, and then tell them about who comes to see you. I have no idea who I would talk to in the department about your visitors." Susan finished the remains of her brandy. "I find this conversation amazing given I just found out today, after six weeks of living here, that you live downstairs. *We* don't run into each other in the hallway."

Susan expected Wanda to be embarrassed. Instead, she gulped her drink and looked relieved. "Just as long as we agree not to gossip about each other." She rose, handed her empty glass to Susan, and headed toward the door. "I'm not like most of the other grad students here. I used to be a faculty member myself and my friendships are more mature than those of the other neuropsychology grad students."

Wanda opened the door to the suite and stepped out into the hallway. "Thanks for the glass of brandy," she called over her shoulder as she headed down the stairs.

Susan shut the door and leaned against the door frame. She looked at the two empty glasses in her hands and laughed. What was Wanda doing that made her so paranoid about department gossip? Susan hoped Wanda was right when she said she was not like the other graduate students. They cannot all be as silly and pretentious as Wanda, Susan hoped. Eventually she would discover what Wanda's visit was all about.

TWELVE

Susan slammed her car door and headed toward her office. It was a brilliant clear Thanksgiving Monday morning and Susan pondered visiting the Butchart Gardens. The brochure on the ferry described it as Victoria's world-renowned tourist attraction, beautiful to visit at any time of year. Obedient to her internal censor, she opted for another day of work instead. She would only feel worse wandering through gardens alone surrounded by festive family groups and couples enjoying the holiday weekend.

Her unrelenting loneliness ached inside her like an infected organ. She could feel its presence as a physical pain. Susan blamed her edginess and morose mood on her solitary existence devoid of physical contact. No one had touched her for months except for Lucas's chaste good-bye peck on the cheek after their dinner together. Her usual optimism was gone, and she was having difficulty concentrating on her work. The last two days had been a constant struggle, and she was not satisfied with the quality of her writing even after the long hours of effort.

She recalled the research with babies raised in orphanages, placed in cribs, and ignored by caregivers. Compared to infants living in families, where they were cuddled, spoken to, and given constant attention, the orphanage babies languished and failed to thrive. Their isolation caused delays in social and cognitive development. Close personal contact was an important part of normal human development, and there were psychologists who argued the need for physical contact with another human was innate. Susan wondered if the same isolation effects happened to adults. Was her cognitive disintegration and desolation related to her solitary existence—never touched, never spoken to, just like the orphanage babies?

When she was married, Paul was always there. They enjoyed each other's bodies and touched a lot both in and out of bed. After the divorce, she was surrounded by men in the lab group who were happy to hold her hand, give her a hug, and join her in bed if the mood hit. Julie was a hugger, but even that human contact was gone and Susan missed it—all of it.

In the absence of a sex life and with the lingering memory of a brief kiss on the cheek, Susan was fantasizing about Lucas. She put herself to sleep imagining the two of them together. Each night these hypnotic dreams grew more explicit. She felt drawn toward Lucas, but her attraction was becoming an obsession fueled by hours of miserable solitude. She wanted their friendship to evolve into an affair. At the same time, she longed for her desire to subside, chiding herself that her fixation was the product of loneliness. An affair with a colleague was not a wise way to start at JDU. Susan's casual affairs in the months after her divorce were temporary. The graduate students at the Institute knew they would move on to another place, another life, and another partner. No one took these brief couplings seriously. After her visit from Wanda Martin, Susan suspected personal relationships among members of the department were not treated as casually here as at the Institute.

Susan's daydreams were interrupted by Jim Kracknoy's voice ricocheting down the empty hallway when she entered the building. "Susan, what are you doing here on a holiday?" Jim stood in front of his open office doorway with a carafe of water in one hand. "I thought I'd be here alone today. Come into my office for a few minutes. I was just about to make a pot of coffee."

"I could ask you the same question, Jim. What're you doing here on a holiday?"

"Come in, come in." Jim gestured toward the loveseat opposite his desk while he fussed with the coffee maker. "I have to finish the department undergraduate curriculum revisions. As usual, Giles did nothing after the department vote and so I'm here to do what I usually do—clean up the administrative details Giles avoids. I'm sure he's sailing somewhere and could care less about whether these changes get into next year's calendar. Students are not a high priority for Giles." Jim slumped into the chair behind his desk and retrieved two coffee mugs from a desk drawer. The aroma of brewing coffee permeated the office.

"How're things going? I haven't seen much of you since the day you arrived. The start of the term is always hectic for me. Giles either neglects a lot of administrative things or he does them so incompetently I have to redo them in order not to offend the dean. Our dean is a stickler for filling out forms correctly—he sees that as the primary responsibility of a department chairman." Jim poured two mugs of coffee and slid one across the desk toward Susan.

Susan took a sip and relaxed against the cushions. She savored the intimacy of being one of two people in an empty building on a holiday weekend. "Jim, could I ask you a few questions about the department?"

Jim smiled at Susan over his coffee mug and nodded. "Sure, what do you want to know?" Susan was grateful he seemed willing to talk.

"I was wondering how Giles became chairman. He's negative about psychology and research, and he doesn't seem to like being chairman."

"It didn't take you long to pick up on the enigma of Giles," Jim said, chuckling. "Let's see, where can I start? Giles has been in the department about fifteen years. By the time I got here six years ago he was one of JDU's most controversial faculty members. He had the reputation of being an awful teacher who would verbally berate his students. Students complained that his course content was light, and they didn't learn anything. Bill Forsyth, who was chairman at the time, was tired of the chronic complaints about Giles and his teaching." Jim stopped and took a sip of coffee. "Giles's research also caused some damage to his reputation. He sought permission from the feds in Ottawa to study the effect of marijuana on classical conditioning. The feds turned him down, and this caused a public scandal—got written up in the local and campus newspapers, that sort of thing. I don't know whether the publicity was about Giles wanting to do research with marijuana or that the feds wouldn't allow the research. The upshot of all of this made Giles bitter about the whole research process."

"How did Giles get tenure and promotion?" Susan asked.

Jim gave Susan an ironic grin. "Good question—I wasn't here at the time and Bill Forsyth doesn't talk about Giles and his tenure. I can only speculate that the department and university were expanding back then, and they needed faculty. The standards of evaluation were much looser when he arrived, and this is another source of bitterness for Giles. He frequently complains that he wouldn't cut it under today's more rigorous tenure evaluation procedures."

"Yeah, I've heard him say that," Susan agreed.

"But I haven't answered your original question—how did Giles become chairman?" Jim furrowed his brow. "Bill Forsythe wanted to step down as chairman. Otto wasn't interested—he's too wrapped up in his research and students. The other senior faculty weren't interested either. Giles was the only likely candidate left. The department voted him chairman for several reasons—the reasons differ depending on whom you talk to. Since the chairman gets a two-course teaching release, a few department members thought this perk would get Giles out of the classroom and cut down on the student complaints about his teaching. Others thought the job would be therapeutic and stop Giles from spending almost every evening drinking at the faculty club. Another group thought being chairman would improve his attitude toward psychology because he would have to represent the department's interests to the administration in a positive way. Put all these groups together and there were enough votes to make him chairman."

Jim waved his hands to emphasize his point, and then continued. "Giles used this opportunity to push for promotion to full professor. He claimed he couldn't be an effective chairman as an associate professor. The department obliged and put him up for promotion. Since Giles was the only alternative for chairman at the time, the president promoted him."

Jim added, "I know all of this may sound odd to a newcomer, but Giles has been chairman for about three years now and between the two of us we do a pretty good job of handling things." Jim leaned forward and patted the stack of papers on his desk. "He can't do too much damage because I keep close tabs on him. Since he has little interest in the job, he usually takes my suggestions on what to do." Jim turned thoughtful. "And some faculty members were right—Giles doesn't drink as much these days and there are certainly fewer student complaints about him. He still has a negative view of psychology, but most people around JDU ignore that."

Jim sat back and smirked. "Giles does love the title of chairman, though. He had a big button made—the one he wears at student registration—to make sure everyone knows he's chairman of the psychology department. If he didn't think it would look too ridiculous, my guess is he'd wear it all the time."

"That's quite a story. Are all decisions around here made like that?" Susan asked.

Jim laughed. "Well, we *are* psychologists, aren't we? Therapeutic motivations are part of our training and heritage. They're in our blood."

"I've another question. Giles told us at the meeting of new faculty that the department expected all of us to teach Introductory Psychology, but neither Lucas nor Jack is teaching Intro this term. Giles said one thing, but the actual teaching loads are not what he said they would be."

For the first time during their conversation Jim hesitated. "Jack taught Intro in Nova Scotia, but you're right, he hasn't taught it here yet. We're looking toward starting a graduate program in gerontology, so we preferred that he teach developmental courses for a few years. We think we're well situated to go in that direction because Victoria is a retirement community with lots of retirees as potential subjects for research. There's an old saying around here, 'Victoria is the place for the newlywed and nearly dead.' We're interested in the 'nearly dead' part of the local population."

Susan nodded. "I've heard Victoria called that—it's not a flattering description, but I can see how the demographic is useful from a research perspective."

Jim chuckled, and then continued. "Lucas was hired to add another researcher to the neuropsychology group. Lucas is willing to teach Intro, but we thought he would fit our needs better if he taught graduate neuropsychology courses and undergraduate abnormal psychology. Besides, I'm quite sure he's being bombarded with grad student requests to be on dissertation committees and to supervise research."

Jim smiled at Susan. "That leaves you to explain. Your situation as far as the department goes is more complicated. Our undergrad students don't have much interest in classic experimental psychology areas. But the department recognizes we need faculty members like you to give methodological guidance to the neuropsychology grad students and to serve on their dissertation committees. We need faculty who understand the new research techniques the grad students must use to complete their dissertation research. We justified your appointment to the dean by saying you could advise grad students and you could teach high enrollment undergraduate courses, like Intro. We couldn't have hired you otherwise. Your specialty doesn't attract a lot of undergraduate student interest and we don't have a graduate program in experimental or cognitive psychology."

Despite Jim's soothing tone, Susan's self-esteem ebbed. She did not see herself as someone to be justified. "Is that why the department didn't invite me for a job interview before I was hired?" Susan asked.

Jim gave a hearty laugh. "No, no—not interviewing when we hire was Larry Goldblatt's idea. We've had trouble keeping new faculty in the past few years. Candidates are hired and then leave after a year or two or we hire them with the commitment they'll get their PhDs within a year and then they don't, and we must terminate them. We had a hell of a mess two years ago when we lowered the boom on a guy after one year and he complained all over campus and went to the press. There were student protests in the department because he was quite popular—it was very unpleasant." Jim scowled. "It was after this incident that Larry Goldblatt…have you met Larry yet?"

Susan shook her head.

"Well, you will eventually. Larry's antisocial. He sails a lot, too, like Giles, although that's about the only thing the two have in common. Larry's a radical behaviorist, and he's always been critical of our hiring practices. He argues the department would have the same success rate hiring new faculty and keeping them if we took all the applicants for a position and chose one at random—no interview, no research colloquium—nothing. Usually, Larry's mutterings about the uselessness of the search process are ignored, but last year the time must've been right. Many of the faculty, especially Giles, were still upset about the student protests and the bad publicity of the year before. So, the department voted to change the search procedures to eliminate campus interviews. We agreed that the various search committees would choose the top three candidates for each position and the job would be offered to the top candidate first."

Anticipating Susan's next question, Jim added, "We followed this procedure for all three vacant positions. Lucas and Jack didn't visit campus for interviews either. I guess time will tell whether or not this experiment is any better than the old way of doing things." Jim shrugged.

Susan stared at Jim. It unnerved her to learn that she had to be justified to the dean *and* she was part of a department experiment. Susan was desperate to ask if she was the top candidate for her position, but she lacked the courage to hear the answer. Instead, she looked at her watch. She and Jim had been talking for over an hour.

"Thanks for taking the time to fill me in on the department." Susan pursed her lips and exhaled in a long sigh. "You certainly have given me a lot to think about."

Jim stood up behind his desk. "Are you alright? I didn't upset you, did I? Sometimes I worry I reveal too much to new faculty about the skeletons in the closet around here."

Susan looked up at Jim. "I guess I'm just used to a department that takes psychology and scholarly work more seriously than seems to be the case here."

Jim frowned and cocked his head to one side. "People in the department take psychology seriously, but many don't let it dominate their lives. I know what you're used to, especially since you work with Dan who is a driven guy—he was like that even as a grad student at Stanford. There are faculty here who don't do research, but there are others like Otto who have an active lab with lots of grad students. The dean and the president want to increase the university's research profile—more grants, more high-profile research projects, that sort of thing. That's why new hires like you, Jack, and Lucas are important. You'll move us away from JDU's old teacher's college tradition toward the research university that the dean and president want."

Susan gave him a wan smile. She would have appreciated compliments like "We're happy you're here" or "You're a wonderful addition to the department," but Jim just stood there sipping his coffee.

Susan rose and placed her empty mug on Jim's desk. "Has Laura come home from Stanford for the holiday weekend?" she asked.

"She's coming over to the island this morning. We're having our family Thanksgiving dinner tonight, and she'll probably stay a few more days and then fly back to California," Jim answered. "Laura's dissertation advisor asked her to consult with Dan on her research methodology, so she's spent the last couple of days in Vancouver talking with him. When she called me last night, she said Dan's been extremely helpful."

The image of Dan and Laura snuggling on the tiny sofa in Dan's office was more than Susan could bear. "Well, thanks again." Susan waved good-bye and hurried out of Jim's office. Rather than run up the stairs to her office,

Susan reversed direction and marched out of the building. Her throat burned with frustrated rage and tears stung her eyes. She had spent the weekend trying to write, while Dan was in Vancouver enjoying the company of Laura Kracknoy. She would deal with this ache in her throat and Jim's aggravating story with a good belt of brandy. No work today.

THIRTEEN

The sky was a cloudless gray, and the trees lining the sidewalk swayed with the promise of an impending storm. A downpour loomed. Susan clutched her upturned jacket collar to her throat as she hurried across campus. She had not yet recovered from her conversation with Jim Kracknoy. Last year she was a graduate student at the top of her class with a completed publication-worthy dissertation. Then the downslide started. She and Paul divorced, and her job search failed. Dan lied about arranging this job for her, and Jim Kracknoy explained she was hired to teach high enrollment courses to justify her presence in the department. She was condemned to a future of hundreds of indifferent students in a massive lecture hall as an assistant professor on the lowest rung of the faculty ladder. She was angry and felt used. At the last department meeting, Susan inspected the faculty around the table and realized why most of them were oblivious to her presence. If her appointment had to be justified to the dean, they only cared that she do what she was hired to do. Anything else was irrelevant.

Susan spied Lucas doing his Tai Chi forms on the lawn next to the Angus building. Usually he was alone, but today there was another man with him. Susan, shivering, halted and watched their synchronized movements. Their eyes were fixed in meditative gaze, oblivious to the wind and to the blowing leaves swirling around their feet. Susan and Lucas had exchanged only cursory hellos in recent weeks. They greeted each other in the department hallways, but Lucas often looked preoccupied. Susan wondered if he felt as pressured as she. Teaching was like feeding an endless fire—the process never stopped. Occasionally, she would congratulate herself for finally mastering her class preparations only to realize there was an exam to write or another article to read or discussion questions to prepare. The next class always posed an urgent demand she had to meet.

Susan sighed. She was lying to Dan about her progress on the book chapters. When he called, she cheerfully assured him her promised chapters would be finished by the end of December. She was mortified to tell him the truth about her struggles to write—only a scant few pages of one chapter lay completed on her desk.

Susan hurried into the building and headed up the stairs to the faculty mail room. As she grabbed the stack of papers from her appointed slot, she felt a tap on her shoulder. She turned to find Giles Plimley-Jones looming over her. "Can I have a word with you in my office?" He did not wait for a response but strode across the hall through his open office door. Susan followed him, her stomach churning. She remembered Giles's ominous comments at his meeting with the new faculty. "If I don't hear student complaints, you're probably okay, otherwise you'll hear from me."

Susan sat down facing Giles across his desk. Although terrifying, a meeting with the chairman about student complaints was not unexpected, she reassured herself. If her appointment had to be justified to the dean based on her ability to teach large classes, and she was failing in that requirement, then she assumed it was the duty of the chairman to speak to her. Susan clasped her hands in a white-knuckled grip and waited for the blow to fall.

"I have some good news for you," Giles said, leaning back in his chair and crossing his hands over his belt buckle. "The president's given you five thousand dollars as part of his grant program for new faculty."

Susan gushed with relief. "Giles, that's great! I know exactly how I'll use the money."

Susan waited for some sign of congratulations, but instead Giles growled. "Good. I don't want you to embarrass the department by squandering the money or giving it back unused. We've had enough of that nonsense."

"Oh, no, that won't happen. Don't worry, Giles."

Giles began shuffling through a stack of file folders on his desk. It was obvious the meeting was over. Susan rose to leave.

"I wish females would wear dresses. I don't like females wearing trousers. It's not feminine. Men like to see women's legs," Giles muttered, never lifting his eyes.

"If you're talking about me, I wear slacks because they're comfortable," Susan snapped as she left the room. She marched down the corridor, fuming at the audacity of Giles's remark. Leave it to Giles to turn a congratulatory meeting into an unpleasant encounter. As she turned the corner, she saw Lucas beckon to her from his office. He was sitting at his desk, and his Tai Chi companion was slouched in one of the office chairs. "Susan, I want you to meet Rick. He's a friend from Tai Chi class."

Rick stood and took Susan's outstretched hand in both of his. "Pleasure," he crooned, then turned toward Lucas. "I have to go, but I'll see you soon." Rick bent and kissed Lucas on the cheek. Lucas rose to give him a warm embrace. The two men kissed a second time, then Rick waved good-bye and trotted down the corridor.

Susan sunk into the chair vacated by Rick. Was Lucas expecting her to comment on the scene she had just witnessed? Not knowing what to say or what Lucas wanted her to say, Susan asked instead, "Can you come to my place for dinner sometime?"

"Sure, I can come over on Saturday," Lucas answered.

"Great. How about seven o'clock?" Susan scribbled her address on a slip of paper torn from her class notes and handed it to Lucas. "I saw you and your friend doing Tai Chi on my way back from my Intro class. The two of you look beautiful moving together."

Lucas smiled. "I like doing Tai Chi with Rick. I'm moving in with Rick and his girlfriend at the end of this month, so we'll have lots of time to practice together. They have a house in James Bay with an extra bedroom."

Susan teased, "So you're finally moving out of the suburbs and into Victoria's dreaded hippy neighborhood. What would Giles say about that?"

"Oh, he'd probably say I was being true to his image of me by moving to James Bay with the other hippies. Giles has told me a few times to stop dressing like a hippie. He sometimes mutters comments about my clothes when he passes me in the hall. It's a very passive-aggressive thing to do, but being passive-aggressive is typical Giles." Lucas laughed.

Susan agreed. "Giles does have fixed ideas about appropriate dress. He just told me he doesn't like females to wear trousers." Susan cleared her throat and tried to mimic Giles's tone of voice. "Women should wear dresses and be more feminine—show their legs—men like that."

Lucas shook his head, a look of disgust on his face. "Giles wants us to know, in his passive-aggressive way, he has power over us. He uses these offhand comments about how we dress to make us uncomfortable. He's telling us he's the boss and pleasing him is important if we want to keep our jobs."

Susan nodded and grinned at Lucas. Giles would certainly make an interesting case study for an abnormal psychology class. Unfortunately, Lucas was right. Giles was the chairman with power, so she had to tolerate his bizarre behavior. Probably a good tactic was to stay out of his way.

FOURTEEN

Susan and Lucas sat at a small folding table near a window. After Wanda Martin's visit, Susan was acutely aware of the shabbiness of her apartment. Peeling wallpaper and a grab bag of secondhand furniture did not compare to the cheerful chic of Lucas's suite. Instead, she planned to impress Lucas with the twilight view of Victoria. "It's like living in a nest," he exclaimed, and Susan nodded, pleased at his response. The windows were just above the upper reaches of the trees lining the street below. Her suite was the highest point in the surrounding neighborhood. Susan smiled. This was her comfort—her nest above the trees with her view of the city and mountains beyond.

Lucas talked enthusiastically about his move to Rick's house in James Bay. With Rick as his guide, he had discovered Beacon Hill Park, Goldstream, and the Malahat, places Susan knew about from tourist brochures on the ferry but had never seen. Her world beyond the JDU campus and her suite was the local shopping center, her source for groceries, wine, and more recently, brandy.

"What have you been doing besides working?" Lucas asked through mouthfuls of vegetable lasagna.

"Nothing," Susan answered. "I go from here to campus and back. The most interesting thing that's happened was a visit from a psychology grad student who lives downstairs." Susan described her puzzling encounter with Wanda Martin.

"The rumor is Wanda's having an affair with Carl Thorndike. If it's true, that's probably what she's worried about," Lucas offered. "Have you met Carl yet?"

"No, I've just seen him at department meetings."

Lucas settled back in his chair. "He's the one Giles was talking about at our new faculty meeting. Carl decided he was bored with studying classical conditioning in rats and pigeons and returned his grant to the government. A great embarrassment to the department and the university president but, personally, I admire his honesty. It took a lot of integrity to do what he did and not care about the consequences."

"How do you know this?" Susan asked.

"I've been to a few neuropsych grad student parties, and they love to gossip about the faculty."

"That's good to hear," Susan grunted. "I was beginning to think the JDU department was filled with social isolates indifferent to everything and everyone. I'm used to gossiping psychologists—to me it's the norm."

Lucas responded, "If you believe the grad students, there's quite a bit of gossip-worthy activity in the department."

Susan poured two glasses of brandy. She handed one to Lucas who had left the table to stretch out on the threadbare carpet. Susan took a cushion from the sofa, tossed it on the floor, and sat facing him.

"Speaking of department gossip, let me tell you about my long conversation with Jim Kracknoy." Susan repeated Jim's story about Giles's research problems and how he had come to be chairman. Susan was stunned by the incongruous chain of events, but Lucas was amused and chuckled several times while Susan talked.

"That story tells a lot about Giles and why he is the way he is," Lucas said. "Unfortunately, a guy like him can be destructive. Giles could become a bottleneck when it comes to department business, either through unintentional incompetence or intentional malice. It sounds like he's capable of both."

"Jim told me why the department didn't bother to have us visit campus for job interviews," Susan offered.

Lucas listened again and sniggered, "Jim may have told you the interview thing was a department experiment, but the grad students have a different view." Lucas sipped his brandy. "The grad students' version is that the faculty is lazy. Most of them don't like the hiring process—attending colloquia, lunches and dinners, you know, the whole interview round of activities. There are long-standing grudges between factions of the faculty, and they don't want to interact with each other more than necessary. The grad students believe the so-called department hiring experiment is just an excuse for eliminating social interactions with colleagues."

Lucas paused. "The grad students have lots of stories around the theme of faculty asocial behavior. Supposedly, a few years ago, Joyce and Ari Petras circulated a memo instructing the grad students and their faculty colleagues to stop inviting them to department parties."

Susan quipped, "The grad students can invite me to their parties. I wouldn't write any memos of refusal."

"The grad students are intimidated by you," Lucas responded. "They've heard you're working on a book, and Otto Hartmann has been singing your praises about your research potential. Otto's not easily impressed, so the grad students take his comments seriously. If you want, I'll take you with me to the next party. A group of grad students rent a house together a few blocks from here—that's where most of the parties are held."

Susan answered with surprise. "I didn't think the great Otto Hartmann knew I existed."

Lucas laughed. "According to the grad students he does, if that's any comfort."

Susan looked at the bottle of brandy and saw it was half empty. She did not remember pouring the second and third glasses for each of them.

Lucas yawned and reached out to run his fingers over Susan's hand. "Can I stay with you tonight?"

Startled, Susan studied Lucas's face. How casually he asked the question, as if it was a natural thing to do after a pleasant dinner and a few drinks. She looked at Lucas stretched out on the floor beside her. She was not drunk enough to shed her misgivings about an affair with a colleague, but she was loose enough with drink to push them out of her mind.

"I'd like that," she replied.

Without a word, Lucas rose and walked into the bedroom. Susan followed and found him standing in front of the window looking at the distant lights of downtown Victoria, his back to the room. Finally, he turned to face her and slowly pulled his caftan shirt over his head. The faint illumination from the moonlit night cast enticing shadows over his bare chest. Lucas kicked off his sandals, unzipped his jeans and stepped over them as they fell to the floor. His eyes were fixed on Susan's face, his expression was meditative. He stood naked in the shadows, waiting. Susan unbuttoned her blouse and tossed it to the floor. She fumbled with the clasp of her bra, her eyes on Lucas while he watched her undress. She dropped her slacks and faced him, naked, from across the room.

Lucas crossed the room to the bed, flung back the quilt, and lay down. Susan's eyes roamed over his body—he was not aroused. She stretched out beside him, molding her body to his contours as she pulled the bed covers over them. He turned his face toward hers and his lips touched hers. His tongue was languid as it parted her lips. Susan tingled with excitement when she returned his kiss. Her fingers slid across his abdomen as she reached for his groin, but Lucas clasped her wrist to stop her hand as she moved to caress him. He sighed, nuzzled her neck with his lips, and maneuvered his body so he could tuck spoon-like into her contours. Susan lay against him—he was still not aroused. Instead, there was a gentle rhythmic breathing on her neck, and she realized he was asleep. Susan ran her fingertips along his arm flung across her hip. His warm breath soothed her. They both had drunk a lot, Susan thought, as she dropped off to sleep.

Susan woke to the sound of choking. It was six-thirty according to the clock on the nightstand. She shivered in the morning cold and wrapped herself in the quilt. The choking sound was coming from the bathroom. Susan rubbed her eyes to wake herself when Lucas appeared, naked, at the bedroom door.

"Are you sick?" Susan asked. "Did you have too much to drink last night? I hope my cooking didn't make you sick."

Lucas crossed the room, picked up his jeans, and started to dress. "No, I'm not sick and dinner was fine. Vomiting every morning is some of the body work I do as part of my therapy. Its purpose is to clear the remnants of the previous day from your system each morning so you have a fresh start."

Susan huddled under the quilt and watched Lucas pull his shirt over his head. He sat down beside her on the bed to buckle his sandals.

"What sort of therapy do you do?" Susan was curious. Most of the psychology graduate students at the Institute had been in some sort of therapy but she had never heard of one that included daily vomiting.

"There's a psychiatrist in town, Bernie Chan, who runs groups. He uses a combination of traditional insight and talk therapies along with nontraditional body work like the morning vomiting ritual. We use aids—benches, pillows, things like that—to help release pent-up tensions stored in body parts like the neck and shoulders. We pound on pillows and push against benches and scream as part of the therapy. It's cathartic."

Lucas turned toward Susan. "I was too caught up in the East Coast academic competition to be smart and publish a lot. My ex-wife was and is incredibly ambitious, and her disdain when I decided to drop out was hard to take. I don't know how to explain it, but I have a sense of defeat I'm trying to work out. I want a new start here and to lead a more genuine life."

"Isn't it hard on your body to vomit every day?" Susan asked, mystified by this unknown therapy.

"It takes practice, but you get used to it. Putting two fingers down the throat usually starts things going."

Lucas clasped Susan's hand and stroked it. "I seem to have lost my sexual power, as Bernie puts it. It wasn't anything about you last night. I'm in a sort of transition phase right now when it comes to sex. Bernie assures me I'll come through this eventually."

"You and Rick were very affectionate in your office the other day. Is being with men part of what you're working on?"

"Did that bother you—Rick and I kissing each other?"

Susan shook her head. "No, I lived in the West Village in New York when I was a grad student and I'm used to seeing men together. I only brought it up because you said you came here to start a new life—" Susan shrugged. "I just thought maybe that was part of your new life—being with men."

Lucas smiled. "Rick and I belong to a men's group. We try to break down the barriers men have between them like not being affectionate in public for fear of being called gay. I guess you could say it's part of my new life—breaking down barriers, trying new things—new ways of personal expression."

Susan closed her fingers around Lucas's hand. "I don't care about the sex part—really, I don't. I'm grateful for your company. It's been a long time since I've been physically close to anyone."

"I'm grateful, too. It's important for me to be around ambitious people like you. I need to face my envy—my conflict that I'm probably not like you but a part of me still wants to be like you—wanting career success, publications, tenure, and fame. It's part of my therapeutic work to face my ambivalence and, hopefully, to come out on the other side okay."

Susan stiffened. "If I'm part of your therapy, then you've got the wrong person, because I'm as confused as you are and about the same things. I'm just trying to survive."

Lucas put his arm around Susan's shoulder and pulled her toward him. "I'm sorry. I put that badly. I'm not using you as a therapy prop. I know you're questioning things, too—in that way, we connect." Lucas kissed the top of her head. "It sounds like all you do is work, Susan. Maybe you'd be less burdened if you balanced your life a little—did other things. Tell you what—there'll be grad student parties at the end of the term. I'll make sure any invitations I get include you, too."

"Thanks, Lucas, I'd like that." Susan leaned her head against his chest, enjoying the firm feel of the muscles under his thin shirt.

They sat in silence for a few minutes, and then Lucas closed his eyes and began slow and methodical breathing. He slid across the bed and rolled his head from side to side with each exhaled breath. When he opened his eyes, he smiled at Susan, put his arm around her shoulder again, and gave her a light kiss on the cheek. "I have to go. I do Tai Chi with Rick on Sunday mornings." Lucas stood and moved toward the door.

Susan wrapped herself in the quilt and followed him. With a last wisp of a kiss, he left the suite and hurried down the stairs. She closed the door and walked to one of the windows to watch him drive away on the street below. When his car turned a corner and disappeared, she shuffled into the kitchen to make a pot of coffee. The familiar gurgle of the coffeemaker was comforting. Susan returned to the bedroom and stretched out on the bed to wait for her first cup.

She rejected being called ambitious, a word she associated with being grasping and shallow. Dan was the ambitious one. He was the one who worried about his position in the field and what his colleagues thought of him. She was *not* ambitious, not in the way Dan was. She agreed with Lucas about balancing her life. She understood her need, but she did not know how to achieve it. There was no lull in the constant onslaught of demands. Fear, not ambition, motivated her every day. Fear of falling behind, of appearing foolish in front of a class, of being unable to complete her chapters, of disappointing Dan because she could not live up to his expectations.

Susan hugged the quilt to smell Lucas's presence. He was troubled, and she felt protective. She understood why he often looked distracted when she saw him around the department. The image of Lucas standing naked in the moonlit shadows of her bedroom, his body, lean and muscular, still fueled her fantasies. She clung to a tiny hope that someday they would make love. But the new reality of an emerging close relationship was reassuring. She knew now they could at least be friends, and she needed a friend.

FIFTEEN

The phone rang. Dan's phone calls had a distinctive ring. It was not the sound itself but Susan's reaction to the tone that made the quality seem different than other calls. She had left a message for Dan earlier in the morning before she went to supervise a final exam. She could not deliver her chapters at the promised time, so Susan had no choice but to tell Dan the truth about her inability to write. She decided to tackle this dreaded moment today because her mood was better than it had been in months. The term was over, and tonight she was going to a party. Lucas had invited her to an end-of-term celebration thrown by the graduate students. Susan opted to ignore her lingering misgivings about Lucas using her as a therapy surrogate for his ambitious ex-wife. She preferred to believe he wanted to connect as a friend and considered tonight's invitation as a companionable date.

"Hi, Dan. Thanks for returning my call."

Dan laughed. "You must not get many phone calls if you can tell who it is before you pick up the phone."

"It's just a sixth sense I have about hearing from you," Susan teased.

"Well, what's up? Why did you call?" Dan sounded to be in a good mood. Everyone's mood lifted at the end of the term, so the timing made it easier to tell Dan the truth she had been hiding for months.

"I called because I wanted to talk to you about my book chapters."

"Great," Dan was enthusiastic. "I was going to call you about the chapters. You remember we agreed I'd go over all the chapters and do a final editing to make the writing sound consistent. I hate textbooks where you can tell that different people wrote the separate chapters. If you can get your chapters in the mail to me today, I'll have time to go over them before I shoot them off to the publisher."

Susan's voice began to shake despite her efforts to remain calm. "I can't send them today, Dan, because only one of my chapters is written—and it's only partially written. I'm hoping to finish it over the holiday break."

"What about the second chapter?"

"It won't be done by the end of December." There was silence on the other end of the phone.

"What's the problem? Why aren't you writing?"

Susan had never discussed anything personal with Dan. When her marriage was dissolving, she kept her personal trouble out of the lab. She would never have considered discussing her marriage breakup with Dan. Panicked about revealing the personal reasons for missing the deadline but too exhausted to be anything but honest, she swallowed her fear and plunged ahead.

"Teaching and lecture prep took up a lot of time this term. I really underestimated how much work it would be." Susan hesitated. "I had some rough spots in class with my students and that took an emotional toll on me. I'm doing better, but the first months were rough." The silence on the line pulsated in her ear, stoking her anxiety. She tried to gauge Dan's response. She did not expect empathy from him because she knew he had never struggled, but would he at least understand her predicament.

"The department here isn't very sociable and I haven't made friends," Susan added to fill the void. "I feel lonely and isolated. Sometimes it's been so bad I can't concentrate and, so, I can't write." Susan's voice trembled. Now that she was talking, she could not stop her confession. "I got a grant from the president's fund for new faculty, so I bought the Iconix four-channel tachistoscope I need for the millisecond timing of my experiments. When it arrived, the department technician made it clear that his priority was the equipment in Otto Hartmann's lab, which, as far as I can see, consists of a few tape recorders and slide projectors. The technician looked at the three-hundred-page manual and basically told me to forget about his help until the end of the spring term. I have this wonderful piece of state-of-the-art equipment sitting idle in my lab because I have no technical help and I'm too overwhelmed to tackle the set-up alone." Susan's voice cracked. She was close to sobbing, but she exhaled with relief. She had finally told Dan the truth.

At last, Dan spoke. "Well, Sue, I think you need some company. Are you going back east to visit your family over the holidays?"

"No. I thought I needed the time to write these chapters." Susan paused. "What do you mean I need some company?"

"Mona is taking the kids back east to visit her folks. They'll be gone until early January. Why don't I come to Victoria for a week or so, and we'll work together on your chapters like we've done with our two research papers. I'm finished with mine so I can help you with yours. If we work hard, I think we can make the deadline of December thirty-first—or come close. I can help you with your t-scope set-up, too."

Dan's offer was casual enough, but Susan's mind raced over the implications of his suggestion. To buy time she said, "As always, I'd appreciate your help. You do help me focus on my writing, and you always were a wizard with equipment."

"Well, then, it's settled," Dan answered. "I'll come to Victoria on December twenty-sixth and we'll work on your two chapters and, if there's time, on your lab equipment."

"Will you stay at the Empress again?" Susan was wary.

"I'd like to stay at your place. I want to enjoy the view of downtown Victoria you've told me about."

Susan stammered. "My suite has a great view, but it really is quite rundown. I haven't had the time to do much to it. I don't think you'll be comfortable staying at my place—not for a whole week."

Another silence fell over the phone line. When Dan spoke, he sounded impatient. "I'll be okay. I'm not a person who requires luxury accommodations." When Susan did not respond, his voice softened. "You know, Sue, sometimes having a personal connection with a colleague can lead to enhanced scholarship and productivity. It can be a good thing."

Dan's obvious intent chilled her like a dousing of ice water, and she shivered. Susan cleared her throat, aiming to take charge of the conversation. "I know the Empress is expensive and you probably can't afford to stay there for a whole week, but I can try to find a cheaper hotel."

Dan interrupted. "Sue, you just told me you're lonely and haven't made any friends. A house guest for a week will do you a world of good. Don't worry about how your suite looks—I'll get by."

Susan froze, unable to force out more words, but Dan broke the silence. He sounded cheerful and determined. "Okay, plan on my arriving sometime on December twenty-sixth. See you soon."

With a click, Dan was gone, and Susan lowered the phone receiver into her lap. With dread, she remembered Julie's warning. Susan looked at her watch and calculated the time difference. She might catch Julie at home at this time of day, so she dialed the New York area code and Julie's number. There was immediate relief when she heard Julie's business-like hello on the other end of the line.

"Julie, hi, this is Susan—bet you're surprised to hear from me."

"Susan!" Julie exclaimed. "I *am* surprised to hear from you. I guess I've been thinking no news is good news because you haven't felt the need to talk. So, what's happening—something's happening—I can hear it in your voice."

Susan sighed gratefully. Julie had not lost her clinical instincts. With a sense of release, she launched into a monologue. Extreme loneliness was changing her, she thought, as she unburdened herself. She was no longer the independent and self-possessed friend Julie knew in New York. Susan could picture Julie's smirk as she ended her story explaining the phone call from Dan.

"*Well*," Julie exhaled. "I thought you and Dan would be lovers by now. In fact, when I answered the phone and you sounded so tense, I thought you were going to tell me you were pregnant. It's a relief to know you're still in the pre-sex phase." Julie continued, "Now that I think about it, I'm not surprised Dan would put writing the book before sex. You're acting like a normal person. You're having trouble adjusting to major changes in your life. Dan is not a normal person, so moving to the West Coast, to another country, and starting a new faculty position doesn't faze him. He just keeps on doing what he always does—work."

"Julie, what should I do? Should I book a cheap hotel room? There's a nice bed and breakfast inn about two blocks from my place—I could get him a room there. Or should I agree to let him stay at my place?" Susan scolded herself—her panic and uncertainty were signs of her pathetic emotional deterioration over the past few months.

"As I see it, Sue, you have two choices. Either you sleep with him until the book is done, or you tell Dan you've changed your mind and tell him to find another co-author. You could try the hotel idea, but you may look ridiculous when he refuses to stay there and ends up at your place anyway."

"Each of us signed the contract, so I don't know if I can back out. I guess I could ask a lawyer about it—if I knew a lawyer and could afford one—which I don't, and I can't."

Julie snapped. "Look, Sue, if you continue to work with Dan, you're eventually going to sleep with him. Get used to the idea. That's how he operates. I told you months ago—Dan worked that way with Jennifer Evans, and now he'll work that way with you." Julie softened her tone. "Look, you told me being a co-author with Dan on a textbook would launch your academic career. Sex with Dan probably is the trade-off for that chance."

"I thought you told me last summer to stay away from sex with Dan. What's made you change your mind now?"

There was a long pause. "I didn't believe you last summer when you told me you weren't interested in Dan. I thought you must've strong feelings for him—maybe even be in love with him—otherwise you wouldn't be turning your life upside down to follow him to the West Coast. I thought you'd be hurt by getting involved sexually with someone as callous as Dan. I was right about him. From what you told me, it didn't take him long to make a move on you once you arrived in Vancouver. But I was wrong about you—Dan made the move, and you resisted, and you've continued to resist even though you've been desperately lonely. I'm proud of you."

"Julie, why didn't you believe me when I told you I wasn't interested in Dan?" Susan felt a twinge of betrayal.

"I found it hard to believe that someone would leave New York for an out of the way place simply for career reasons." Julie hesitated, then continued, "Last summer I didn't believe you when you said you were going to Canada because of your career. I thought you were moving for love and I was wrong. I misjudged you, Sue, and I'm sorry."

Susan heard the contrition in Julie's voice. She could not be angry with her friend for thinking she was lying about Dan. A lot of people at the Institute probably thought the same thing. She followed Dan to British Columbia because she was in love with him. She had a sudden sinking feeling—maybe Dan was one of those people.

"I've never thought of Dan in a sexual way. Sometimes he turns me on because he's said something brilliant but it's not a sexual turn-on—it's more of an intellectual rush."

"Sue, you've set yourself on a particular course, and sex with Dan may be part of the trip. You're lonely and you're horny. You had an active sex life after you and Paul divorced—but you're not a grad student any more with a ready supply of lab partners eager to hop into bed with you. It sounds like you're living a pretty isolated life. If you're not emotionally involved with Dan, maybe some regular, casual sex will be a needed diversion."

"You make it sound so simple and, maybe it is, except going to bed with Dan might interfere with—" Susan stopped.

"Interfere with what? Have you met someone you're not telling me about?"

It was impossible to hide anything from Julie even from three thousand miles. "No, not really—there's a guy in my department, another new faculty member—we've had dinner together a couple of times."

"Is he good-looking? Do you like him?"

"Yes, he's very attractive and, yes, I like him, but he's eccentric. He's caught up in a strange therapy where you do body work as he calls it."

"Yeah, oddball therapies abound on the West Coast—screaming, pillow punching, massage—that sort of thing." Julie sniggered.

"He's very busy, so we haven't seen each other much, but I'm going to a party with him tonight."

"Have you slept with him?"

Susan hedged, hoping Julie would not notice. "No, we haven't had sex."

"Well, given this new guy, keep any personal stuff with Dan out of the department. From what you've said that shouldn't be hard to do. Your colleagues sound like a disinterested bunch. Besides, Dan's married, you and he live in different cities, realistically, how often are you going to get together? Maybe this trip will be it for a while, or maybe forever—he could lose interest after the thrill of the chase is over."

"Julie, it can't be as easy as you make it sound."

Julie laughed. "When the book is in press, you can move on with your life—just don't sign any more contracts."

Susan laughed, too. "I get the picture."

"Let me know how things turn out. If you don't call me, I'll call you after the holidays."

Susan replaced the receiver after Julie hung up. Talking to Julie calmed her, but the nagging dread of dealing with Dan was as powerful as ever. She took a deep breath and exhaled to restore some internal equilibrium. It was time to forget about Dan. Tonight was party night, and she would see Lucas again.

SIXTEEN

Susan heard Lucas's car door slam and the start of his climb up the stairs. She opened the door to her suite before he could knock. Lucas laughed as he rounded the corner of the stairwell and saw her standing in the doorway. "You must be really looking forward to this party," he said, bending to brush her lips with his.

"Is it that obvious?" Susan made a gesture of helplessness. "I guess I was getting anxious you wouldn't show up—it's close to ten o'clock." Susan turned to grab her jacket and a bottle of wine.

"The party will just be getting started," Lucas answered. "We'll be right on time. The house is only a few blocks from here." Lucas helped Susan with her jacket.

Susan followed Lucas down the stairs while he explained. "The party is at a house run by a couple of grad students, Danny and Vic. They live in one of these classic Victoria mansions with lots of bedrooms they rent out to other grad students. I don't know how many students live there because the couples in the various bedrooms come and go. Danny and Vic have been at JDU for a while, so they act like house parents—organize the rent, set down the house rules, that sort of thing."

"Sounds like you've been there before," Susan said as she settled into the front seat of Lucas's car.

"Yeah, I've been to a couple of parties. Danny and Vic like to share their drug stash, and because so many students live in the house it's almost like the place is a constant party. Tonight will be a big event because it's the end of the term and everyone wants to celebrate."

After a short ride Lucas parked his car in front of two stone pillars at the entrance to a sweeping curved driveway. Susan sighed. "I guess I've been out of things—not being involved with grad studies this past term." She grimaced at the memory. "Other than the dreaded proseminar, of course."

Lucas turned off the ignition and smiled at Susan. "I told you the grad students are a little intimidated by you. Maybe tonight will break the ice and you'll get regular invitations to these parties—if you want regular invitations." Lucas laughed. "One experience and you may join Joyce and Ari Petras in the group of department loners."

Lucas and Susan walked up the driveway. The house was an imposing three-story stone structure. Its ornate Victorian elegance was apparent even in the dark. The oak front door was huge, and Lucas struggled to open it. A deafening burst of ABBA's, *Waterloo*, greeted them when they entered the paneled hallway. Lucas waved to a cluster of students standing in front of a massive stone fireplace in the living room. He abandoned Susan and crossed the room to join the group. Except for a coat rack and a gigantic stereo system on the wall opposite the fireplace, the room was bare. There were window seats crammed with chattering students beneath the panes of the leaded glass windows at the front of the house. A lavish crystal chandelier hung between the wooden beams that crossed the ceiling in a checkerboard pattern. The smell of marijuana was intense.

"Hi, I'm Danny." Susan turned to find a tall, willowy woman with wild brown hair streaked with grey standing at her elbow. She wore black tights and an oversized black sweater with frayed sleeves. The stained fingers of her right hand held what was either a self-rolled cigarette or a joint. Danny shouted in her ear as ABBA blared from the stereo. "We're glad you could come tonight. We would've invited you before, but time slips away and before you know it the term's over." Susan held up her bottle of wine in a lame gesture of greeting. Danny motioned Susan to follow her to the kitchen.

The room was packed and noisy. Everyone was clustered around a large plank table strewn with bottles of beer and open bottles of wine. Puddles of the various beverages made haphazard patterns on the table surface. Danny handed her a plastic cup and a corkscrew and then disappeared. As Susan poured the wine, she looked up to find Bob Van Holland standing across the table. He grinned, gesturing he wanted to talk with her. At least she knew one student at the party. Relieved, Susan maneuvered herself through the crowd around the table.

"I got the final exam print-outs from the computer center and everything's okay," Bob slurred. Susan saw he was a little drunk. "I don't think we'll have the mess-up we had at mid-terms. The computer center actually listened to our complaints, and the exam scoring appears to be error-free this time."

"Good news—that is something to celebrate." Susan touched Bob's beer bottle with her wine-filled cup in a toast of triumph.

Bob leaned toward her ear. "You probably don't know many people here," he said, waving his beer bottle around the room. "Most of the mob in the kitchen is neuropsychology grad students. They're always close to the booze despite the lip service they give to alcohol-related brain damage." Steadying himself against the table, Bob was about to launch into a more detailed description of the party guests when an attractive, plump woman appeared at his elbow.

"It's time to go, Bob," she said with an apologetic smile in Susan's direction. Bob took another sip of beer and leaned against the woman's ample chest. "This is my wife, Millie. Millie, this is Dr. Barron. I'm the teaching assistant for Dr. Barron's Intro course," Bob explained with another spastic wave of his beer bottle. Millie placed her arm around his waist to steady him against her hip.

"Pleased to meet you, Dr. Barron," Millie laughed as she held Bob in place against her body. "I trust you've seen Bob in a better light than tonight. He always gets drunk at these end-of-term parties. He hasn't said anything too outlandish or insulting, I hope." Bob finished his beer oblivious to the conversation.

"No, not yet," Susan replied. "Bob probably deserves a good drunk, though, after the term we've had—a lot of computer problems with the exam grades, which didn't make the students very happy."

The noise level in the kitchen erupted to new levels with the arrival of a boisterous group from the living room. Susan watched Millie turn Bob toward the door to struggle through the throng converging on the kitchen. Bob waved his empty beer bottle at Susan in a flamboyant gesture of farewell. Left alone at the table, Susan scanned the crowd for another companion. She was about to leave the kitchen to search for Lucas when she spotted a colleague leaning against the refrigerator. He was cradling a beer bottle in both hands. Susan crossed the room and took over the opposite corner of the large refrigerator.

"Hi, you're Carl Thorndike—I've seen you at department meetings, but we've never had a chance to talk." Susan feigned more confidence than she felt.

Carl peered down at Susan through his wire-rimmed glasses and took a sip of beer. "Well, Susan," he said, "now's a good time to get acquainted."

Searching for something to say, Susan blurted out the first thing that came to mind. "Probably a lot of people ask you this question, but are you related to the psychologist Thorndike of the puzzle box fame?"

"I'm asked that question occasionally but only by psychologists who are aware that Edward Thorndike ever existed. So, that's a point in your favor—you know about Thorndike and the cats in the puzzle box." Susan suddenly remembered Carl was the department's expert on psychology's history. She hoped he would not test the limits of her scant knowledge about Thorndike and his research. She took a gulp of wine.

"To answer your question, no, I'm not related to Edward Thorndike, although his work influenced me to choose animal learning for my doctoral dissertation topic. Unfortunately, I found the research didn't suit me.

I returned a government grant when I decided I wasn't interested in animal learning anymore." Carl gave Susan a devilish grin. "I'm sure by now you've heard that story from somebody in the department. It has become one of the great department scandals, and I don't think Giles has ever forgiven me—not that I care much."

"I think someone has mentioned it," Susan nodded. "Giving up a grant and publicly saying I'm not going to do this anymore is a courageous thing to do—a lot of researchers wouldn't have the guts to do that."

"That's generous of you, Susan. Do you want to repeat that sentiment to Giles?"

Susan laughed. "I stay as far away from Giles as possible. I don't think he likes me very much."

"Giles doesn't like anyone in the department very much. He's strange, though. He has this iconoclastic anti-academic façade but he's quite traditional in the way he kowtows to conventional status hierarchies. That's why he's so angry about my grant. He thought it made him look bad in the eyes of the chain of command—the dean, the president. I chalk his attitude up to his days in the military—being in the Royal Air Force in World War II."

"Giles was in the RAF?"

"Yeah, he's one of those Canadians who volunteered in the early days of the Battle of Britain. He's very proud of his British heritage—I guess he thought he needed to go over there and defend the homeland. It's rumored he was one of the few pilots in his squadron who survived the war."

"That explains why he's so anti–draft dodger. He's mentioned draft dodgers to me a couple of times—about how there're draft dodger hippies in Victoria, at JDU, in the department." Susan took a chance. "Are you one of them?"

Carl grinned. "Well, I am and I'm not. I got my grad degree at the University of Alberta during the height of the draft years. After living in Canada for a while, I wasn't much interested in returning home. I don't know whether I ever got a draft notice in the States—I never went back to find out. Giles calls me a draft dodger, but me and the others like me at JDU like to think of ourselves as objectors to an irresponsible war. As it's turned out, we were right."

Suddenly, Wanda Martin appeared at Carl's elbow. "Hi, Carl," Wanda flirted as her shoulder brushed the arm of Carl's shirt. "Hi, Dr. Barron, glad to see you could make the party. We like to have faculty members at our parties—Carl's a regular." Wanda turned her body. It looked like she was trying to trap Carl against the refrigerator, but he sidled sideways to put some distance between them. Susan watched the amusing ballet between the two of them. If there was an affair going on, Wanda had far more romantic energy for it than Carl. Sensing that Wanda was going to monopolize Carl's attention, Susan raised her cup in farewell and went in search of Lucas. She spotted him huddled on one of the window seats with a woman. Her blond hair glowed against the dark oak wainscoting on the wall behind her. Their postures toward each other were intimate. Susan got the message—she was not about to interrupt their conversation.

Left alone, Susan stood in the hallway between the kitchen and living room, leaned against the wall, and surveyed the party. Wanda had success-fully isolated Carl in a corner of the kitchen. He was hiding behind his beer bottle as he watched Wanda's face—she was making wild gestures with her plastic cup. Carl's expression was one of resigned patience coupled with slight annoyance. He looked over Wanda's head, saw Susan watching them, and shrugged with a gesture of stoic endurance. *Trapped by a student, what can you do?*

Susan blushed at being discovered and turned to find Lucas approaching her with the golden-haired woman in tow.

Lucas looked sheepish. "Susan, I'm taking Janice home. She lives quite far out of town and needs a ride. Anyone here can give you a lift home since you live just a few blocks away."

Susan examined Lucas's face, wondering if Janice was another of his self-discovery projects. She guessed there would be no sexual hang-ups with Janice because of unresolved conflicts about his ex-wife. She cringed at the pang of jealousy twisting inside her as she studied the two of them standing hand in hand. The dim hope she nurtured that she and Lucas would spend the night at her place was more powerful than she wanted to admit.

"Yeah, sure, no problem—I'll find someone. Thanks for bringing me, I'm enjoying myself." Susan gulped the last of her wine. "I think I'll go in search of a refill."

Susan started toward the kitchen, but Lucas caught her arm. "I want to wish you a happy holiday. You deserve a break. You've worked hard this term."

"I'm going to be working over the holiday. I have book chapters to write," Susan snapped.

"Well, don't work too hard and try to have some fun." Lucas looked hurt at her gruff response.

Susan spun around and walked toward the kitchen. She was dejected, angry, and cold, as cold as the gust of wind blown into the hallway when Lucas escorted Janice out the door. Susan searched the room for more wine. Wanda and Carl were still in the corner—Wanda gesturing and talking and Carl sulking behind his beer. She could ask Wanda to drive her home. After all, the two of them lived in the same building. As Susan watched Wanda's coy maneuverings, she felt empathy with her hapless plight. Susan, too, was lonely and deprived so she decided not to intrude on Wanda's pursuit of Carl. She would walk home alone.

SEVENTEEN

December twenty-sixth, Boxing Day—Susan frowned at her rain-soaked office window. The campus was deserted. At the last department meeting Susan overheard conversations about annual holiday trips to Hawaii and to ski resorts in the States. Other colleagues mentioned travel to the BC mainland to visit family and friends. An aura of eerie abandonment hung over the department. It was odd how silence was distracting, and Susan's mind drifted from the blank page curled in her typewriter. She sighed. Last Christmas she was window shopping on Fifth Avenue with Julie and enjoying the holiday atmosphere of New York's most expensive stores. If she was back east now, she would be visiting *her* family and *her* friends. But she was in Victoria, alone over the Christmas holiday, pitifully grateful for an invitation to a graduate student party that ended in disappointment.

The only positive in her holiday happened when Susan, ready to leave the party, by chance met Carl and Wanda at the door. Carl insisted she could not walk home alone and bundled her into his car along with Wanda. Susan still giggled over Wanda's self-conscious embarrassment as she said good night to the two of them at the door of Wanda's suite. Wanda's cheeks flamed when Carl said, "I had no idea you lived here. That's great—we'll get together for dinner one night—the three of us. I'm not a bad cook when I put my mind to it." The episode with Carl and Wanda almost compensated for the dismal memory of watching Lucas leave the party with Janice.

After the party, Susan had plenty of time to think about Dan's impending visit. She was skeptical of Julie's idea that sex with Dan was inevitable if she wanted to finish the book with as little conflict as possible. She mulled over the idea that intermingling personal with professional life leads to higher levels of productive creativity. Susan could see how this notion worked for Dan. His career progress was of paramount importance in his life. He also liked regular sex. What could be better than to sleep with your colleagues? If Mona became suspicious of the time spent with other women, Dan could point to the research papers and books as the products of the time spent away from her. The sex would be easily hidden, especially if Mona was not interested in academic life aside from regular lunches with faculty wives.

Susan was not sure this type of arrangement would work as well for her. Maybe she should be flattered that a man as intelligent, hard-working, and ambitious as Dan was pursuing her. She still smarted with the sting of Paul's disdainful dismissal of her PhD work. "I don't want to be married to someone with more degrees than I have," he had shouted during one of their arguments about their future. Susan did agree with Julie on this point—Dan liked to sleep around, and sooner or later she would become just one of his many women. How would a probable temporary liaison with Dan impact a future long-term relationship with another man? This question with an unknown answer nagged at her.

On Christmas Eve, Susan took stock. She stood with her back to the door of her suite, surveying it, trying to visualize being there with Dan. There were no doors to any of the rooms, so you could walk from the living room to the bedroom with no chance of privacy. The bathroom was tiny, as was the kitchen with its ancient appliances. She could not imagine being in this space with Dan for an entire week.

To clear her head, Susan took a walk around the neighborhood she had grown to love. She enjoyed inspecting the mansions nestled among the stately trees surrounding Craigdarroch Castle, the centerpiece of the area. The Castle was perched on a rise overlooking Fort Street, a main artery leading into the center of town. The Castle housed the Victoria Conservatory of Music, and occasionally she heard someone playing a complex classical piece on the piano as she strolled past the building.

Most of the houses in the region were converted into rental suites like the one where she lived except for a bed and breakfast, The Castle House Inn, a few blocks from her place. She stopped to examine its exterior. An enormous wreath of fresh pine boughs adorned the carved oak door. When she entered the lobby, she found a cheerful, multi-colored tree trimmed with pine cones. Instead of a star, the treetop sported a ribbon printed with the greeting, *Welcome to Victoria, BC.* The room was inviting, with a crackling fire under a mantle adorned with holly leaves and red ribbons. The warm ambience and the enticing scent of fresh pine emphasized the barrenness of Susan's suite. Holiday decorations were an amenity she had forgotten.

The owner was friendly, delighted to have a visitor to the university as a guest for a week. She showed Susan several spacious rooms done in a Victorian style with flowered carpets and tasseled drapes at the windows. Susan chose a room with a fireplace and a slightly less garish décor. She wrote a check for the first night's rent and left with a sense of relief. It was obvious Dan would be more comfortable staying here than with her.

Susan sprang to attention when a crash echoed through the empty hallway. Dan had arrived. Susan positioned herself in her desk chair with her fingers poised over the typewriter keyboard. She managed a few sham pecks on the keys, her face artificially composed into an expression of concentration, when Dan appeared at the door of her office.

"Hi, Sue." Dan's voice boomed through the emptiness. He placed his briefcase and typewriter on the floor next to the door and slumped into the spare chair in Susan's office. He looked fatigued, and his eyes had a hollow expression. He pointed at Susan's coffee carafe. "That coffee smells good. I definitely need some good coffee—the stuff on the ferry is terrible."

After a few sips, Dan exhaled. "I didn't realize Boxing Day is a national holiday in Canada. There was so much traffic at the terminal I almost didn't get on the nine o'clock sailing. The cafeteria lines were enormous. I barely had time to grab some coffee before we arrived here—lots of traffic on the highway even before it started to rain, which made things worse. I see the campus is completely deserted. I knew you were here because I saw your car in the parking lot. It wasn't hard to miss since it was the only one there."

Susan laughed. "I didn't realize today is a holiday either. I was feeling nervous in this eerily empty building, so I'm glad you're finally here."

Dan leaned back in his chair and slurped his coffee. "I struck up a conversation with one of the passengers on the ferry who told me today is called Boxing Day because, during Queen Victoria's time, the wealthy gave boxes of gifts to their servants on the day after Christmas as a sign of appreciation—hence the name, Boxing Day. Nice tradition for extending the holiday that we don't have in the States."

"And, hence, the deserted campus—everyone's still celebrating Christmas," Susan quipped as she refilled Dan's mug. She picked up his typewriter and briefcase and motioned him to follow her. "I fixed up a workspace for you in one of my lab rooms downstairs." When they reached the basement, Susan unlocked the largest of her three research rooms where she had set up a makeshift office with a small desk. By design, Susan had chosen the same room that housed her new, and yet unused, tachistoscope. It sat majestically on a table in the center of the room next to an impressive stack of user instruction manuals.

"This is great, thanks." Dan opened his briefcase and removed a thick file. "Time to get to work. I brought my outline and notes on your second chapter, so I'll start fleshing that out." Dan approached the tachistoscope with a sense of awe. "This is quite the machine," he said as he stroked the blond wood of the case. "With four channels to present stimuli with millisecond timing, you should be able to set up some interesting experiments."

Susan sighed. "My wonderful new t-scope will remain silent unless I get some help with the electronics set-up that programs the timers on each channel. I told you the department technician's time is devoted entirely to Otto Hartmann and his students."

Dan laughed. "Yeah, new faculty are always at the bottom of the list when it comes to staff assistance. I'm having the same problem at U of V. I'll see what I can do with this baby after I spend a few hours writing."

* * * * * * * * * * * * * *

"I think the air is starting to thin." Dan gasped as he trudged up the last few stairs to the landing in front of Susan's suite. Dan leaned against the wall, panting, as Susan unlocked the door. He staggered into the living room, placed his briefcase on the floor, and rotated to inspect the room. Dan darted to the windows, crossed his arms over his chest, and peered through the glass at the growing darkness. "I can see the lights of the Parliament buildings from here. If it wasn't so dark, I bet you'd have a good view of the Olympic Mountains, too." Dan turned a corner and stepped into the bedroom to take in the view from the window. "You've got an even better view from here." Susan followed, turning on lamps to break the gloom while Dan completed his tour. Staring out the kitchen window, he gave his final assessment. "You didn't lie about the view—it's magnificent."

"You can see why I thought you wouldn't be comfortable here, Dan," Susan said. "The suite has no privacy, and it's too dark now to see the glaring flaws. The view is worth the discomfort to me but probably not for you."

"Yeah, I can see that. How do you put up with the cold?" Dan asked as he rubbed his arms.

Susan was relieved when Dan did not object to staying at The Castle House Inn. At check-in, the owner made a huge fuss over a professor from the University of Vancouver gracing her humble establishment. She became even more effusive when Dan mentioned writing a book. Dan loved adulation, and the owner's attitude was enough to win him over. She was glad his tour of her suite was cementing the arrangement.

"Let's have a drink before dinner." Susan retrieved a bottle of white wine from the refrigerator.

"I have something better." Dan put his arm around Susan's shoulder and gave her a playful squeeze. "I brought a bottle of scotch—the same brand we used to drink at the parties at the Institute. I thought we could toast the old days back in New York." Dan bustled into the living room and clicked open the lock on his briefcase to extract a magnum-sized bottle of Johnnie Walker.

Susan improvised a dinner of cold cuts served on her folding table by a window. In tribute to the season, she flung a multi-colored shawl over the surface, and placed two Christmas candles in the center of the table. The room had a makeshift festive air when they sat down to eat. The glow of candlelight was a welcome respite from the damp gloom outside.

Dan congratulated Susan on her three large lab rooms. The scotch loosened his tongue, and she began to understand the depth of his resentment over U of V's exaggerated promises of research space and equipment. The hollowness around his eyes could be signs of stress, Susan thought, as she listened to Dan brainstorm about possible future research projects located in her lab if she was willing to continue their collaboration beyond the textbook.

The scotch was having its effect on her, too, and her attention wandered back to a distant conversation with Howard Lloyd, one of Dan's colleagues from NYU. Howard was a frequent visitor to the Institute labs, and over the years he had shown an interest in Susan's research. Last summer Howard invited her to lunch—for Susan, an unexpected treat.

"I'm glad we're having this opportunity to talk before you leave town." Howard smeared butter on a bread roll and took a bite. "I want to warn you about the future out there on the West Coast. It's one thing to write a textbook with your dissertation advisor. Lots of senior people have their students work on textbook chapters and then list them as co-authors on the text. I've done it myself. Writing a textbook is an attention-getting device to get name recognition among researchers, especially those that use your text. But textbook writing isn't serious scholarship, and no one considers it to be. Continuing to do research with your advisor early in your career is another matter and a bad idea. The field expects you to establish your own research independence. If you pay any attention to your advisor at all, it should be to publish papers refuting his theoretical positions—show how he was wrong in his research approach and how you're right in yours. That's the way the game is played if you want to be taken seriously."

Susan protested. "Don't you think that's old-fashioned, Howard? If your advisor is doing interesting research and you want to be involved, isn't there more to be gained by being cooperative rather than competitive? I mean, it's the work that's important, not the status of the researchers."

"You've got a point, Susan, but unfortunately the field doesn't work that way. It's tough enough for a woman to be accepted as a serious cognitive psychologist without the added burden of being seen to lack independence of thought." Howard paused to take a bite of his sole fillet. "Don't get me wrong. There's nothing wrong with Dan. He does high-quality work. But he's an ambitious workaholic interested in becoming a household word in the field like Leonard Wesselman, his role model."

"Wait a minute, Howard." Susan protested a second time. "You just mentioned Dan and Leonard. The two of them are a good example of what I'm saying. Leonard was Dan's dissertation advisor, and Dan came with him to help set up the lab at the Institute. This hasn't hurt Dan's career—he's publishing, getting grants, and now he's got this new position in Vancouver. These all seem like signs of respect to me."

"Susan, I've been around a long time and I know how the field works. In the case of Dan and Leonard—yes, Dan was Leonard's student and came with him to the Institute." Howard hesitated. "I'm not so sure Dan's career has remained unscathed by his lingering association with Leonard. Yes, he received a number of job offers, but the one from the university in Vancouver was by far the best. I don't know what it means when you have to leave your own country to get a reasonable offer when you go out on the job market."

Susan squirmed, realizing Howard's comments about Dan described her situation, too. Howard must have sensed her alarm because he added,

"I mean, I don't know what it means when you're someone of Dan's vintage who's been out in the field for a while. Maybe that's why he's leaving—he realizes he must break his ties with Leonard. Maybe that's why he's chosen West Coast obscurity in another country rather than sticking around the East Coast where most of the cognitive psychology action is right now."

"Sue, you look like you're falling asleep and you haven't heard much of what I've said in the past little while, have you?" Dan refilled her glass with scotch. Susan noticed with alarm that the bottle in Dan's hand was almost empty.

"No wonder I'm having trouble concentrating," Susan muttered, gesturing at the bottle. "I think we've had a lot to drink. You can clearly handle it better than I can." Susan rose and steadied herself against the table, then turned and marched toward her bedroom. She pulled back the quilt and dropped into bed with relief, not bothering to undress. She fell asleep—her head swimming in an alcohol haze.

Susan woke to a strange sensation. Someone was stroking her cheek. She opened her eyes to find Dan kneeling beside the bed, his face close to hers. Before she could speak, he plunged his tongue snake-like in and out of her parted lips. The pressure of his kiss stifled her breathing, and she groaned in protest.

"Dan, we've had a lot to drink," Susan whispered, pushing him away. "Go back to the inn and sleep it off. Come back tomorrow morning for breakfast."

Dan grunted, rose to his feet, and shuffled toward the door. Susan heard him fumble with his coat and the click of the lock as he shut the door to her suite. She stared at the variegated shadows shimmering across the bedroom ceiling as she licked her lips to soothe the soreness left by Dan's insistent exploration of her mouth. Her head ached—a hangover was blossoming. She turned and buried her head in the pillow to placate the pulsating waves of pain. She hoped Dan would find his way back to the inn but was too tired to care if he got lost.

EIGHTEEN

Dan crammed his suitcase into the trunk of his car and slammed the trunk lid. He turned and pulled Susan toward him, brushing his lips down her cheek. Susan shifted her head to one side, so his kiss missed her mouth and grazed the side of her neck.

"Thanks for your help this week. I know I'll have a better second term now that I have my writing rhythm back—and your help with the t-scope means we can get started on some data collection—so thanks with that, too," Susan said as she wiggled out of his grasp.

"We got a lot of work done. Our editor will be pleased we met the deadline." Dan lowered his face to try again for a kiss, but Susan backed away.

"You better get going. There could be a lot of ferry traffic today with people traveling at the end of the holidays."

Dan tried one last time for another kiss, then gave up and got into his car. With a wave, he was gone. Susan shivered in the early morning chill as she watched him drive away. When his car disappeared, she made the long climb to her suite.

"It's New Year's Day, 1975," she announced to the empty rooms. The remnants of their New Year's Eve celebration lingered in the empty champagne bottles lying in the middle of her living room floor. Too tired to start a clean-up, Susan looked out the window over the treetops. There would be little respite from the gloom today—just a gradual brightening as the day dawned.

Susan admitted reluctantly that her attitude changed when Dan was around. Her lethargy toward writing—her disappointment with academic life—abated under the influence of his unstoppable work ethic. Her tendency to procrastinate and obsess over small flaws in her writing vanished. Dan's enthusiasm for experimentation and his ability to generate interesting research ideas were contagious and restored her confidence in the value of the path she had chosen. There was at least one psychologist in her life with an intense focus on generating new knowledge in contrast to the barren intellectual environment of her department. The result, after months of delay, was that Dan arrived in Victoria and her two chapters were finished in a week—and her t-scope was operational with experiments in the works to test its potential.

Their joint effort worked so well they took a break one afternoon to visit a pub rumored to be favored by the psychology graduate students. They found a corner booth with a view of the strait and distant mountains, and Dan, over his pint of bitters, became reflective. "According to colleagues in the field, I took a professional hit when I left New York. They warned me about going to an obscure place and losing touch with the cutting edge of cognitive psychology. I'm going back to New York in March for the Eastern Psychological Association meetings. I want to show those critics I'm still a force to be reckoned with even if BC is not the epicenter of the cognitive psychology universe—not yet, anyway."

Susan countered, "The West Coast isn't a backwater. You went to Stanford, the top-rated psychology department in the States, if not the world. There's UCLA, USC, the University of Oregon—all these departments have good cognitive programs."

"It's not the West Coast they see as a problem—it's the University of Vancouver." Speaking more to himself than to Susan, he said, "U of V may not be a powerhouse now, but that doesn't mean it won't be in the future. Stanford people always keep score with each other and count the plastic badges—who's getting them and who's not getting them. Right now, most think I've lost ground coming to BC."

She asked, "What're plastic badges?"

Dan rattled off, without hesitating, "Faculty positions at major universities, articles in top journals, academic promotions, elections to prestigious societies...."

"Sounds exhausting. Can't you just do what you want?"

Dan laughed. "Sure, but every conference you go to, every time you meet one of your grad student classmates, you'll feel the sting of their subtle patronizing attitude—poor Dan, he couldn't quite make the grade."

Last night on New Year's Eve, Dan opened up again. "My parents didn't want me to go to Stanford. They thought I'd lose my Jewish identity on the West Coast. They saw California as the home of liberals, heathens, and godless movie stars and insisted I needed a good Jewish wife to protect me from California's temptations. My parents and Mona's parents got together and arranged for us to meet. I wanted to go to Stanford, and Mona wanted to get married. I knew the only way I was going to make my parents happy was to take Mona with me to the West Coast."

"Why was it so important to make them happy?" Susan asked.

"I got an appointment to the Naval Academy when I was graduating high school. My parents were thrilled at the honor, but I'd only gone through the appointment process to please them. I had no interest in the military. I didn't tell them I'd applied to other places and wanted to go to Cornell. Eventually, they accepted my decision, but I spent four years suffering under their grudging disapproval, which got worse when I switched my major from physics to psychology. I couldn't handle more years of unrelenting criticism, so I did what they wanted and married Mona. I was in graduate school only a few months when Mona got pregnant. I was the only married grad student in my lab group, and I soon became the only grad student parent in the department. It was not a distinction I'd planned to achieve. But Mona wanted kids, and I try to make her happy when I can."

Emboldened by the champagne, Susan asked, "What about your affairs? What does Mona think about them? They can't make her happy." Dan stared at her. She had never seen this blank expression before. It was as if a curtain fell, turning his blue eyes to grey and his face to stone. "We all make bargains to get through life," Dan replied, his tone flat. Susan wondered who had made the bargains, Dan or Mona or both. That question remained unanswered because it was obvious that topic of conversation was over.

The living arrangement at the Castle House Inn lasted one day. Dan arrived at her suite early on the first morning and circled her in his arms. They moved toward the bedroom together. Other than the brief encounter with Lucas, it had been months since Susan had been naked in bed with a man. She was stiff at first—still getting used to the new Dan, to the new relationship, and to sex again. Soon she relaxed and let herself enjoy that first morning. Dan's lusty enthusiasm made up for his speed. After months of celibacy she refrained from being judgmental about Dan's approach to sex. Eventually, he will slow down, she told herself that first morning.

Susan did not object when Dan told her he wanted to wake up next to her every day. He returned to the inn, gathered his belongings, said good-bye to the adoring owner, and moved into her suite. But after the first day, the sex changed. Exploring her sleeping, inert body each morning was his foreplay, and sometimes she was not fully awake when he moved on top of her. Often, by the time she was awake and ready to take part, Dan was done. The sex was frequent but short. She tried coaxing him to relax, telling him she needed more time, but his sexual urgency did not diminish. Dan liked swift morning sex—over and done with and on with the day. There was no nighttime sex. Dan crawled into bed and was asleep in a few minutes with his back turned toward her. On the first few nights she fondled him and whispered her intentions in his ear but with no response. Eventually, she kept to her side of the bed and stared at the ceiling until she fell asleep.

Exhausted, Susan yawned, smoothed the rumpled sheets on her bed, and curled up under the covers. It was still too early to start the first day of the new year. When she considered the events of the past week, she wondered if 1975 was off to an auspicious start. Susan was confident about the truth of what she told Dan. She had her writing rhythm back and would complete the remaining chapters to meet the editor's deadlines. Their work relationship was strong and flourishing. Dan was driven to prove something to his Stanford classmates so their work would move forward at a fast pace. Her only worry was keeping up.

The sex part was another story. Julie's view that casual sex might provide some release turned out to be a fantasy. Instead, a conversation Susan had with a graduate student friend at the Institute popped into mind. The two of them were having coffee and musing about relationships—what worked, what did not—when her friend said, "Having bad sex is worse than having no sex because it's a teaser. Bad sex leaves you hungry for the good stuff. It's better to be celibate—have no sex. After a while, you don't miss it." There was truth to what her friend had said. Before this week Susan feared she was withering away from lack of physical contact. Now, after a week of frequent sex, she did not feel better. She was sore, too much bad sex, not enough caring, not enough fun. Dan's businesslike release of physical needs was not her idea of intimacy.

She hoped Julie was right about Dan seeing Susan as another sexual conquest, soon forgotten when a new woman appeared. She would stick with the positive. They worked well together. They were colleagues, maybe eventually friends, but not lovers. Susan wanted to finish the book in the old way—the lover part explored and then abandoned. Comforted by these thoughts, Susan started to doze. What bargain had Dan and Mona struck? was her last thought before she fell asleep.

N I N E T E E N

January was damp, dark, and windy. Susan succumbed to the temptation to hide in bed, her face buried in the pillow with the quilt pulled over her head to block out the unrelenting sound of rain. It was a joke, but Susan checked each morning for mildew between her fingers and toes as part of her dreaded five o'clock wake-up ritual.

By six thirty, Susan was in her office, behind her desk, waiting for her coffee maker to brew the comforting brown liquid. She poured her first cup and pressed her fingers against the warmth of the mug's ceramic surface. An unexpected childish whine at her open office door broke the morning silence. "Your coffee smells so good. Can you spare a cup?" Her phantom colleague, Penny Carson, slid into view, coffee mug in hand. Startled, Susan motioned her toward the spare office chair and filled the large cup.

Penny squeezed her ample frame into the chair. "Thanks," she said. "I need a caffeine fix. My coffee maker died yesterday, and I haven't had time to buy a replacement." Penny sat back in the chair and surveyed Susan's office. "So, you're an early bird like me. Most days I'm here by five. I like to work in the morning quiet when no one's around. Is that why you're here so early?" Penny scanned the notepaper and books scattered across Susan's desk.

"I have a nine o'clock Intro class. I've never taught Intro Psych before, and I need lots of preparation. That's why I'm here."

"Oh, of course, teaching—that explains the early morning hours." Penny sipped her coffee and eyed Susan. "Has Giles talked to you about your teaching evaluations yet?" Penny thrust her mug toward Susan who poured the dregs of the carafe into her cup.

"No." Susan shook her head.

"He'll probably talk to you sometime this week. I don't think he'd mind my mentioning the evaluations. I'm on the department executive committee, and we'll be meeting this week to talk about the teaching evaluations of the untenured faculty."

"What's the department executive committee?" Susan asked, wary of the presence of an official-sounding department committee she knew nothing about.

Penny looked surprised. "Didn't Giles go over this with you during your new faculty orientation meeting?"

"I don't remember," Susan hesitated. "I know he told us to read the faculty handbook." She gestured toward the blue binder sitting on one of her bookshelves. "I haven't read the handbook, actually," Susan admitted. "Should I have?"

Penny guffawed. "It's not exactly a riveting piece of writing. Our current dean wrote it and he's very proud of it, especially the part about options available for faculty evaluation. Our department executive committee is one of the options outlined in the handbook."

"Who's on the committee?" Susan asked. Her anxiety was mounting—not a good way to start the day.

"Giles and Jim in their capacities as chairman and assistant chairman—and three other faculty members elected by the department. This year it's me, Joyce Petras, and Carl Thorndike." Penny stopped. "Wait a minute. Did you attend the faculty meeting where we elected the executive committee members?"

Susan flushed. "I may have missed a faculty meeting or two last term."

Penny frowned. "I've pushed for us to elect the executive committee with ballots distributed through office mail so everyone can vote in the election for such an important committee." She leaned toward Susan, lowering her voice to a conspiratorial whisper. "Giles opposes the idea of mail ballots. He is against giving everyone the chance to vote because it's easier for him to manipulate the election if a person can vote only at a department meeting."

Penny gave a wistful glance into her coffee mug, but, noticing the empty carafe, she rose from the chair. "Giles will talk to you after the executive committee meets. Members of the committee will visit your class to observe your teaching. We'll decide on this year's schedule when we have our meeting this week."

Susan slumped in her chair. She should have been better prepared and chided herself for not reading the handbook.

"Don't look so tense. The teaching evaluations aren't as bad as they sound. Just be glad Ari Petras isn't on the executive committee this year. He likes to stand in the hallway outside of open classroom doors. That's his method of evaluating faculty teaching. He insists you can tell a lot about how a person teaches by listening to what they say when they don't know an evaluator is listening." Penny giggled. "You'll be happy to know this year's committee does not use Ari's method."

As soon as Penny left her office, Susan lunged for the handbook binder. She stopped short when Penny stuck her head around the door jamb again. "I forgot to mention something." Penny looked at Susan—her eyes had an amused gleam. "It will probably be either Joyce or me who does your classroom visit. Giles will think it's more appropriate for a woman to evaluate another woman. He'll think he's being progressive, but I know it's because he doesn't want to be the person to bring bad news to a female faculty member. He's old-school when it comes to relationships between the sexes. That's not to say there'll be any bad news—in your case, anyway." She gestured farewell with her now empty coffee mug and disappeared.

Susan thrust her head out the door—Penny was continuing down the corridor away from her office. Reassured, she grabbed the binder and opened it to the page marked Tenure Document. Her cursory scan of the pages verified that the psychology department was following one of the options outlined in meticulous detail in the document. Penny said Ari Petras stood and listened outside open classroom doors to evaluate faculty teaching. Her heart raced. Anyone could enter the foyer of the large lecture hall where she taught her Intro class and stand by the door, in the shadows, listening. The hundreds of seats arranged in sloping tiers blocked her view of anyone entering the hall. She would never know if someone came through the rear doors to observe her class. The thought was chilling.

* * * * * * * * * * * * * *

"I see you have office hours now." Joyce Petras gestured toward the sign hanging on Susan's open office door. "I'll leave if a student comes, but I wanted to stop by and say hello." Joyce smiled as she settled into the same office chair inhabited by Penny Carson the day before. Susan was astonished. Joyce Petras was another phantom colleague and not a person she expected to make a casual, unannounced visit to her office.

Susan blurted, "I know you want to talk to me about evaluating my teaching. Penny was here yesterday and told me members of the department executive committee would be visiting my classes sometime this term. And, of course, I read the evaluation procedure in the faculty handbook." Susan waved her hand toward the blue binder now resting on the corner of her desk.

"We haven't had our executive committee meeting yet." Joyce giggled. "I came to invite you to dinner. Ari and I want to take you to our favorite Greek restaurant."

Remembering what Penny had said about Ari Petras and teaching evaluations, Susan wondered why Joyce was inviting her to dinner. Was she being paranoid to connect the two events—a visit from Penny and now a rare social invitation from the Petrases? She ordered herself to relax—Joyce was just being friendly. Besides, she sensed the invitation did not contain an option for refusal. "Thanks, I'd like that," Susan responded.

"I feel guilty that Ari and I haven't been more welcoming to you since you arrived. We don't socialize with people in the department. We keep to ourselves and rarely go out. But we love Mykonos. We know the owner, and we're regulars there. We think you'll like it." Joyce appeared nervous—casual social chitchat seemed not to be her forte. "We feel a kinship to someone with Stanford roots, so we can catch up on old times over dinner. How about a week from Saturday?"

"Fine," said Susan, regretting the speed with which she agreed to the date. The barren landscape of her social life was hard to hide. Hesitant, she added, "You realize, Joyce, I did my PhD at the Institute for Research in the Social Sciences, not Stanford."

"Oh, we know that," Joyce chuckled. "Dan Kavline went to Stanford. He and I were grad students together there. I remember him well, and I'm sure he remembers me."

Susan returned a weak smile, wondering why Dan had never mentioned his graduate school connection with Joyce. Had he kept silent because he and Joyce had been sexually involved? Joyce's simpering tone hinted at the possibility that she was yet another woman in Dan's life. Joyce rose from the chair. "Don't worry about the teaching evaluations. Giles will explain everything after the executive committee meeting." Joyce giggled as she disappeared through the open doorway. "It's not as bad as it sounds. It's just a rite of passage we all have to endure."

The week rolled toward Friday, the designated day of the executive committee meeting. Susan glanced at her watch, surprised to find it was already four-thirty. She looked up to see Giles at her office door. "Can I have a word?" He settled himself into her office chair without waiting for a response. She retreated behind her desk.

Giles coughed. "The executive committee met this morning." Giles cleared his throat and tried again. "We discussed the teaching evaluation process for new faculty." His voice steadied, and he continued with more confidence. "I assume you've read the faculty handbook." Giles peered at Susan, and she nodded.

"Jolly good—then you know members of the executive committee will visit one of your classes to observe your teaching. We'll also distribute teaching evaluation questionnaires to the students in each of your classes."

Giles paused and Susan blurted, "Mrs. Wong gave me a copy of the questionnaire given to students."

"Oh, jolly good—so you're up on the game—you've seen the bloody questionnaire." Giles shifted position to cross one leg over the other. His obvious discomfort increased her anxiety.

"Joyce Petras will observe your class. She volunteered to do it, so there's no reason why she shouldn't do the observation unless—" Giles suddenly looked panicked as if something had occurred to him for the first time "—you object to Joyce doing the evaluation. You don't object, do you?"

"No," Susan reassured him.

Penny Carson was right—women faculty would evaluate women faculty. Penny said Giles would think it the appropriate way of doing things. Susan wondered if Joyce volunteered or if Giles hinted that one of the women committee members should evaluate her teaching and Joyce then volunteered.

"Oh, jolly good," Giles was relieved. "Observations have to be done by the end of February. Thought we'd get an early start this year since there's three new faculty." Giles frowned. Discussing teaching evaluations with faculty members was a duty Giles obviously despised. He slapped his two hands on the arms of the chair. "Well, I guess that's that."

"Giles, before you go, I have a question." Susan knew she was on shaky ground because Giles looked anxious to bolt for the door. "Why were no teaching evaluations done last term?"

Giles's face blazed. He replied, "This teaching evaluation thing is a bloody nuisance. Few people at JDU cared about students evaluating faculty teaching." Giles leaned back and rolled his eyes. "Then there was a big blow-up in the bloody English department. One of the faculty members was denied tenure. The department said he wasn't a good teacher, so they voted against him for tenure. His students protested—he was very popular with students—went out drinking with them, that sort of thing—so he appealed and called in the bloody CAUT."

"What's the CAUT?" Susan asked.

"Oh, of course, you wouldn't know about the CAUT. You're from the States. CAUT is the Canadian Association of University Teachers." Giles grimaced. "They poke their nose into things when faculty members claim unfair treatment. They're a bloody nuisance. When the CAUT gets involved, it usually means a scandal will develop. The English department was accused of unfair treatment, and JDU was put under CAUT censure."

"Which means?"

Giles sniggered. "A CAUT committee publicizes the unfair treatment. They sometimes recommend against faculty accepting positions at universities under censure—things like that. The censure is lifted when the situation is corrected in the eyes of the CAUT. The censure of JDU lasted for three bloody years." Giles sighed—his displeasure was evident. "The upshot was our new president hired a bloody new dean for the Faculty of Arts and Sciences."

Giles glared at Susan. "Our new dean wants us to 'clean up our faculty evaluation act' as he puts it, so we're now required to do formal evaluations of the teaching of untenured faculty members at least once each academic year. In my opinion, the dean's trying to turn JDU into one of those bloody Ivory League universities like the one he came from—all this talk about the legal rights of faculty to have fair performance evaluations. It makes no sense to me."

"Sorry to ask another silly question, but what's the Ivory League?"

Giles's eyes widened with petulant irritation. "You're from the States and you've never heard of the Ivory League universities? I'm astonished.

Surely, you've heard of Harvard, Yale, and places like that. Our bloody dean comes from Dartmouth, I think."

"Oh, you mean, the *Ivy League* universities," Susan chuckled but stifled the urge to break into laughter when she saw the flush of embarrassment creep over Giles's face. She cleared her throat instead. "Yes, of course, I've heard of the Ivy League universities."

Giles rose from the chair, straightened his shoulders, and stretched himself to his full six-foot-plus height. This gesture seemed to restore his confidence. As he turned to leave Susan's office, his voice was unusually bitter even for Giles. "Ivy League, Ivory League, what the hell bloody difference does it make, except our Ivy League dean," he turned and made an awkward bow in Susan's direction, avoiding eye contact, "is forcing us to do things we're not used to doing at JDU." Giles stepped out into the hallway and gave Susan an awkward military-style salute. "Got to go—this conversation has cut into my Friday afternoon drinking time at the club."

He disappeared, leaving Susan collapsed against her desk shaking with laughter. She appreciated the nuance of his mistake in combining ivory tower and Ivy League. She was not living in the rarified environment of an ivory tower, and JDU certainly did not have the prestigious trappings of the Ivy League. She smiled. She was somewhere in the middle, in a faculty position in the new and, yet undiscovered, Ivory League.

TWENTY

Susan hurried toward Mykonos. She did not want to make a bad impression on Joyce and Ari Petras by being late. It's either feast or famine she muttered as she bent her head against the wind. That old saying certainly described the night.

Julie called around five. "How were things with Dan?" she asked without bothering to say hello.

"We got a lot of work done. My first two chapters are in the hands of the publishers and Dan helped me set up my new lab equipment," Susan answered.

Julie laughed. "Don't be evasive—you know, I'm asking about sex with Dan."

Susan hesitated. "Sex was okay."

"Not a ringing endorsement of satisfaction," Julie sniggered.

"It's hard to describe. There was lots of sex—quick, not much foreplay—businesslike. It reminded me of a conversation I had with someone at the Institute about celibacy being better than bad sex."

Julie laughed again. "I'm not surprised—someone with his history— lots of partners—sex as a sport—not a winning formula for a warm and loving partner."

"I don't think I'll be seeing much of him, so it doesn't matter whether the sex was good or bad. I haven't heard from him since he left Victoria on New Year's Day."

Julie sniffed. "He's probably drummed up some action in Vancouver by now. I'm not saying this to hurt your feelings—it's just, Dan is what he is—exactly what I told you last summer."

"You're not hurting my feelings. One part of me is mad when I think about him sleeping with other women—I don't want to be compared. I'm like that with all my bed partners regardless of feelings. It's an emotional bad habit I'd like to break. Another part of me hopes he finds other women in Vancouver so there's no more pressure on me."

"There may be one less woman in Dan's life soon. It's rumored around the Institute that Jennifer Evans is getting married."

"Really, that's a surprise."

"One of the guys from your lab group—I can't remember his name— mentioned it to me. He told me about Jennifer and said to say hello to you and to tell you about Jennifer. I asked him whom she was marrying but he didn't know."

"Maybe she's always had another relationship and sleeping with Dan was just a casual thing," Susan offered.

"Who knows—but speaking of relationships, what's happening with the guy in your department—the one who's trying to change his life?"

Susan sighed. "Nothing's happening. I went to a grad student party with him before the holiday, and he left with someone else. I haven't heard from him since except to say hello when I see him around the department." Susan glanced at her watch. "Julie, I have to go. Believe it or not, I'm having dinner with two of my colleagues tonight."

"Oh, yeah, who?"

"They're a married couple in the department, Joyce and Ari Petras. They invited me to dinner at their favorite Greek restaurant so we could swap Stanford stories. Joyce was in grad school at Stanford at the same time as Dan. She seems to think working with Dan gives me a Stanford connection."

"The Stanford mafia—they're everywhere." Julie sneered.

Susan laughed. "It's a free meal and something to do on Saturday night. Besides, there wasn't much of an option to refuse. Ari Petras seems to be a mysterious behind-the-scenes power in the department. He makes everyone anxious at department meetings."

"Doesn't sound like much fun, but Greek food is one of my favorites so at least you'll eat well. Keep me posted about Dan—and the other guy, too, if anything happens there."

Susan realized when she hung up the phone that, without perfect timing, she would be late for dinner. She grabbed her jacket and purse, locked the door to her suite, and raced down the stairs. She almost ran over Carl Thorndike walking through the front door.

"Susan, nice to see you," he said. "Have time for a drink with Wanda and me? I have a nice bottle of wine here." Carl pointed to the Chianti clutched in his right hand.

"Sorry, Carl, I can't tonight. I'm in a rush to get downtown. Joyce and Ari Petras invited me to dinner." Susan panted as she struggled into her jacket.

"Is that so?" If Carl was surprised, he hid it well. "Well, don't let your guard down around Ari. He may look innocuous in his avuncular way, but he can be treacherous if he takes a dislike to a young faculty member."

"Thanks for the advice, Carl. I'll try to keep the conversation on neutral topics." She fled out the front door, down the steps to her car.

Her watch read six-thirty when she parked. Susan hunched against the wind as she trudged toward the lights of the restaurant. The force of the rain sprayed her face, causing her to regret leaving her umbrella in the car. Being damp all winter was something she would have to get used to. Remembering Carl's ominous warning about Ari, she took a deep breath to calm herself and pulled open the door to Mykonos. Immediately, she saw Joyce waving at her from a table at the rear of the restaurant.

"I'm so sorry I'm late," Susan apologized as she shrugged out of her rain-soaked jacket.

A set of unseen arms lifted it from her shoulders and Ari exclaimed, "Ah, Nikos, our guest has arrived. Now you can bring the food I ordered." Susan turned to see a squat man in his fifties, smiling at her. "Of course, Dr. Petras," he replied. "And what can I bring the young miss to drink?" Susan glanced at the wine glasses in front of Joyce and Ari. "I'll have what they're having, thanks."

Joyce gave Susan's hand a friendly pat. "Don't worry about being late. Ari likes to talk to Nikos about Greece, and Nikos likes to have his chef prepare something special for Ari when we come for dinner. All that takes time." The door to the kitchen opened, and two waiters emerged with large platters. Nikos followed them, carrying a glass of wine that he placed in front of Susan. The waiters busied themselves arranging the platters of food on the table.

"Everything looks delicious." Susan basked in the tempting aromas of the dishes in front of her, realizing suddenly she did not have much of an appetite. She sipped her wine, while Joyce dipped into the platters of moussaka and spanakopita. Ari looked delighted as he spread tzatziki on a shard of warm pita. Susan had been tense about this dinner even before the combination of Carl's warning and being late. Joyce and Ari had a well-established reputation for being an asocial couple, so she could not fathom why they had invited her to dinner. Susan fretted over another complication. It was a couple of weeks since she talked to Giles about her teaching evaluations. Susan was determined to ask Joyce about the evaluations this evening.

Joyce dominated the conversation, bombarding Susan with random facts about life in Victoria and at JDU. There was an occasional monosyllabic correction from Ari. As the dinner progressed, Joyce switched to the story of how she and Ari met at Stanford. Ari was a social psychology faculty member and Joyce a graduate student in the program. Susan now understood the age difference between them. Joyce was twenty years younger than Ari, at least.

"You've heard of the bookshelf game series?" Joyce looked at Susan for confirmation. "Those games were Ari's idea," she bubbled. "Ari told the manufacturer that adults would buy board games if the packaging was disguised as elegantly bound books suitable for display on a shelf with other books—a brilliant idea, I think." Susan smiled at Joyce's delight in Ari's achievements. Ari just grinned in his gnome-like fashion; his eyes twinkled behind his horn-rimmed glasses. He seemed to expect to be admired. He obviously agreed that he was the accomplished person Joyce described.

Joyce continued her monologue of Stanford stories while the plates were cleared, and miniature cups of espresso appeared. "Dan and I were graduate students together at Stanford," Joyce said. "We weren't in the same grad student group—he was with the cognition people and I was social psych—and he was a couple of years behind me—but we knew each other from department social events."

Ari took a sip of coffee and interjected, "Very smart young man—very hard working—worked a lot of late hours. I would see him leaving the lab or the library often at nine, ten at night—crossing campus toward the grad student housing complex."

Joyce giggled again. "I'm not so sure those late hours were totally about his work in the lab, Ari."

"What do you mean?" Susan asked, sensing gossip.

"Dan spent a lot of time with another grad student in the cognition program, Liz Grantley. They were inseparable and, before I met Dan's wife at a department reception, I thought Liz and Dan were married because they were always together. I don't know if Dan's wife knew about Liz. Unfortunately, Liz was killed in a car accident."

Ari nodded. "Very sad—she was a bright young lady and very pretty. She had a promising future ahead of her."

Susan dipped her head over her coffee cup. It was hard to hear that Dan's career was dotted with research collaborators who were also lovers. Liz Grantley, Jennifer Evans, and now Susan Barron—a trio of cozy relationships kept separate from his family life. How many women could Dan hide from Mona?

"How did Dan react to the news of her death?" Susan asked.

"I don't know. I defended my dissertation the following semester and lost touch because I was busy with my research. Besides," Joyce blushed, "Ari and I were together by then and I didn't pay much attention to the other grad students because of my situation with Ari."

Dinner finished, Nikos appeared with coats and jackets and, after much hugging and expressions of affection between Nikos, Ari, and Joyce, they left the restaurant. Susan gathered her courage. "Joyce, I spoke with Giles a few weeks ago and he said you would be visiting my classes to evaluate my teaching. Have you decided when that will be?"

"Sorry, I meant to talk to you about the class visits. I've been so busy writing a grant proposal, I forgot. I can visit your Intro class this coming week. Penny Carson will probably come with me." Joyce looked exasperated. "Giles wants us to make these evaluation visits on a completely unannounced basis. He likes to trap new faculty—give them little chance to prepare and then sock them with poor evaluations—not because they're bad teachers but because they haven't had a chance to put their best foot forward. In my opinion, the poor procedures used to evaluate new faculty are the reasons JDU has a bad record of keeping people and a reputation for causing scandal and turmoil around tenure cases."

Joyce turned to see if Ari was listening, but he was already seated in their car parked in front of the restaurant. She whispered, "Don't tell Giles I gave you notice of our class visits. He wouldn't like that I told you." She patted Susan's arm. "Thanks for joining us. See you next week." Joyce slid behind the wheel, waved to Susan, and maneuvered the car out into the street. Susan watched the Petrases' car disappear, then turned in the opposite direction to walk the few blocks to her car. The evening had gone well. She had not made any social mistakes besides being late, and Ari seemed friendly.

Bad luck, she thought. Joyce would visit her class when Susan planned to lecture on personality theory, Joyce's area of expertise. She knew what she would be doing for the rest of the weekend—reading up on theories of personality. She did not want any factual errors in her lecture for Joyce to pounce on and criticize. Susan felt a rush of panic imagining the faculty evaluators watching her in class next week. She quickened her stride in anticipation of the glass of brandy waiting at home. She needed it to calm her nerves.

Lost in thought, Susan climbed the stairs to her suite. As she passed Wanda Martin's door on the second-floor landing, it suddenly flung open and Carl Thorndike emerged slamming the door behind him. Next there was a shattering crash as something fragile smashed against the closed door. Susan assumed Wanda had thrown a glass. Carl stared at Susan. He seemed startled to find someone in the hallway. Without thinking, Susan motioned him to follow her up the stairs.

Once inside her suite, she said, "I'm going to pour myself a glass of brandy. Want one?"

Carl exhaled. "Yeah, sure, I could use a drink."

Susan grabbed two glasses and the brandy bottle from the kitchen counter and ushered Carl into the living room. Carl did what the visitors to her suite had done before him. He went to one of the windows facing the city and reveled in the view. When Carl finally left the window and sat down, Susan handed him a glass of brandy.

"Aren't you going to ask me about what just happened?" Carl began.

"If you want to tell me, I'll ask," Susan replied.

Carl took several deep breaths. It looked like he was trying to calm himself. A sequence of loud crashes from the suite below broke the silence. This time it sounded like china being thrown to the floor. Carl shook his head—his expression a combination of disgust and dismay. "It was a mistake to get involved with a student," he muttered. "It sounds like she's having another one of her temper tantrums. In the past, she's just thrown pillows—sounds like she's switched to harder stuff tonight."

"Why is she angry?" Susan asked.

"Wanda's obsessed with her dissertation—that's all she talks about. She's constantly asking me for advice about methodology or to read articles she's having trouble understanding. Finally, tonight I told her if things were to continue between us, she had to stop dragging me into her dissertation research. I'm not on her committee, and I have students and work of my own to do." Carl paused to sip his brandy.

"All grad students are obsessed with their dissertations. I was like that, too. It may be one reason why my husband is now my ex-husband."

Carl looked up from his glass. "You're closer to that shit than I am, being a new PhD, so you're more understanding. Frankly, I was getting bored with the whole thing."

Carl rose and walked to the window. "Wanda got angry tonight because she accused me of using her—for sex, for comfort—and that I didn't want to give anything in return."

"Is she right?" Susan asked.

Carl remained at the window. "Maybe—loneliness can lead one down a strange path. My ex-wife moved back to Alberta after our divorce and took the kids with her. I'm paying so much child support I can't afford to visit them very often and she's not about to pay the plane fare for them to visit me. I'm lonely—I miss my kids. I started going to the grad student parties for something to do on weekends. Wanda seemed willing—more adult than most grad students—able to handle the situation. Boy, was I wrong about the last part."

Carl turned to face Susan. "I made a mistake, and it was time to break it off."

"Do you think there'll be repercussions around the department?" Susan refilled her glass.

Carl shrugged. "Wanda's paranoid about Otto finding out about us. She was worried after you moved into the building. That's why she didn't tell me you lived here. But who knows what she'll do? Whatever happens, I'll have to handle it." Carl poured himself another brandy. "How was dinner with Joyce and Ari?" he asked.

"Okay. Joyce did most of the talking—about Stanford, about Ari." Susan remembered Carl was on the executive committee, so she added, "I spoke with Joyce about my teaching evaluations. She's going to visit my Intro class next week."

"Joyce's okay. We're active in the JDU faculty association and we're committed to giving new faculty a fair shake when it comes to evaluations that affect tenure. We bucked pressure from Giles and Ari and managed to get a majority of fair-minded faculty on the executive committee this year." Carl chuckled. "I'd like to be privy to Joyce and Ari's private conversations because they couldn't be more different when it comes to evaluating faculty. Ari has the good-old-boy view—if they come from the right school and he likes them, then they should be tenured—that is, after he sneaks around to spy on their classrooms and listen to student rumors. Giles goes along because he's intimidated by Ari and his Stanford connections. Joyce, on the other hand, is adamant about fairness and equal treatment—giving new faculty a chance to perform with open evaluation procedures. In that way, they're an interesting couple."

Carl drained his last drop of brandy. "Things are quiet downstairs, so I think it's safe for me to leave. Thanks for the brandy and for rescuing me. Don't worry about the evaluations—underhanded shenanigans are a thing of the past at JDU."

Susan walked Carl to the door. "I know what loneliness can drive one to do—I've become an expert. Don't be too hard on yourself." Carl looked drained as he waved good-bye and tiptoed down the stairs.

TWENTY-ONE

Susan spent Sunday in the library buried in textbooks on personality theory, carefully preparing her lectures for the upcoming week. Her apprehension increased as the fantasies about her possible classroom failures grew more vivid. She had spent long hours trying to become an expert in an area of psychology not studied since her undergraduate days. It was rotten luck, she grumbled, that evaluators would sit in her class while she lectured on a topic with scant knowledge beyond the textbook. She broke into a sweat as she imagined disastrous scenarios—students asking her questions she could not answer, losing her place in the lecture because the material was unfamiliar. Countless things could happen to make her look bad.

It was obvious why the faculty committee chose to observe her teaching of Intro rather than of Cognitive Psychology, her area of expertise. Months ago, Jim Kracknoy revealed that her appointment was justified by her ability to teach high-enrollment courses. The only teaching of interest to the department happened in the huge Intro Psychology course. Her throat tightened as she recognized a sad fact. Her other teaching assignments did not matter. Her value to the department did not rest on the years spent studying human cognition.

Susan stood at her bedroom window, pondered the distant lights of the city, and sipped her brandy. A year ago, she was desperate for an academic appointment. She envisioned a department with bright, interested colleagues, sharing research ideas over the occasional drink. She dreamed of working with graduate students eager to join her lab group. With an ironic sniff, she shook her head at her naivete. Her ideal of academic life was demolished by the reality of her situation. She was in a department with disinterested colleagues who barely acknowledged her existence, with a department chairman who was openly hostile to faculty, and with grumpy graduate students who viewed the professors as adversaries. If she could talk to her one-year-ago-desperate-to-get-a-faculty-position self, what would she say? Her thoughts tumbled over each other as Susan sorted through the possible bits of advice. She finally settled on warning her one-year-ago self to be careful what you wish for. You may be in your fantasy faculty position with all the imagined trappings—graduate students, a research lab, the title, Assistant Professor, —only to find yourself alone and treading water in a strange place.

If Dan had not thrown her a professional lifeline over the holidays, she would be drowning by now. As it was, she felt she was hanging on by the wisp of a gossamer thread. Howard Lloyd had warned Susan about continuing collaboration with her dissertation advisor. What did Howard know about intellectual isolation? He had spent his career in the research-intensive environment of the East Coast. He could hop on the subway and consult with a colleague at any of a dozen universities dotting the boroughs of New York City. If anything, she was becoming more dependent on Dan as her only source of intelligent interaction about the topics she loved. During his visit she had devoured their debates over the latest publications. She enjoyed the give and take about which research findings were important enough to include in the book chapters. She was thrilled when her tachistoscope came to life with the planning of exciting experiments soon to come. These positives comforted her when she despaired about her stumble into an unwanted sexual relationship.

Monday morning, long before daylight, Susan was in her office brewing a pot of coffee. Both her spirits and her energy level needed a lift. Joyce was not specific about what day this week she and Penny would observe her Intro class, but Susan had a premonition that today was the day. Joyce seemed like the type, who once reminded of an official duty, liked to get it over with as quickly as possible. What if most of the seats in the large lecture hall were empty this morning? Panicked, she slumped into the chair behind her desk. Mondays were not the best attendance days—plus the miserable weather this morning could tempt many students to stay in bed. Joyce and Penny may interpret low attendance as students being too bored to come to class. Susan watched the rain streak across her office window as dawn broke and the sky lightened. Her mood matched the gloomy weather.

The shrill ring of Susan's office phone broke the early morning silence. She jumped at the sudden noise and tipped the hot coffee she held over the lecture notes piled on her desk. She picked up the receiver while trying to sop up the spill with wads of tissue.

"Dr. Barron speaking," Susan growled into the phone as she reached for more tissues to stop the coffee from dripping down the side of her desk.

"You don't sound like you're in a good mood this morning," Dan's voice was jovial on the other end of the line.

"You got that right," Susan snarled as she dabbed at the puddle of coffee. The spill did not smear the ink of her handwritten notes, but the sheets were damp, and a large brown stain covered the center of the stack of papers.

"I've been trying to call you all weekend—at home and at your office. Where've you been?" Dan asked.

"I wasn't home much this weekend. I was working in the library. Members of the department executive committee are coming to my class—I think this morning—to evaluate my teaching." Susan's voice turned shrill as she glanced at her watch. Her class started in less than an hour.

"That's just part of the game when you're untenured." Dan did not sound particularly sympathetic. "I'm sure things will go fine."

"How do you know? You've never been to my class and watched me teach." Susan barked into the phone. She was so agitated that her throat tightened, and her voice was harsh with anxiety.

"Calm down, Sue, I'm just trying to be helpful. It's true, I've never observed you teaching, but I've seen you give talks at conferences and you do a fine job. Sometimes your voice shakes a little, but you generally do okay. Just relax."

"I'm lecturing on personality theory this week in my Intro class, and Joyce Petras is one of the faculty members coming to observe my teaching. As luck would have it, of course, personality is one of her specialty areas—she teaches the upper-level course to majors. As you know, personality theory is *not* one of my areas of strength. I spent all day yesterday reading textbooks trying to put together a set of lectures but, honestly, my knowledge in this area is thin. I hope the students don't ask questions I can't answer." Susan heart raced as she imagined this scenario during class.

"It'll be fine, don't worry." Dan's voice was calm as if he was talking to a child crying over a bruised knee.

Annoyed, Susan barked, "I can't talk long this morning. Why did you call?"

"I'd like to come to Victoria around Valentine's Day. I have a gift for you."

"Really? Since when do you pay attention to holidays like Valentine's Day?" Susan's voice cracked with sarcasm.

"Listen, Sue, this is clearly a bad time to talk to you. Let's just say that I'll come over to Victoria one weekend in mid-February, okay?" Silence hung over the phone line. "Sue, what do you say?" Dan asked again.

"What's the gift?" Susan was curt. She wanted to shift Dan's attention away from a visit.

Dan sighed. "Okay, I wanted it to be a surprise, but maybe it'll cheer you up if I tell you now. I'll soon have the first checks for our shares of the royalty advance on our textbook. Our editor was pleased with the chapters we sent, and so our advances will be here in a couple of weeks." Dan stopped and waited. Hearing only silence, he continued, "I thought I could deliver your check and we could go to dinner at the Empress to celebrate."

Susan looked at her watch, impatient. "I really don't have time for this right now. My Intro class starts soon. Why don't you just send me the check in the mail? If things don't go well for me this week, I won't be in the mood to celebrate, anyway."

Dan's voice went flat. "I'll call you sometime next week and we can discuss it again." He sounded hurt, Susan thought. "Good luck with the teaching evaluations." Susan heard the click as Dan hung up.

Susan was fifteen minutes into her lecture on trait theories of personality when she turned from writing the word *introversion* on the chalkboard and noticed Penny and Joyce sitting in the last row of the lecture hall. Joyce had extended the retractable desk and was writing. Penny gave her a weak wave when she noticed Susan was aware of their presence. Susan's voice quivered as she glanced at her lecture notes for some moral as well as intellectual support. Fortunately, when Susan looked up from the podium, she saw several students with raised hands. Relieved, she answered the questions about introverted behavior and her composure returned.

The room was filled this morning. Dreary Monday mornings in late January were not the optimal days for maximum attendance, but topics like personality and abnormal psychology were of intrinsic interest to students. They were curious about the meaning of their own behavior, or better yet, the motives behind the mysterious behaviors of family members or friends. Susan was nervous about presenting topics in Joyce Petras's specialty area, but she relaxed when the students responded to her lecture. Her spirits rose as class participation became more vigorous—unusual for a Monday morning. She became comfortable enough to ad-lib a few examples. "Introverts are in the library, while extroverts spend their time in the cafeteria surrounded by their friends. Extroverts are more fun on a date, but introverts are the people you want to study with." There was a spattering of laughter from both the students and the evaluators.

At the end of class, Joyce and Penny waited for the students to leave the lecture hall, and then walked down the long staircase to the front of the room. They stood aside as Susan answered the questions of several students who had clustered around her after class. One young woman, who occupied the same front-row seat at each class, lingered until she and Susan were alone. "Dr. Barron, if someone is an introvert, how do they become an extrovert?" Her tone was hushed, and she looked embarrassed at her question. Susan sensed the student was asking about herself. She glanced toward Penny and Joyce and saw they were listening to the exchange. Penny's eyes twinkled with amusement.

Susan cleared her throat. "Well, one theory claims that introverts have an over-active nervous system, so they avoid external stimulation to compensate for the intensity of their internal life. Extroverts are the opposite—their nervous system is under-active, so they need a lot of excitement to get them going."

"So, are you saying someone can't change from one to the other because their nervous system won't let them?"

Susan hesitated. "That's a good question. It just might mean that it will take effort to go against one's physiology. Besides, it is just one theory about the difference between introverts and extroverts." Susan took a chance. "Why, do you want to change?"

"Yeah, I'm the one in the library. I want to be the one in the cafeteria."

Susan wanted to offer comfort—the young woman looked pitifully morose. "I've always thought behavioral change is possible, no matter what the odds."

The student responded with a weak smile. "Thanks, Dr. Barron, I may give it a try." She turned to climb the stairs, leaving Susan alone with Joyce and Penny.

Joyce bubbled. "That was a great class. I could quibble with how you presented the material, but I know that personality theory isn't your area of specialty. Given that, I thought you did a good job."

Penny nodded in agreement. "I admire your ability to handle a class this large. When I first started at JDU, I was assigned one of these large Intro sections. I was so tense about teaching such a large group I would go to the restroom and throw up before each class. After my first year, I told Bill Forsyth, who was the chairman then, that I'd do anything, including taking on an extra class, rather than teach a large lecture section of Intro. Fortunately, Bill agreed, and I was saved from the torture of the long walk down these stairs," Penny turned and waved at the now empty room, "and the scrutiny of three hundred and fifty pairs of eyes. Being back in this room is making me anxious."

Susan wondered if Penny was trying to make her feel good, but Penny continued, "I agree with Joyce. You did a fine job for someone who's just starting out."

Susan felt the color rise in her cheeks. Pleased and relieved, she grabbed her jacket thrown over a chair and followed Joyce and Penny up the stairs and out the door at the rear of the room. As they left the building, Susan asked, "Will you be coming to class again on Wednesday?"

Joyce and Penny looked at each other and a non-verbal agreement seemed to pass between them. "I don't think we need to do more in-person observation," Joyce responded. "We have enough information to write our report for the executive committee. We'll distribute course evaluation questionnaires to the students toward the end of the term. You'll leave the room, and your TA will distribute and collect the questionnaires from your students."

Penny waved good-bye as they entered the Angus building. She headed toward her first-floor office, while Joyce and Susan started the climb to the second floor.

"How's the textbook coming?" Joyce asked.

Susan did not know if this was part of the evaluation, so she paused a few seconds to deliberate. "It's going well. In fact, Dan called me this morning to say our editor liked the first chapters we sent."

"I noticed Dan was here over the holiday break. Did having him around everyday help with your writing?" Joyce asked.

Startled, Susan blurted without thinking. "I didn't see you in the building. I thought Dan and I were the only ones here."

Joyce laughed as she leaned against the wall next to Susan's office door. "I wasn't in the building. I have two dogs, and I bring them to campus on weekends and holidays to give them a chance to run around. I saw you and Dan walking out of the building toward the parking lot a couple of times. That's how I knew he was here. The two of you seemed to be in such intense conversations, I didn't want to intrude on your work by stopping to say hello. I'm sure I'll get to catch up on old times with Dan sometime soon. It's nice to have a collaborator who's more than just a colleague, isn't it?" Joyce winked at Susan as she turned and bustled down the hallway toward her office.

Susan took off her jacket and hung it on the hook behind her office door. She dropped the coffee-stained lecture notes on her desk. She was foolish to think her colleagues would not notice Dan around campus for a week. They may be eccentric and asocial, but they were not stupid. She recoiled at how her colleagues, especially the men, would interpret her relationship with Dan. Susan shook her head, annoyed. She was not going to let a casual remark spoil the success of her day—a good teaching evaluation from Joyce and Penny. She sat down at her typewriter. She had a chapter to finish, and she wanted to enjoy the rare experience of satisfaction with a job well done.

TWENTY-TWO

Susan savored her sense of well-being for the rest of the week. Contentment had been elusive since her arrival at JDU, and she welcomed the feeling back into her life.

Jack Bernoski tapped on her open office door. "Got a minute?" he said.

Astonished, Susan motioned him toward the empty chair beside her desk. Jack usually ignored her except for desultory greetings in the department mail room. According to Bob Van Holland, Jack resented academics from the States. He told the graduate students it was unfair that psychologists educated in Canada were overlooked in favor of those with degrees from universities in the States. If Bob's gossip was true, Jack likely avoided her for this reason.

Jack settled himself into the chair. "Have you had your teaching evaluations yet?"

Susan nodded.

"Mine went okay." Jack leaned back with a broad grin.

"That's great, Jack, tell me what happened." Susan welcomed this unexpected opportunity to compare notes.

"Carl Thorndike and Jim Kracknoy came to my Developmental Psych class this week. The visit was supposed to be unannounced," Jack gave Susan a conspiratorial smile, "but Carl hinted that the evaluation would be this week. Carl doesn't like faculty popping into classes unannounced to do evaluations. I was nervous because Jim is a developmental psychologist like me, but I was over-prepared, and the class went well." Jack grinned, obviously pleased with himself. "I can't tell you how relieved I am. When I taught in Nova Scotia, I always flubbed these types of faculty evaluations."

"Penny Carson and Joyce Petras visited my Intro class this week. I was nervous because I was lecturing on Joyce's specialty, personality theory, but things went well for me, too." Susan added, "Joyce also gave me a hint the evaluations were this week, so I was over-prepared, just like you." For the first time, Susan felt a connection with Jack. Both had conquered their fears and survived.

Jack slapped both knees and rose from the chair. "My wife and I are going out for dinner tonight. I want to celebrate. I'm desperate to keep this job. I won't go back to the Maritimes—too much poverty—it's too depressing. Back east the BC universities have a reputation for favoring faculty with degrees from the States. But I've been treated fairly, and I think I have a good shot at staying here—so it's time to celebrate." Jack walked toward the open door.

"Why do you think this department favors faculty from the States? It seems to me there's lots of Canadians here."

Jack laughed. "Look at the department faculty list in the university catalogue. There's lots of Canadians, but most of them got their PhDs in the States. There's only a couple of us who went to Canadian graduate schools."

Susan pressed. "I find it hard to believe there's discrimination against graduates from Canadian universities. We have a large graduate program— the University of Vancouver has a large graduate program. The students who want faculty positions must go somewhere after they graduate."

Jack replied, "The universities back east are more receptive to Canadian PhD graduates. It's BC with the reputation for a preference for faculty from the States. It's sort of a Canadian thing, anyway, to undervalue a homegrown product in favor of a foreigner, especially from the States or from Great Britain." Jack laughed again. "You look like you don't believe me. There's been lots of news commentary on this topic—read about it for yourself. Not to change the subject, but do you know how Lucas made out?" Jack asked.

Susan shook her head. "No, I haven't talked to Lucas for a while."

"I'm sure things went well for him, too. He's the most experienced of us." Jack swung out the door. "Treat yourself to a celebration," he advised as he left.

Susan looked at her watch—four o'clock. The voices in the hallway were Giles's gang heading to the faculty club for their Friday afternoon round of drinks. She shuffled papers into her briefcase. Jack was right—a good bottle of wine to celebrate her triumph was a festive way to end this special week.

"Hi, how're things going?"

Susan looked up to find Lucas standing in her office doorway. For weeks, she had seen Lucas only in passing. They rarely spoke except for a casual hello. She responded with the authentic cheerfulness she felt, "Things are going well, how about for you?"

Lucas leaned against the door frame. "Are you doing anything tonight?"

"No, why?" Susan was wary.

"There's a pub in the Empress called The Beaver. Want to go there tonight for a beer?"

Susan leaned back in her chair and studied Lucas. It was clear he wanted to talk to her about something serious. She wondered if it had to do with the teaching evaluations this week. If so, he was not happy—his expression was drawn and worried.

"Okay, what time?" she asked.

"Around nine o'clock. I'll meet you at the pub. You can't miss it. Just follow the Friday night crowds." Lucas slid out of the door frame.

Susan joined the throng at the pub entrance. Lucas was right; it was not hard to find. Partygoers reeking of beer and an even stronger scent of marijuana pushed her through the door. She scanned the room and spotted Lucas sitting at a corner table. His hands circled a pint glass of beer. She elbowed her way through the mass of bodies in front of the bar. Lucas saw her and gave a desultory wave of greeting.

Susan settled herself into the chair next to Lucas. "This is quite the place," Susan exclaimed as she shrugged out of her jacket. She was a stranger to Victoria's night life. She had never been to a downtown bar on a Friday night. She was excited to finally be part of a weekend party scene. Lucas gave Susan a weak smile, said nothing, but gestured to a waiter who was mopping spilled beer from an adjoining table. "Do you want another beer, Lucas?" the waiter asked.

"What do you want, Susan?" Lucas leaned over and whispered in her ear. Susan smelled the beer on his breath and wondered how many drinks he had had before she arrived. Susan looked up at the waiter. "I'll have the same thing Lucas is drinking."

"A Labatt's it is, then." The waiter flung the cleaning cloth over his shoulder and headed toward the bar. Susan thought she saw him wink at Lucas.

"You must come here often. The waiter knows your name," Susan teased.

Lucas muttered, "Yeah, I come here a lot. It's just a five-minute walk from my house, and when I can't stand being at home, I walk over here for a beer."

The waiter placed a chilled pint in front of Susan. "I'll put this on your tab, okay, Lucas?" Lucas nodded, and the waiter returned to the bar with the air of familiarity granted to pub regulars.

Susan took a few small sips of the unfamiliar Canadian beer. "How are things working out with your housemates?" Susan asked.

"I'm moving out at the end of this month. Things aren't going well. We've started to get on each other's nerves." Lucas took a sip of beer, licked the foam from his lips, and looked glum. There were dark circles under his eyes, a sign he needed sleep. *He is drunk or soon will be,* Susan guessed.

"Where are you moving?" This is going to be a tough night, Susan thought, annoyed that Lucas was so sullen.

"I got an apartment in James Bay not far from here," Lucas answered as he pulled back from the table and stared at Susan.

"Did you have a teaching evaluation this week?" Lucas crossed his arms over his chest.

Relieved, Susan answered, "Yes, I did." Hearing no response, she continued, "Joyce Petras and Penny Carson came to my Intro class last Monday morning. I was nervous, but the class went well and they seemed pleased." The muscles in Lucas's face tightened. Susan yearned to describe every detail of her triumphant day, but Lucas's expression warned her to be silent. Instead, she asked, "What about you? Who came to your class?"

"Otto Hartmann and Tom Carlisle," Lucas answered.

Susan looked surprised. "They're not members of the executive committee. Why did they do the evaluation?"

"Giles told me no one on the executive committee had expertise in neuropsychology, so he asked two of the neuropsych faculty to do the evaluation. He told me this was a common practice—to go outside the committee if they had to." Lucas leaned over the table toward Susan.

"Well, how did it go?" Susan was curious.

"I'm sure it would have gone okay if there'd been a class."

Puzzled, Susan asked, "What do you mean?"

Lucas replied, "I tried something different with my Abnormal Psych class this term. I gave them forty questions. Each student must provide written answers to each of these questions by the end of the term. We only meet formally as a class when one of the students wants to discuss their work on these questions with the whole group. Otherwise, individual students meet with me in my office to go over their answers."

"Sounds like an interesting idea—a lot of work for you, though." Susan tried to sound encouraging, but the glum look on Lucas's face did not change. "Well, what did Otto and Tom say?"

"The two of them showed up in my office and asked me why there wasn't a class. They'd gone to the classroom expecting to sit in on a lecture. When I told them how I'd organized the class, Otto particularly did not look pleased." Lucas shrugged. "He gets red in the face when he's angry, and that's how he looked when I told him what I was doing."

"What did Tom say?"

"He seemed okay with things. He told me I should've scheduled a lecture session so they could observe my teaching. I told him I would've done that if I'd known they were coming to my class." Lucas's voice was tense.

"You mean you didn't know they were coming?" Susan voice rose with surprise.

"No, of course not—Giles told me the evaluation visits are unannounced." Lucas paused, his eyes scanning Susan's face. His expression was suspicious. "Are you telling me you knew Joyce and Penny were coming to your class on a particular day?"

Susan stared at Lucas. She felt trapped. Joyce did not want her to tell anyone about the advance notice she gave Susan. But Lucas looked so miserable she opted to tell him the truth. "I didn't know the exact day they were coming. Joyce just gave me a rough time frame—the evaluations would take place sometime this week. Joyce said Giles was the only one on the executive committee who liked the idea of unannounced visits. Everyone else wanted to give new faculty the chance to prepare."

Lucas slumped back in his chair. "So, Giles screwed me by not telling me Otto and Tom would visit my class. I thought Tom looked surprised when I told him I wasn't expecting their visit. Now it all makes sense." Lucas's eyes flashed, and his fingers shredded the edges of the paper coaster under his beer glass. They sat in silence as the minutes passed. Susan sipped her drink and waited. She wondered what he was thinking as he stared at his glass of beer. Suddenly, he started to laugh. "I talked with Bill Forsythe, and he told me Otto doesn't approve of experimental teaching methods."

"What are you going to do?" Susan asked, realizing that Giles likely had sabotaged Lucas's evaluation.

"Tom worked it out with Giles. I'm going to hold formal lectures next week with my Abnormal Psych class, and Otto and Tom will come one of those days to watch me teach. However," he mumbled, "I think the damage is done."

"What do you mean?"

"Well, if Otto hates teaching that strays from the traditional lecture, then he knows the classes next week are being staged for his benefit. And, he hasn't appreciated the criticisms I've made about the dissertation topics of a few of his grad students. I'll do my best to prepare, but I don't think Otto is positively disposed toward either me or my teaching," Lucas added. "Fortunately, Tom will be there, too. At least one of the evaluators will be on my side—I think."

"I'm sure things will work out." Susan hated sounding so lame, especially since she was not convinced what she said was true. Silently, she agreed with Lucas—his evaluation outcome was uncertain. She reached over to squeeze his hand. "Things will be fine, don't worry."

Lucas sat silently scrutinizing their entwined fingers as he rubbed the back of Susan's hand with his thumb. Eventually, he asked, "Can I come to your place tonight?"

Taken aback, Susan quipped, "Are things that bad at your house?"

Lucas frowned at her flippant response. "It has nothing to do with that—I'd just like to be with you tonight."

Susan hesitated, uncertain. She had no idea what was happening with him. The feel of his thumb slowly massaging her hand was warm and inviting, but what did this mean?

"Why do you want to be with me tonight? I need some clarity about what's going on with you. It didn't work out that well between us the last time." Susan shrugged. "Well, some part of it worked out, but other parts didn't."

Lucas searched her face. The dark circles under his eyes had deepened. His mumbled response was almost incoherent. "Things are going well for you here, unlike for me. Maybe some of your success will rub off. I think about you and you and me a lot, and I want to be with you tonight."

Susan stared at him, trying to hide her shock. They had not talked in months. It was hard to believe he thought about her at all. Was he in a delusional state caused by the fiasco around his evaluations, or was he drunk and likely to forget this conversation in the morning? Either way, she had little to lose in spending the night with him. It might end like the last time—no sex, just cuddling—and that was okay. Besides, she sympathized with his plight. She would need a friend, too, if she suddenly found out the department elites were aligned against her. "Alright, let's go back to my place," Susan agreed, still not sure she had made the right decision.

TWENTY-THREE

While Susan unlocked the door to her suite, Lucas lowered the collar of her jacket and his lips brushed the back of her neck. The gentle pressure of his kiss surprised Susan and held the promise that tonight would be different than their first encounter.

They entered the dark bedroom. Susan turned toward Lucas. The moonlight had mellowed the lines of his haggard face. She asked, uncertain, "Lucas, what's this all about? You disappear for months and then tell me tonight you think about me—you think about you and me—what do you think about?"

Lucas's smile was warm as he slowly traced the outline of her face with his fingertips. "Sometimes I watch you from my office window. You're walking across campus to your Intro class with a determined look on your face. I know how you've struggled with your teaching, and I admire your courage—you're tough but loveable at the same time. It's a combination hard to resist. I disappeared because I tried to resist, but there in the pub," his voice dropped to a whisper, "you looked so concerned, so endearing, so irresistible."

While he spoke, Lucas unbuttoned Susan's jacket and tossed it on the floor. She realized as he fumbled under her sweater with her bra clasp that she was starting to remove his clothes, too. Their assorted garments dropped like leaves into piles on the floor.

Naked, Lucas bent toward Susan, sliding his lips inch by inch along the skin of her upper thighs and hips to her breasts. Susan ran her fingers through his curls and met his lips when his kisses reached her face. They sank onto the bed. His mouth was inviting as his tongue snaked deep inside her.

Susan stroked Lucas, taking pleasure in the muscular contours of his body and then his arousal. When he entered her at last, she gasped with its anticipation and the warm delight of his feel inside of her.

"Come on top. I love how you look in the moonlight," Lucas said, brushing her nipples with his fingertips. She arched over him, his hands guiding her hips, as they rocked back and forth.

Susan did not want to stop. She closed her eyes overwhelmed by desire, wanting to halt time. It was inevitable—such intensity could not last forever—there were moans and cries of delight, then release. Breathless, Susan slumped onto Lucas's chest.

"I like what we just did," Lucas murmured.

"Me, too," Susan panted. "I wonder if Wanda Martin heard us. I think we were rather noisy."

"Maybe the department will gossip about you," Lucas teased, his lips near her ear. In the moments of calm, his breathing became regular. He mumbled, "—falling asleep—stay close." Susan pulled the quilt over them, settled herself under the covers next to his warmth, and closed her eyes.

Rain spattered the bedroom window. Susan woke with a start to another gloomy morning. She checked the clock on the bedside table.

Lucas stirred. "What time is it?"

"Six o'clock," she answered, stretching catlike along the expanse of his body.

Lucas groaned, "I should leave—I have a Tai Chi group Saturday mornings." He raised himself on one elbow to peer down at Susan. His hair was tousled, his face relaxed. The dark circles under his eyes had faded. He cupped her nipple with his fingers, then his hand started a descent across her stomach toward her groin.

"I'm surprised you're still in bed. It's your morning ritual to throw up, isn't it?" Susan laughed, shivering under his touch.

Lucas smiled. "I do that to get rid of yesterday's garbage." He kissed her breast. "But I liked yesterday so much I don't want to get rid of it. In fact, I want to do it again," he said. Susan giggled before his mouth closed over hers.

* * * * * * * * * * * * * *

"It's eight o'clock, I really do have to go," Lucas said, picking out his clothes from the disheveled pile at the foot of the bed.

Susan sat huddled in the quilt. "Do you want me to drive you home? It's raining, and you don't have your car here."

Lucas shook his head. "I had a lot of beer last night. A walk through the rain will clear my head." He buttoned his jacket. "A friend from my men's group gave me the key to his place at Shawnigan Lake. He's gone to Mexico for a few weeks. Can I pick you up around noon? We'll go and check the place out. I haven't been there yet."

"Sure, I'd like that." Susan grinned. "Where's Shawnigan Lake?"

"North of Victoria—not far, about a forty minute drive," Lucas answered.

Susan draped the quilt around her and walked Lucas to the door of her suite. He cupped her chin and ran his fingers over her lips, a brief kiss, and he disappeared down the stairs. She returned to the bedroom window to follow his progress. Lucas had drawn the collar of his jacket around his ears, and his hands were shoved into the pockets against the damp chill of the dismal morning. Susan hugged herself to prolong the delicious sensations of love making. It had been a long time since joyous, satisfying sex. She tingled with the sensual pleasure of her body.

* * * * * * * * * * * * *

Lucas inserted the key into the lock and gave the door a shove. It creaked open, and Susan followed him into the cottage. The interior was a large, narrow room with the living room adjoining the kitchen much like a railroad car. There was a continuous wall of windows facing the lake. Susan surveyed the view. A cement patio circled the exterior with stairs down a bank to a narrow wooden pier. A battered rowboat was upturned on its planks. A tiny island of rocky outcroppings lay about a hundred yards from the end of the pier. The cottages dotting the opposite side of the lake were visible, but the dense forest obscured the sight of any of the adjoining properties.

"It's pretty here," Susan said, admiring the tranquility of the water shimmering under the dull winter sky. "Do people live here year-round?"

Lucas joined her at the window. "Some do. One of the neuropsych grad students lives across the lake. I was here once before when she invited me to dinner. There's a village and a private school about a mile down the shore. The grad student's husband works at the school," Lucas said, waving his hand toward one end of the lake. "My friend told me he inherited this cottage from his grandparents who lived in Vancouver. They used it as a weekend getaway, but my friend lives here permanently. The places around the lake are probably a combination of permanent and part-time residences."

Lucas rubbed his arms. "It's freezing in here," he complained. "I saw a stack of wood outside. I'm going to build a fire." He checked the flue in the rustic flagstone fireplace across from the windows. "Great, it looks like the fireplace is in good condition."

While Lucas arranged the logs, Susan explored the kitchen. She found a well-stocked liquor cabinet nestled in one corner. "Do you think your friend would mind if we drank a bottle of wine?" Susan asked.

"Choose the one you want. I'll replace it before he gets back," Lucas answered, looking pleased when flames started to smolder. He threw pillows from the couch onto the floor in front of the hearth. "Let's sit here," he motioned toward the pillows. "This'll be the only warm place in the room until the fire catches hold." Susan opened the bottle of wine, poured two glasses, and gave one to Lucas who shivered and moved closer to the blaze. "I can see why my friend goes to Mexico every winter. It's really cold in here."

Susan toasted Lucas. "Here's to a successful teaching evaluation for you next week."

Lucas scowled. "I was upset last night, especially when it became clear Giles sabotaged me by not giving me advance notice of the class visits. Walking home this morning I realized I'm starting not to care what happens. I'm tired of jibes about the way I dress, how I teach my classes, how I conduct neuropsych assessments at the hospital, how I criticize dissertation research proposals. I came here because I thought it would be a free, less conservative environment, but the department is turning out to be a repeat of what I wanted to escape." Lucas paused. "I like Victoria and I want to stay, but I need a job until I can find other work that suits me better." Lucas looked at the flames and muttered. "One part of me says my pride will be hurt if I'm fired after my first two-year contract—I'd rather leave on my own terms—but another part of me says I'll be happy to go because I don't really fit in and I don't want to try to fit in."

"Talk to Carl Thorndike about what happened with Giles. He told me that people in the department are tired of the dirty tricks played on new faculty and they want them to stop," Susan implored. "The students like you. That must count for something."

"The students aren't the problem. It's the outdated attitudes of the faculty I have trouble with. Otto and I haven't clicked as colleagues, and that's a fatal error on my part. He's critical of everything I do—at the hospital for consultations, at grad student research meetings, and now my teaching." Lucas put his arm around her shoulders. "Don't look so troubled, Susan.

I'll talk to Carl, but whether that will help or not, who knows? One way or another it'll all work out in the end."

Lucas paused to sip his wine. "But what about you? I think it's ironic that this isn't your dream job, but you seem to be adapting well. I see the 'Do not disturb' sign on your office door, so you're getting on with the book and now a good teaching evaluation—what's your key to success here?"

Susan leaned her head on Lucas's shoulder and sighed. "I don't have a key to success. Joyce Petras and Dan were grad students together at Stanford. She may be positive toward me because she sees me as part of a Stanford connection, unrealistic as that is. My best friend in grad school, Julie, coined the term, Stanford mafia. Stanford grads are obsessively proud of their elite status, and they stick together. Now that I think about it, I may owe my good teaching evaluation more to Dan and his Stanford roots than to my own ability. As far as my research goes, no one in the department is interested in what goes on in my lab—that will be my own doing without any help from anyone but Dan."

Susan sniggered, "As you recall, Giles told us we had to publish. He didn't tell us we would be on our own to figure out how to do that." She raised her head and peeked at Lucas. "Speaking of research, are you making any progress on the mind-body problem?"

The fire glimmered with a seductive crackle, and the icy chill in the room started to lift. Lucas grinned, slipped his hand under Susan's sweater, and traced the outline of her breasts with his fingertips. "At the moment, I'm more interested in the body side of the problem. I think you didn't let yourself go last night—you were worried about Wanda Martin eavesdropping," he teased.

"Silly, wasn't it?"

Lucas pushed his hand beneath the fly of Susan's jeans. His fingers searched between her legs. "You don't have to worry about anyone hearing us here. The lake is on one side, and the other cottages are hundreds of feet away. We can make as much noise as we want." They settled onto the pillows scattered across the floor in front of the fireplace.

Susan chuckled as Lucas stretched his body over hers, their hips pressed together. "If I'm not mistaken, Lucas, I feel you have definitely recovered your sexual energy."

Lucas murmured. "Bernie, my therapist, has a retreat on Quadra Island called Tranquility Farm—primitive and peaceful. I've been there a couple of times for group sessions. Bernie told me my sexual energy would come back if the circumstances were right—I guess these are the right circumstances."

Removing each other's clothes became a game. Finally, naked in front of the blazing fire, Lucas nibbled Susan's ear and whispered, "It's only Saturday—we have the rest of the weekend. I think I'm well on the way to becoming Bernie's most successful cure."

* * * * * * * * * * * * * *

"I wish you weren't so conscientious," Lucas chided. "Canceling a class now and then makes the students appreciate you more. We could have stayed at Shawnigan until tomorrow morning. Another night in front of that fireplace would have been nice—there were other erotic possibilities of foot massage to explore." Lucas smiled and reached across the car seat to fondle the back of Susan's neck.

"Promise me you won't brag to your therapist about your miracle recovery," Susan pleaded with a laugh, remembering the massage possibilities they had explored.

"Bernie's so intuitive, he'll figure it out when he sees me—I won't have to say anything. Besides, Bernie's not responsible for our weekend. It's the connection between us that unleashed all that…," Lucas struggled for the right word, "passion." His expression softened as he continued to caress her neck.

"Maybe someday I'll be casual about teaching." Susan groaned under the gentle touch of his fingertips. How could she tyrannize herself into abandoning a remarkable day with the image of three hundred blank faces waiting for her the next morning?

Lucas's eyes danced with a devilish gleam. "I'm being cooperative because you said you had to get up at four AM to do the lecture prep you didn't do this weekend. If I stayed with you tonight and we got up at four, you would not be preparing lectures."

Susan laughed and nodded agreement, then reluctantly opened the car door. "Good luck next week and, please, talk to Carl. He has good insights into Giles and what motivates him. He may be able to tell you what Giles's dirty tricks are about."

"I'll talk to Carl, but it's not just Giles, it's Otto, too. He's set in his ways and rigid about what he thinks is the correct way to do things." Lucas shrugged. "I think inflexibility is just Otto's style."

Susan gave Lucas a lingering farewell kiss. She faked a light-heartedness she did not feel. "The only mistake we almost made this weekend was thinking about rowing to the island off the end of the pier. It was good luck you noticed the holes in the bottom of the rowboat before we tossed it in the water."

"This is not the time of year for a swim in Shawnigan Lake," Lucas agreed, while his fingers stroked her cheek. Their eyes met in a silent pact. It was so hard to say good-bye—to each other…to the weekend.

Susan jumped from the car to fend off the temptation to stay. She waved good-bye and scurried up the stairs to her front door. When she turned around, Lucas's car was swallowed by the darkness of the Sunday night.

TWENTY - FOUR

The pages of Wanda Martin's dissertation proposal lay scattered across Susan's desk. Otto Hartmann wanted an opinion on the merits of the manuscript, but Susan was struggling to find positive things to say. Wanda should stop worrying about her neighbors gossiping about her sex life and spend more time mastering the basics of experimental design, Susan grumbled, as she penciled another comment in the margin.

It was Friday, Valentine's Day, and Dan would arrive soon. Her attempt to dissuade Dan from a trip to Victoria to deliver the royalty check failed. Dispirited, she pushed Wanda's proposal aside and stared out the window. She resented coping with Dan when what she really wanted was to savor the memory of her weekend with Lucas. Or better yet, to spend another weekend with Lucas.

Lucas and Susan had embraced each other with starvation-like fervor—the passion between them intense. Susan understood her side of the powerful attraction. She had endured months of deprivation except for the unsatisfying interlude with Dan. Her body craved sexual fulfillment. Lucas also acted as if he was deprived, which surprised Susan. She had assumed his life was filled with willing partners, with many women attracted by his seductive appeal. Susan tipped an imaginary hat to Lucas's therapist. He had, without a doubt, recovered his sexual energy.

Eventually the two of them agreed to do something other than huddle under the blankets by the blazing fire. They discovered a few tins of tuna fish and some Ritz crackers and had a makeshift picnic on the pier. The warmth of the Sunday afternoon sun prompted a momentary plan to row to the island until Lucas noticed the jagged holes pierced through the bottom of the upturned rowboat. Their outing thwarted, they returned to the comfort of the pillows and blankets in front of the fire. Susan sank back in her chair and closed her eyes to relish the sensual memories of her weekend with Lucas.

Suddenly, Dan was standing at her office door. "Hi, Sue." Dan hustled into the room, slammed the door, and set his briefcase on her desk. He reached down and pulled her from her chair. Once in his arms, he crushed his lips against hers. His tongue darted into her mouth, while he pressed her against his body. She felt his arousal as he pushed against her hips.

"Dan, please," Susan sputtered. "Not here—I have student office hours now, and I must keep the door open," she lied.

Dan's arms circled her shoulders. He murmured, "I missed you, Sue." Stunned, she maneuvered out of his embrace. His eyes twinkled as he reached into the pocket of his blazer to pull out an envelope "Here's your royalty share, as promised." Susan tore open the flap to inspect the check. It was real. She gave a sigh of relief that Dan had not fabricated an excuse to visit her. Dan chuckled and reached for her again, but Susan evaded his grasp.

"I need to keep my door open during student office hours," Susan explained. "The department takes faculty office hours for students very seriously."

Susan swung open the door to find Lucas standing in the hallway outside. "Lucas, what're you doing here?"

"Hi, Susan, I didn't know you were in your office. I was just leaving you a note on your door to ask—"

Lucas's eyes drifted upward, and Susan guessed that Dan was standing behind her. She gestured, "Lucas, this is my colleague, Dan Kavline. Dan—Lucas Selkirk—Lucas is new this year like me." Susan's voice faded.

Dan extended his hand, but Lucas did not respond. Instead his hand crumpled the scrap of paper he was holding. "How's the book coming along?" he asked, his voice stiff.

"Great," Dan exclaimed curling his arm around Susan's shoulders and pulling her toward him. "I'm here this weekend to deliver the first of our royalty advances. We're going to celebrate tonight with dinner at the Empress." Dan cupped Susan's neck with his hand.

Lucas's face froze, his expression unreadable. "Well, congratulations." He turned and started walking toward his office.

Dan called out. "We're not finished with the book yet, so I'm here to keep Sue writing until we finish those final chapters."

Lucas stopped and retraced his steps. "I don't know Susan as well as you do, but it seems to me she doesn't need outside encouragement to work. She drives herself pretty hard on her own." Susan scanned his face. There was the familiar intimacy that had grown between them but also disappointment.

"Lucas, what did you want to tell me?" Susan asked as she twisted out of Dan's grasp. She pointed at the wad of paper in his hand.

"Nothing important—I'll talk to you next week." Lucas turned, saying over his shoulder, "Have fun or don't work too hard, you two, whatever fits the situation." Susan watched as Lucas crammed the note into the pocket of his jeans and disappeared into his office, slamming the door.

* * * * * * * * * * * * * *

Susan huddled under a quilt on her bedroom window seat. Sleep was impossible, so she sought solace in the distant Victoria skyline shimmering in the gloom. Dan was sprawled across her bed. She had encouraged him to drink several pre-dinner cocktails and a bottle of wine at the Empress. There were brandy night caps waiting when they returned to her suite. Fortunately, Dan needed little encouragement to drink heavily. When his head started to nod, she led him to the bedroom, helped him remove his shirt and slacks, and tucked him under a blanket. Her plan for the evening had worked. Dan was asleep or passed out, she did not care which, so there would be no sex tonight.

Susan shifted her eyes to the distant city. She could not erase Lucas from her thoughts. She was haunted by his reaction when he found her with Dan. What was in the note he was about to leave on her office door? She was tortured by the look on his face and the sound of the slam of his office door.

Susan curled into a ball and circled her knees with her arms. She had not felt this way since the early years of her marriage—the warmth of the chemical bond that results from sharing delicious intimacies. The uninhibited exploration of two bodies caused a special closeness between two people. She yearned for Lucas. She rested her head on her knees because she feared he would now shut her out. Their weekend together made a return to solitary isolation a thought hard to bear.

"Why aren't you asleep?" Dan wobbled out of bed to sit beside her. He rubbed his temples—a sign of a hangover, Susan guessed. He fumbled for her hand under the quilt.

"Why didn't you tell me you knew Joyce Petras at Stanford?" Susan snapped.

Dan mumbled. "To tell you the truth, I'd forgotten about her. I didn't know her that well in grad school. Back then she was a knockout—long blond hair down to her waist—tight jeans and even tighter tops. She got involved with Ari Petras, and they started to live together, causing lots of gossip. Some people in the department didn't like a faculty member living with a grad student. Others didn't like Ari walking out on his wife." Dan smirked. "I saw her on campus one day, and I couldn't believe the change. The long hair and tight jeans were gone. I thought she was trying to look older because she's so much younger than Ari." Dan coughed to clear his throat. "I heard Joyce and Ari got married and left Stanford, but it was Jim Kracknoy who told me they were here at JDU."

"Joyce told me she knew you at Stanford. She said you spent a lot of time with a grad student named Liz who was killed in a car accident."

Dan nodded. "Her name was Liz Grantley. We planned a lot of experiments together and helped each other in the lab. Graduate school wasn't quite the same after she died." Dan's eyes gleamed in the dim moonlit room. "Lab work can be very lonely. Working with collaborators reduces the isolation, and collectively you can accomplish a lot more. Liz and I worked well together. After she died, I just wanted to finish my degree and get the hell out of there."

"Dan, what does your wife think of the other women in your life—Liz, Jennifer, me?"

"What do you mean, what does she think?" Dan was guarded.

"Well, is she jealous? Does she know you're unfaithful to her?"

"Who said I'm unfaithful?" Dan growled. Realizing how ridiculous his reply sounded, he laughed. "Other than the obvious present situation, of course."

Susan struggled. "You spend a lot of time away from home. You work with women colleagues. Does Mona ever get angry or jealous or ask what you're doing when you're not with her and your kids?"

Dan stared at Susan. He looked indecisive, as if he was at a crossroads, uncertain of the path to follow. Finally, he answered, "Mona was jealous of Liz. When Liz died, Mona claimed she'd used witchcraft to put a curse on Liz that caused the accident that killed her."

Susan jerked her hand from Dan and gasped. "What're you talking about, Dan—that's crazy—you don't believe Mona can put evil curses on people, do you?"

"No, *I* don't. I'm telling you this because you asked if Mona was ever jealous and I'm telling you, yes, she was—she was jealous of Liz. Her story about the curse was just her way of expressing her jealousy and she was trying to frighten me."

"Why would Mona want to frighten you?"

"She told me she didn't want me to get involved with any other women again or the same thing would happen to them—she'd curse them, and they'd die."

"Dan, this is ridiculous. You're a scientist. You can't believe in curses and sticking pins in voodoo dolls or whatever is done to place a curse." Susan was stunned.

"No, I don't believe in curses, but Mona does."

Susan tightened the quilt around her. "Dan, you're still involved with other women. Are you saying we should all fear for our lives?"

Dan wrapped his arms around Susan. "Of course not. None of this is real. Mona just thinks it's real. Everything's under control—I used her own tactics against her to stop her silliness."

"What did you do?"

"I went to see one of the older, well-respected witches in Palo Alto. I asked her to put a protective mantle around me so that any evil done to me or to people I cared about would backfire on the person who placed the curse. She did what I asked and gave me a talisman I wear as a protection. I told Mona what I'd done. She was surprised. I guess she didn't realize I was picking up a lot about witchcraft from being around her and her friends—but she understood. The jealous rages and talk of evil curses ended."

Susan pushed Dan away. "You can't be serious. I've never seen you wear any occult talisman. You're making this whole thing up."

Dan sighed. "I knew you'd have this reaction. That's why I've never told anyone about this before." Dan tried to guide her back to the bed, but Susan resisted. "I knew Mona was convinced she'd used witchcraft to cause Liz's death, so I used her own beliefs to stop her from thinking she could manipulate and threaten me. As far as the talisman goes, I wear it to remind her that I'm protected and those I care about are protected. Mona believes in its power and that's all that matters." Dan held up his left hand to display the broad silver band around his ring finger.

"I always thought that was your wedding ring." Susan examined Dan's hand with new curiosity.

"It was designed to look that way," Dan explained. "In the occult world a large mass of specially crafted silver wards off evil—so I wear it and Mona knows I'm protected."

"So, you think what happened to Liz was a genuine accident?"

"Of course, I do. Liz went to Lake Tahoe with her family. Liz's brother had a serious drinking problem, and Liz convinced her parents a ski vacation, when they were all together, would help him face his problem. He was driving the car that skidded off the road. They were both killed. The autopsy showed her brother had high levels of blood alcohol at the time of the accident. I wish I knew why Liz got in the car—I'd warned her to be careful around him."

"Dan, if your story is true, how can you stay married to Mona?" Susan was mystified.

Dan looked resigned. "Mona and I had Sarah less than a year after I started grad school. We were naïve—didn't know much about birth control—but we learned fast enough. It turned out, Mona couldn't tolerate the pills and before we knew it, she was pregnant again with Leah. By this time, I was friends with Liz, but I didn't think Mona knew anything about her. After she made her threats when Liz was killed, we didn't have much physical contact, but she was already pregnant with Jacob." Dan paused. "Mona and I haven't divorced because our parents wouldn't know how to handle it. There'd be lots of fuss over the grandchildren and who knows what else."

Susan sat in shocked silence. Either Dan's crazy or Mona's crazy or they are both crazy—whatever the truth, she did not like it. Dan walked across the room and got into bed. Susan remained on the window seat, staring at him.

"Come on, get some sleep—you look exhausted. We can talk more about this tomorrow."

Susan shook her head. "No, I'm not tired. I want to sit for a few minutes more." She heard him sigh and roll over. Soon, there was the heavy breathing of a deep sleep. Eventually, she carried the quilt into the living room and fell asleep on her sofa.

* * * * * * * * * * * * * *

Susan woke to the smell of brewing coffee. She rolled over and saw that Dan was dressed. "Glad you're awake." A moment later he was standing above her with two mugs of coffee in hand. Susan wrapped herself in the quilt and accepted one of the cups. The unfinished conversation hung between them.

"How much of what you told me last night is true?" Susan asked.

"All of it," Dan replied.

"It's hard to believe there are people who practice witchcraft and who believe they can harm others by placing curses on them. This whole thing gives me the creeps—it's so unreal."

"Look. Witchcraft is a religious belief, and I'm using Mona's beliefs against her for my own benefit. That doesn't mean I think any of it is real. It works because Mona thinks it's real. I'm proud of myself for coming up with, what I think, is a pretty clever solution."

"What's your marriage like? When I saw you with Mona, the two of you seemed okay together, but what you're describing now is more like an occult war zone. Were you putting on an act for my benefit?"

Dan laughed. "The situation with Liz happened a long time ago. Mona got over it, and we've been cordially distant for years. She has the kids—that's what she wants, and they keep her busy."

"And, of course, she has her side business dealing with curses," Susan snapped. "When you told me that you and Mona have a bargain, what you meant was that she has her playthings—kids and magic—and you have yours—other women."

"Yeah, that's our bargain," Dan agreed, looking sheepish. Then he added, "I told you all this because I don't want you to worry. Mona's under control." Dan sipped his coffee, but Susan sensed his tension. "I hope you'll keep my secret. I wouldn't want my colleagues to get wind of this. It could make me look pretty ridiculous."

Susan recoiled. She stared at Dan with the hatred she had felt a year ago when he berated her into applying for the job at JDU. She resented him, and she was angry at letting herself be dragged into Dan's sordid life. Obviously, he was not aware of the disdain she felt for his unbelievable story. If he was, he did not care. His only concern was his professional image—his standing among his colleagues.

Susan hissed, "Don't worry. I'll keep your secrets. We both have a vested interest in maintaining your credibility—at least until the textbook is published. After that, who knows?"

TWENTY-FIVE

Susan arrived on campus Monday morning and searched for Lucas. A note on his office door announced he was ill and away from campus for the week. Disheartened, she walked to The Castle to take comfort in a cup of coffee. She found a copy of the local newspaper on a cafe table and grabbed it to distract her from her glum mood.

"Mind if I join you?" Susan looked up. Carl Thorndike settled into the chair across from hers, a cup of coffee in hand.

"Not at all." Susan was grateful for the company. She pointed at the newspaper. "The headline is the annual Victoria flower count. What's that?"

Carl laughed. "It's Victoria's gloat over the rest of Canada shivering in the bitter cold of February and March. Victorians count the number of daffodils and other flowers blooming in their gardens, the total is tallied, and the result is broadcast nationwide. It's a way to advertise Victoria's balmy climate to Canadians freezing in Alberta, Saskatchewan, and points east."

Susan was skeptical. "But it's not warm here. In fact, it's gloomy and wet."

Carl laughed again. "If you were sitting in Saskatchewan right now where it's -40 degrees Fahrenheit, +40 degrees in Victoria would look pretty good."

"Yeah, I guess it would," Susan frowned. She had never experienced temperatures that extreme. Still, she found it hard to imagine that reading about flowers growing in Victoria would provide any relief.

Carl smiled at her lack of enthusiasm. "Every place has its pretensions. Victoria's pretension is that it's one of the warmest places in Canada and, therefore, one of the most desirable places to live." He chuckled, and then leaned across the table and lowered his voice. "I assume you heard about Lucas's teaching evaluation disaster."

Susan sipped her coffee, not wanting to reveal how she knew about Lucas's dilemma. Fortunately, Carl misinterpreted her hesitation. "Don't worry, I've already talked to Jack Bernoski and I'm glad to have this chance to talk to you." His tone was reassuring. "We want to do something about Giles's attempts to sabotage new faculty he doesn't like. A few of us want these dirty dealings to stop."

"Why should Giles have something against Lucas?" Susan asked. "He's popular with students—he knows his neuropsychology—I don't understand."

"Departmental politics, my dear," Carl responded. "Ari and Otto have taken a dislike to Lucas, and Giles is in their pocket when it comes to deciding who stays and who goes. Lucas's unorthodox teaching practices haven't helped, but the three of them have no right to condemn Lucas on flimsy gossip and innuendo. Disliking his personal style should not be the reason for trying to torpedo his career here."

"What's going to happen?" Susan asked in a shaky voice.

"I'll sit in on Lucas's reevaluation to make sure he gets a fair shake. Then I think we'll start a movement to get rid of Giles as chair. He was a stop gap choice when there was no one else, but now Jim Kracknoy can take over and we'll all be the better for it." Carl downed the last of his coffee. "I trust we'll have your support when the coup occurs."

Susan was naïve when it came to the intrigue of a department revolt. She had no idea how a department disposed of its chairman. If Giles was elected, did the department just wait until his term was done? That would be a peaceful and orderly way to do it—the way political terms worked. Or, do members of the department march into his office and tell Giles he's through as chairman—a junta-like overthrow—with the replacement, Jim

Kracknoy, ready to take charge? Taking sides in a department rebellion was not something she had anticipated as part of her first year at JDU. She should be flattered—being treated like an insider and not a newcomer on probation—being invited to join an inner circle of conspirators. The truth was she was alarmed by Carl's request. She could only stare at him, too baffled to know what to say.

"Good," Carl seemed to assume her silence meant agreement. "By the way, thanks for the brandy a few weeks back and for providing a respite from my relationship problems."

"Have there been any repercussions?" Susan asked.

"No, Wanda was civil finally. She realizes that finishing her dissertation is more important than stirring up gossip in the department. It would only backfire on her—she's too vulnerable right now. I recommended she consult you for methodological advice about her dissertation research."

Susan laughed. "So, I have you to thank—Otto gave me a copy of her dissertation proposal to read. I understand your frustration now. She needs a lot of help when it comes to proper science."

Carl nodded. "Wanda's not our brightest student, but she has a job waiting when she finishes her degree, so she's motivated to work hard, and she'll follow whatever guidance you give. As for Wanda and me—what's the saying—don't dip your pen in the company inkwell. We both agreed that was good advice we should've followed. Don't mix your personal and work life." Carl smirked as he waved good-bye. "Actually, it's advice other people in the department should take, too."

Susan watched Carl hurry out of the coffee shop, leaving a wave of anxiety in his wake. Was Carl's last remark directed at her? She had been focused on Wanda's concern about department gossip and had not included Carl in a possible surveillance equation. How many times had he seen Lucas or Dan when he was in the building or in Wanda's suite? Susan mentally cycled through the occasions of these visits. Neither Dan nor Lucas mentioned running into anyone, but it could have happened. Susan cringed, knowing her pen was awash with company ink—another thing she had not planned for her first year at JDU.

After several weeks, Susan found Lucas alone in his office. "Hi, Lucas, how're you feeling?" She tried to sound casual.

Lucas raised his head from the papers strewn across his desk. "Hi, Susan, come in. I haven't seen you in a while. How're things going?"

"I want to ask you the same question. The note on your office door said you've been sick." Susan relaxed into the chair beside Lucas's desk, relieved by his friendliness.

"I'm fine—just a bad cold."

"How about the evaluation visit to your Abnormal Psych class—how did that go?"

"I think it was okay. Carl was there with Tom and Otto. I got the impression he was some sort of watchdog over the process. Tom was positive—gave me some good feedback. As far as Otto goes, who knows?" Lucas shrugged. "He took a lot of notes during my class but left as soon as the class was over. Tom did all the follow-up. I don't know whether Otto's leaving was a good or a bad sign, and Tom didn't mention it when we talked."

"I guess we'll all know in a month or so when Giles gives us feedback on our first year performance," Susan responded.

Lucas leaned back in his chair, stretched his legs, and crossed his arms over his chest. "I'm happy to wait until then," he said.

Susan summoned her courage. "Do you want to do something this weekend? We could go back to The Beaver for a beer."

"I spend my weekends on Quadra Island at Tranquility Farm, Bernie Chan's retreat I told you about. I'm going there this weekend for a drumming session."

"What's a drumming session?"

"A group of men sit around in a circle and pound on drums. It's a symbolic reenactment of male tribal rituals. Bernie uses these sessions to foster male bonding. It's a way to reassert feelings of power and mastery."

Susan controlled a sarcastic urge. "Does it work—the mastery and power thing?"

"I feel better after these sessions. Whether I feel more powerful, I don't know." Lucas looked thoughtful. "I like going to Tranquility. Being there helps me get perspective on the rest of my life. It's not a question of whether something works or not. It's not like a switch where you're either comfortable and feel your personal power or you don't. It's a gradual process of self-discovery—learning more about the various dimensions of what you're capable of doing." Lucas looked at Susan. "Someone like you probably thinks I'm talking nonsense."

Susan bristled. "Why do you say that?" she countered.

"Well, you seem to have your life figured out—publishing, academic success, tenure sometime in the future. You don't seem to have the doubts that I do."

"I wouldn't be so sure about that. I've struggled with a lot of things this year."

"I know about some of your conflicts, but are there others?" Lucas asked.

Susan was taken off guard and hesitated. Lucas was waiting for revelations of vulnerability, but she was reluctant to speak further. She sensed the closeness between them was gone. He was judging her again, and the intimacy of the weekend at Shawnigan Lake seemed to be forgotten. Defensive, she answered, "Oh, a lot of things. Maybe I should come to retreats at Tranquility Farm, too."

Lucas nodded, but his voice was guarded. "Sure, it might be a good idea. I'll leave a brochure in your mailbox."

An awkward silence followed. Finally, Lucas asked, "How was your weekend with Dan?"

"Fine, we had our royalty celebration Friday night, and then we worked for the rest of the weekend. We set up an experiment in my lab, and then outlined chapters for the textbook." She tried hard to convince Lucas that Dan and she were only colleagues. She flushed at Lucas's amused expression when she met his gaze. It was obvious he saw through her flimsy facade. Susan wanted to shout that she had made sure Dan was too drunk for sex the two nights of his visit, but Lucas's expression revealed that such a confession would make no difference. He had made his judgement about her relationship with Dan and had closed off.

"Sounds hectic," Lucas's voice was flat. His hand swept over the papers scattered on his desk. "Speaking of work, I need to grade these essays from my Abnormal Psych class." He picked up the paper on the top of the pile. "See you around, Susan," he murmured as he began reading.

Susan rose from the chair. She decided on one last foray. "Lucas, the weekend Dan was here you were going to leave me a note. What did you want to talk to me about?"

Lucas looked up at Susan standing at his office door. His eyes were sad as he scanned her face. After a moment, he shook his head. "No need for us to talk now. I figured everything out for myself."

* * * * * * * * * * * * * *

Susan sat curled in her quilt on her bedroom window seat, listening to the rain and studying the distant city lights. The lights looked different when it rained, inviting yet blurred and mysterious. If she was a bird, she would fly over them and immerse herself in their mindless beauty. Instead, she sipped her brandy. The bitter taste lingering on the back of her throat matched the bitterness of her mood. Susan's eyes glazed with tears, and her throat ached with a frustration the brandy could not relieve.

It was clear Lucas had removed himself and no longer saw her as his ally, his friend. Making love in front of a fire at the cottage on Shawnigan Lake would not happen again. Dan's presence in her office, his possessiveness—fondling her neck, bragging about royalty checks and celebration dinners, how Susan needed him to motivate her writing—all this had driven Lucas away. And for what—for Dan to have another selfish fling with a female colleague? She despised Dan for what he had done, even though she knew a future with Lucas was fraught with uncertainty. Even so, uncertainty with Lucas was preferable to Dan's reality. Lucas was an eccentric—daily vomiting, constant body work, male bonding sessions, and whatever other weird therapy he practiced at Tranquility Farm was part of his exotic appeal. Dan's occult standoff with his wife over the right to have serial extramarital affairs made Lucas's life seem less off-beat and more normal—at least more understandable.

Susan gulped the brandy and rested her forehead on her knees to ease her throbbing headache. A relationship with Lucas would have been perilous. The sex was monumental—there were definite sensual advantages to all that body work—but the two of them diverged in crucial ways. Lucas sought self-discovery, while she wanted an academic career he saw as grasping and ambitious. She would never know if they could have overcome that void. Her career was her top priority. That was her daily mantra. Was her dream of a career worth the pain of losing a relationship before it had a chance to grow? Was it worth the self-betrayal she felt when in bed with Dan? These questions haunted her because she did not have an answer.

Susan craved her former simple graduate student existence. She wanted Julie to lecture her about sex, men, and life—to use her for practice therapy. She was nostalgic for the short-lived sexual romps with fun-loving partners living for the pleasure of the moment. Her life had become too complex and incomprehensible. Dan cheated on beautiful Mona because he was trapped in an arranged marriage with a jealous wife who held him captive to her strange religion. Other women like Jennifer Evans must seem mundane—so reasonable compared to Mona and her witchy tricks. She winced when she imagined Julie's scolding if she ever revealed Dan's story. She could hear Julie's angry cry, "Get the hell away from him. He's figured out a new way to manipulate women into bed—he's nuts."

Susan sighed, wrapped the quilt around her shoulders, and walked through the dark to the kitchen to pour another brandy. What worried her was that Dan might not be nuts. He might be more sincere than his constant philandering suggested. Julie insisted Dan used his collaborations and his long work hours to seduce women and to conduct multiple shallow affairs. Maybe he was working on an overall plan to seek someone he preferred over Mona—Liz Grantley was killed, Jennifer Evans was in New York, so now Dan had turned to her.

Susan took a gulp of brandy and shook her head. Julie was right. Dan was a chronic womanizer who would get tired of her eventually. Like Carl and Wanda, she and Dan would agree they made a mistake and move on with their work—no more sex. That decision would be an enormous relief only dampened by her regret at losing Lucas before the two of them had a chance to start.

TWENTY-SIX

Susan was mesmerized by the large map of Vancouver Island and the Gulf Islands on the wall outside the ferry cafeteria. She studied the names of several of them—Mayne, Galiano, Salt Spring, Pender. Her TA, Bob Van Holland, had mentioned camping trips to Salt Spring, so she inspected this section of the map closely. Ganges was the major town on Salt Spring. Why did a village on an island in western Canada carry the name of a river in India? She vowed to visit Salt Spring and find out. She searched the map for the location of Quadra Island and finally found it off the coast of Vancouver Island far north of Victoria. She saw there was a ferry to Quadra from a town called Campbell River—another future trip, she promised herself.

The cottages scattered along the rock-strewn coasts on both islands bordering Active Pass were so close to the ship they beckoned her to come ashore. The blustery wind stopped her from stepping outside, but a group of camera-laden tourists braved the winds and rocking deck to photo the two shorelines as the ferry steamed out of the narrow passage and into the broad expanse of the Strait of Georgia.

The term was over. A celebratory weekend and a room at the Sylvia Hotel in Vancouver waited for her. "The Sylvia is a Vancouver landmark. It's dated, but it's a *must* place to stay because of its location overlooking English Bay at the entrance to Stanley Park," Jim Kracknoy had gushed when Susan asked him for a Vancouver hotel recommendation. Susan felt cocooned in Victoria for months, but she began to shed the constraints of island life as the ferry chugged toward the mainland coast. She was meeting Dan for lunch at

U of V before starting her weekend escape. Dan had unknown urgent business to discuss, and he insisted they meet. She would get the lunch meeting out of the way, and then start exploring Vancouver, especially Stanley Park.

Susan parked her car and joined the stream of professors flowing into the imposing U of V faculty club for lunch. Her only familiarity with faculty clubs was the JDU version lodged in one of the leftover WWII army huts on campus. A misguided architect had struggled to reproduce a décor of oaked grandeur, but the outcome was a shoddy imitation of the sought-after effect. The JDU faculty club was a dramatic example of how a silk purse could not be made from a sow's ear.

Susan's most recent visit to the JDU faculty club was a lunch with Penny Carson. The meal started well with Penny praising Susan's courage in tackling the large Intro Psych course. Susan appreciated the compliment. Impressing Penny and Joyce with her teaching was one of the few treasured achievements of her first year.

"Let me give you some advice," Penny said as she covered her Cobb salad with mounds of bleu cheese dressing—hardly the diet lunch Penny claimed she needed to lose weight. "Get rid of the sign on your office door."

Susan looked puzzled. "You don't know what I'm talking about, do you?" Penny chuckled while Susan shook her head.

"The 'Do not disturb' sign that shows up some afternoons—Ari Petras won't like it."

Susan frowned. Who cares what Ari Petras thinks? Then she remembered her conversation with Carl Thorndike. Ari was the backroom power in the department, saying yes or no to the careers of new faculty. An ominous chill crept up Susan's spine.

Penny chattered, oblivious to her effect on Susan. "Look, Ari likes you right now and that's important. But he doesn't like faculty putting up barriers to office visits from students. He thinks we all should have an open-door policy when we're on campus—students can stop by our offices at any time. I don't think he's seen the sign yet, but my advice is to toss it."

Susan stammered, "I had a hard time writing last term. I thought regular writing hours would help me focus. The sign is more a discipline for me than to keep students away."

"I understand what you need to do," Penny cajoled. "But faculty who don't publish anymore resent someone announcing they need time to write. I want to warn you that broadcasting your work ethic may disturb some powerful people in the department. Be careful, that's all."

Susan distrusted Penny smiling at her from across the table. Penny spent hours in Giles's office in what looked like friendly chats. Did Giles suggest that Penny talk to Susan about the sign on her door? Susan wondered if her colleagues were offended, or if Penny was doing Giles's bidding by trying to increase her anxiety. Susan did not know the truth, but, angry, she ripped the sign in half and tossed it in the trash when she returned to her office.

Fragments of faculty chatter surrounded her as she entered the U of V faculty club—editors, grant funds, publication deadlines, post-docs, and graduate students—the conversational stuff of a real research university—topics she rarely heard discussed in the JDU psychology department. U of V was an academic environment where faculty took intellectual work seriously. It was not just JDU's dismal faculty club that paled in comparison. Even the casual lunchtime conversation showed a level of scholarly sophistication beyond her experience at JDU. She suspected that U of V was not a place where colleagues were told to remove "Do not disturb" signs from their office doors.

Dan waved at her from the sofa in front of the enormous rock-faced fireplace that dominated the club's lobby. He rose as she approached and pulled her toward him. Susan accepted a kiss on the cheek, and then sidled out of his arms to walk toward the wall of windows at one end of the entrance hall. The view of the white-capped waters of the Strait of Georgia captivated her. Dan stood behind her, molding his body to hers. His lips grazed her ear. "Rumor has it U of V has recruited many faculty members based on the beauty of its faculty club. I know I was impressed when the psychology faculty brought me here during my interview."

"It definitely beats the rundown remodeled army hut JDU calls a faculty club," Susan agreed, admiring the view.

"Let's go downstairs to lunch." Dan motioned toward the stairs leading to the cafeteria on the building's lower level. He waved at a group of men seated around a table as they entered the spacious room. "That's the psychology faculty table," Dan explained. "A rotating group of colleagues eat lunch here every day. I usually join them, but today I want to talk to you alone." The psychology faculty lunch group was devoid of women, Susan noticed, as she took a tray and followed Dan through the lunch line.

They found a table in a corner sheltered from the din of the noisy diners. Dan got down to business immediately. "I'm going back to New York this summer. A new publishing house specializing in psychology is starting up. They approached Jennifer Evans about writing a book on the latest memory research. She agreed as long as I'd co-author it with her." Dan had a self-satisfied grin. "The publishers want up-and-comers in different areas of psychology to write books to help launch the company—rising star authors to get things off the ground."

"Can you handle working on two books at the same time?" Susan asked, knowing the answer before Dan confirmed it.

"Sure, I've done my chapters. All that's left is to edit the chapters you write so there's continuity of writing style in the book."

"I have two more completed chapters in the trunk of my car," Susan answered, secretly relieved to be left alone this summer.

"If you finish your chapters by September, we'll meet our final deadline and we'll get another royalty advance. I spoke with the editor, and she wants a 1976 copyright on our book. She's guaranteed top priority production and a completed textbook for the spring of '76—on time for course adoptions for the fall term. If you send me your chapters as you complete them, my editing should move right along."

"I think I can make that schedule," Susan answered, warming to the idea of seeing her name on the cover of a textbook in a year's time. Silently she calculated. If the book is published next spring, she could either wait a year to see how book sales progressed or she could start a job search in the months following publication. Either way, she estimated that in two, maybe three years, she would find her dream job and leave JDU behind.

Lunch finished, Susan and Dan climbed the staircase toward the lobby. "When are you leaving for New York?" Susan asked.

"In a few weeks—mid-May," Dan answered. "I need to nail down a place to live for the summer."

Suddenly Dan stopped. "Mona, you didn't tell me you were coming to the club today." Susan tensed when she saw Mona Kavline standing in the middle of the lobby at the top of the stairs. She looked elegant and stunning in a form-fitting sheath dress that emphasized her slim figure. Her jet-black hair was tied away from her face and flowed in a silken mass to the middle of her back. Susan noticed the stares of a few of Dan's colleagues, as they departed the cafeteria, when Mona approached Dan to greet him with an enthusiastic kiss.

"I don't tell you everything, Dan." Mona's tone was coy but ominous. "I thought I'd surprise you." Mona's eyes swept over Susan. "Nice to see you again, Susan. Dan didn't tell me you were coming to Vancouver."

Susan faltered, "I came for the weekend with a friend from Victoria. Dan and I were discussing our book over lunch." She wondered if Mona was in the club when Dan greeted Susan. Had she seen Dan's body pressed against hers as they stood at the window? She hoped she did not appear as nervous as she felt.

"Dan, come and have a drink with me in the bar," Mona simpered. "I want to talk with you about family matters." Her hand slipped through Dan's arm. Her expression was possessive when she smiled at Susan.

Dan surveyed Mona, his face stony. "Okay, just this once. You know I don't like to be disturbed during work hours. I'll just walk Susan to her car and be back in a few minutes." Dan clasped Susan's elbow and hurried her through the lobby and out the door. At her car, Susan opened the trunk and handed Dan the envelope with her chapters inside.

"I thought you were coming to Vancouver by yourself," Dan hissed.

"I *am* here alone," Susan whispered. "I didn't plan to run into Mona, and I didn't know what to say. I felt more comfortable letting her think I was here with someone else. I have no experience as the other woman, and I'm not used to running into wives. I thought I had to explain why we were together." Susan muttered, "I hope she didn't see us in the lobby before lunch."

Dan rubbed his forehead, looking stricken. Susan realized he was wondering the same thing—what had Mona seen? Dan's facade about having Mona under control was shattered. He was as unnerved as she was to find Mona in the faculty club. Susan slammed the trunk closed. "I'm going downtown to check into the Sylvia Hotel, and then I'm going to take a walk in Stanley Park."

Dan's marital intrigue was starting to bore her. While Dan struggled to compose himself, Susan remembered a conversation with Julie about having affairs with married men. Experienced in these matters, Julie was philosophical about the inevitable course of lies. "They all have some variant of the story that their wives don't understand them, and they have an arrangement—they don't sleep together anymore—they stay together for the kids or for family reasons. And, then, if you manage to meet the wives, they turn out to be reasonable if not very nice women who think everything is perfectly normal between them and their husbands. And, the irony is it *is* normal. I'm the outsider, the sucker who believes the line 'our marriage is just a shell.' That's about when the affair ends—when I realize I'm a fool and he's a manipulative, two-timing jerk." Susan chuckled to herself. She missed Julie.

"I love the Sylvia," Dan mumbled. "It has a bar with a great view of English Bay. Can I join you for a drink there around six tonight?"

Susan glared at him. Dan's version of his marital story had a unique occult twist, but Julie was right, he was just another two-timing, manipulative jerk, who could not handle the mixing of wife and lover.

"Please," Dan pleaded. "I won't see you again for the rest of the summer and I want to talk to you about a few things."

"Okay," she relented. She felt generous because of the impending, welcome separation. "See you at six."

TWENTY-SEVEN

Susan found a table by the window in the hotel bar. The room was crowded, and tables were scarce. She sipped her scotch, feeling content after her hike along the Stanley Park seawall. The Friday night drinks-after-work crowd continued to pour into the bar in chattering clumps. The men loosened their ties while they ordered drinks. The women gravitated to the bar where they could expose an expanse of thigh as they perched on the stools. The bar was a Friday night pick-up place—a singles bar. She watched the flirtatious maneuverings with detached interest and wondered if there were similar haunts in Victoria.

Susan motioned to a waitress. "I'm expecting someone to join me. Could you bring me a refill and also a double scotch for my friend?" As the waitress headed toward the bar, Susan spied Dan at the door and waved. Dan weaved through the crowd and flung himself into the chair opposite Susan. "I've ordered you a drink," Susan shouted over the rising noise level.

"Hi, Dr. Kavline, it's nice to see you again." The waitress crooned as she set the drinks on the table. Dan gave her a weak smile and took a gulp of scotch. The waitress returned to the bar, and Susan watched Dan's eyes scan her departing body.

"It seems like you're well known here," Susan said.

Dan shifted uneasily in his chair. "Yeah, I've been here a few times— mostly with job candidates and guest speakers. The department uses this hotel for out-of-town visitors." Susan suspected Dan was lying from the

195

sultry way the waitress eyed him from the bar. This was a singles hang-out after all, and the promise of casual sex hung in the air. Dan leaned forward, cradling his drink between his hands. "I spoke with Jennifer this afternoon. She's leaving the Institute and moving to Boston. She's accepted a position at Boston University starting in January of next year." Dan sounded grumpy.

"Why is she leaving the Institute?"

"She's getting married—someone at MIT," Dan answered. "She's moving to Boston so they can live together and eventually marry." So, the rumor Julie heard was true. Jennifer Evans plans to marry.

"You don't look happy. Is it because of the book or because Jennifer's getting married?" Susan asked.

"Both," Dan sounded surly. "Jennifer moving to Boston may delay the progress of our book. I'm not surprised she's marrying this guy, but the timing is bad."

"Maybe you're upset because you're in love with her?" Scotch always loosened Susan's inhibitions.

Dan looked startled. "I'm not in love with Jennifer. How can you say that? I'm—" Dan stopped.

"You're what?" Susan was curious.

Dan stared at Susan. He took a sip of scotch. "I was going to say I'm glad she's doing what she wants and what will make her happy—she's a good friend and collaborator."

"But the two of you are lovers. You must have some feelings for her," Susan persisted.

Dan slammed his glass of scotch on the table, and the amber liquid splashed over his hand. "You're determined to ask me about women I've known, aren't you?"

"Yes, I'm determined to ask you about them." Susan stood her ground.

Dan sighed. "I'm very fond of Jennifer, and I think she feels the same about me. We have a comfortable friendship."

"A comfortable friendship that includes sex," Susan snapped.

"A comfortable friendship that *did* include sex. That's been over for a while—months before I left the Institute." Dan slumped back in his chair. He waved at the waitress and motioned for another drink. When it arrived, Dan sipped it in silence watching the sidewalk traffic stream toward Stanley Park. Susan waited—something else was on his mind.

"Mona and the kids are going back east for the summer, too—in June when the school year's finished. They'll stay with her parents in New Rochelle."

"You don't seem very happy at the thought of having your family close by." Dan was scowling and tapping his fingers against his glass.

"It'll cause additional pressure I don't need."

"How so? If they're staying with your in-laws, you won't see them every day."

Dan stopped his nervous tapping and looked squarely at Susan. "Mona and the kids may not return to BC at the end of the summer."

"Why won't they come back? Is Mona suspicious? Is that why she showed up at the faculty club today?" Susan tensed. Images of a Liz Grantley-like disaster raced across her mind.

"It doesn't have anything to do with that." Dan looked embarrassed. He coughed, struggling for a more measured tone. "Mona doesn't like it here. Vancouver is not the right place for her to practice her Jewish faith, in her opinion. She thinks the religious education for the kids is inadequate and they'll stray from their Jewish roots if they stay here."

"What about you?"

Dan quipped. "My only attachment to Judaism starts when I can't find a decent bagel. I want my kids to learn to read, write, and do math. I'm not interested in their religious education, especially if it interferes with learning the basics." Dan shrugged and stared out the window. "When she visited her folks last December, they probably pressured her to consider moving back east. Knowing Mona's mother, she would say something like—your children miss their grandparents and their father's not very attentive because he's too wrapped up in his career—the kids are too much for you to handle alone. Mona's mother tolerated me but never liked me much."

"You told me Mona liked Vancouver because she could practice her witchcraft. You said she was in demand," Susan countered.

Dan nodded. "Yeah, that's about the only thing she likes, but it isn't enough."

"Will you leave U of V because of this?" Susan panicked at the prospect of Dan leaving before their book was published. That would be an ironic twist. She moved to BC to write a book with Dan so she could get the attention she needed to find a better faculty position. It would be easy for Dan to leave for another job back east. He had colleagues all over the continent and he had his Stanford connections. It would not be the same for Susan—not before the work with Dan was done.

"No, I like it here," Dan responded. "The department's treated me well. I got immediate tenure and promotion, which I'm told is rare at U of V. My lab space isn't great, but the situation will improve over time. I plan to stay."

Dan reached across the table and entwined his fingers through hers. "If we play our cards right and the textbook is a success, I could get the U of V department to offer you a job." Susan laughed. Dan face paled at her unexpected response.

"I think I've had enough to drink." Susan pushed her glass away and signaled to the waitress for the check.

"Can we talk in your room?" Dan asked. "It's too noisy here to carry on a conversation."

"Okay, but that's all we'll do—talk."

* * * * * * * * * * * * * *

Dan immediately encircled Susan in his arms after she closed the door to her room. His kiss was urgent, but Susan pulled herself from his grip. "Wait a minute. We're here to talk." She sunk into the chair beside the bed, suddenly fatigued from the combination of scotch and her long walk. Dan sat on the corner of the bed facing Susan.

"How will it work if Mona and your children stay back east and you stay here?" Susan asked. "That's quite a commute."

"Mona and I may divorce." Dan's eyes searched her face.

"You told me divorce was not possible—family ties were too important." Susan leaned her head against the back of the chair and stifled the urge to yawn.

"Mona's talking about it. She's really unhappy."

Susan snorted with derision. "That's not surprising. She has a husband who has multiple affairs and uses her witchcraft against her, so she'll leave him alone. Finally she's realized she's unhappy. What took her so long?"

"This isn't funny, Sue, it's a major disruption." Dan looked agitated and hurt.

"Yeah, you might have to stop working to take care of your life. That does happen sometimes."

"I wish you wouldn't be so flippant," Dan groaned. "I was serious about what I said downstairs in the bar. I could get you a position at U of V, and we could be co-authors and collaborators and a couple—*if* I was divorced."

Susan placed her hands on the armrests of the chair and pushed herself upright. Her eyes locked with his. The only sounds in the room were the street noises outside the window. Finally, Susan said, "Dan, you and Mona have to decide about your marriage. Don't make me part of that decision. I will *not* make any commitments about being with you when and if you get a divorce."

"That's not exactly the answer I wanted to hear." Dan bit his lip, looking frustrated.

Overcome by fatigue and wanting this conversation to end, Susan moaned, "Dan, I'm exhausted. I shouldn't drink scotch on an empty stomach."

Dan reached out to grasp her hand and cleared his throat. "Sue, let's get serious for a minute."

"Okay, what do you want to get serious about?" Susan covered a yawn with her free hand.

Dan hesitated, and then murmured, "Sue, you're the love of my life."

Susan sniggered. "Dan, that's a corny line from a B-movie. You've had a lot of loves in your life. I'm just one of many."

Dan shook his head. "No, that's not true. I've never felt the way I feel about you for anyone before."

"Not even Liz Grantley?" Susan asked.

"It was so long ago—being with Liz. All I remember about my time with Liz is how I enjoyed being with someone who was smart and who understood my work. When she died, I didn't know whether I would ever find that combination again—but I've found what I've wanted with you." Dan's eyes scanned Susan's face, looking for reassurance.

Susan removed her hand from Dan's grasp. "Let's finish the book."

"Are you saying you don't want the same thing—with me?" Dan pleaded.

Susan remembered Julie's advice. Go along until the book is published. "Dan, I'm saying I don't want to talk about the future. You're married, you have children, and you have a lot to deal with. I've been through a divorce, and mine was simple. No kids—a mutual agreement to split—and it still took two years. If you and Mona go through with this, it could take a very long time with all the complications you have. It's much too soon to talk about anything after a divorce."

Dan rose from the bed. His demeanor screamed his need for affection—an invitation to spend the night or at least a hug. He turned toward her. "I'd like some encouragement," he insisted.

"Sure," she said. "I'll be here at the end of the summer when you get back from New York. I'll have my chapters finished and new data from my lab for you to look at." She leaned back in the chair and closed her eyes. She heard the click of the lock as Dan closed the door behind him. Then she fell asleep.

Susan woke with a start and looked at her watch—ten o'clock. Her stomach growled with hunger pangs. She headed back to the bar in search of snacks and a glass of wine. This time she would avoid the soporific effects of scotch. The room was nearly empty, and the window table was free again. Outside, the street scene around English Bay was festive with crowds wandering the sidewalks and bumper-to-bumper traffic lining the street. It reminded her of the streets of New York on a Friday night, and a wave of nostalgia washed over her. The urban din of Vancouver was refreshing after the stuffiness of Victoria. Maybe it would not be so bad at U of V. Living in a big city would be more fun than being stuck in a small town on an island. Life in Vancouver would be more her style. Too bad Dan was part of the deal.

"Where's Dr. Kavline?" Susan looked up. The waitress, who had served her hours before, placed a bowl of peanuts on the table. Susan grabbed a handful and ordered a glass of wine. The waitress teased, "No scotch this time? It's Dr. Kavline's favorite drink."

"Dr. Kavline went home. I think I'm better off with the gentler effects of wine," Susan answered. "You seem to know Dr. Kavline pretty well. Does he come here often?"

"Yeah, professors and grad students from the U of V psychology department come here almost once a week. I'm getting a master's degree in history at U of V, but I know a lot of psych grad students and I sometimes join them for a drink when my shift is over. The U of V psych department is well-known on campus for its partying ways. The professors are younger and better looking than the old guys in the history department—maybe that's the reason." The waitress hustled to the bar to retrieve Susan's wine. As she set the glass in front of Susan, she said, "That's how I know Dr. Kavline. He's always part of the group that comes in. Are you a friend of his?"

"I'm a professor at James Douglas in Victoria. Dr. Kavline and I are writing a book together. We had a meeting today to talk about the book." Susan answered before remembering that she and Dan had been holding hands, a definite sign their meeting was about more than a book. She chuckled at the skeptical frown on the waitress's face as she hustled to service another table.

Susan was not surprised Dan was part of a department party crowd. Dan loved and lied at the same time. The gatherings at the Sylvia bar were regular social events and not the occasional hosting of a department visitor. How many of the women grad students had a crush on Dan—how many had slept with him—maybe even the waitress? His energy, his rising star status, and his exotic New York City background would make him irresistible, especially to the locals.

Susan sipped her wine. It was hard to understand Dan's perception that he was in love with her. She sympathized with his desire to have a psychologist and collaborator as a wife or partner. Leonard Wesselman was married to a psychologist, and there were other prominent couples working together in the universe of cognitive psychology. Maybe Dan wanted to imitate his mentor and other major figures in the field by marrying a colleague. Did he see this as another pathway to entering the respected ranks of the colleagues he so doggedly admired?

She could not imagine Dan as her department colleague, partner, and lover. Her only experience with such an arrangement was watching Joyce and Ari Petras. Department lore hinted that Ari insisted on a job for Joyce before joining the JDU faculty. If this was true, it would explain her forced assertiveness at department meetings—under constant pressure to show she was good enough to be there without Ari's help. If Susan agreed to Dan's plan, Joyce's fate would be her fate. She would be Dan's playmate, hired to keep him happy. The department would view her as his appendage, and she would struggle to gain respect as an independent colleague as Joyce Petras did.

It would not be long before Dan was telling her, not Mona, he was working late or staying extra days at an out-of-town conference. Dan's deceptions and his casual affairs would not change. Her mind wandered through these scenarios while she pondered Dan's interpretation of love. Dan was not in love with her. He was in love with a plan to live his life—work and sex combined into one convenient relationship—seamless and without disruption. Liz Grantley died, and it appeared Jennifer Evans had rejected him. It stung a little to be third in line, but Susan had no desire to share Dan's dream life. Dan might not realize it, but Susan knew he would never love anyone as much as he loved himself.

TWENTY-EIGHT

Giles Plimley-Jones eased his lanky frame into the chair beside Susan's desk. "The executive committee met and asked me to convey their approval of your progress this year. They instructed me to tell you to keep up the good work." Giles glared at Susan over the rim of his glasses. Susan grinned despite Giles's threatening expression.

"That's good to hear, Giles. Will I get a letter from the committee?"

Giles sneered. "That sort of thing is too formal for us. Although Joyce Petras is pushing for us to put things in writing, the rest of us are happy with just an informal chat."

Susan felt devilish and could not resist pushing the point. "Giles, at the start of the first term you told us to read the Faculty Handbook. I took your advice, and the Handbook says faculty are entitled to formal, written notice of their progress evaluations."

Giles glared at her. "It says that, does it?" Giles sat silent for a few minutes staring at her bookcase where the Faculty Handbook stood prominently. "These damned new regulations—hard to keep track of them. I'll talk to Jim and the executive committee. They'll know what to do." He slapped both hands against his bony knees and rose from the chair. "That's that, then—keep up the good work, jolly good, cheerio." With a desultory salute, he disappeared out the door. Susan shook her head. Poor Giles. Even when his news was good, he was uncomfortable. He just did the minimum to get the job done.

A successful evaluation demanded a Friday night festivity to cele-brate the end of a difficult year. Before she could decide what her solo party would be, she heard a light tap and turned to find Lucas standing in her office doorway.

"Let's go for coffee."

"What a nice surprise," Susan bubbled. "I haven't talked to you in weeks."

"It's been a while. Let's go down to The Castle, get a coffee, and enjoy the sun and the view."

Once at The Castle they took their coffee to a table on the outdoor veranda. The students had scattered for the summer, leaving Susan and Lucas alone on the deserted terrace. She joked about her visit from Giles and how ill-at-ease he was when discussing her evaluation.

"Giles came to see me, too," Lucas offered. "My news was not as positive as yours, but my meeting was also pretty funny."

"What happened?" Susan asked.

"I can't remember the exact phrasing—Giles has a unique way of put-ting things—but the gist went something like this. Your lecturing is fine, but you should avoid using nontraditional teaching practices. The department views anything other than lecturing as a sign of laziness—a shirking of one's teaching responsibilities." Susan giggled as Lucas imitated the hapless chairman. "Giles mentioned Otto's disapproval of my unprofessional attire and said that the neuropsychologists in the department have a huge say in whether I stay or go, so I should make every effort to keep them happy until I get tenure."

"Giles said *that*," Susan blanched.

"The 'stay or go' part is a direct quote," Lucas chuckled. "I didn't say much, just thanked him for the feedback. The conversation rapidly deteri-orated into a series of 'jolly goods' and 'cheerios' and 'things will work out after all it's only your first year'…you know, the rambling random words

Giles conjures up when he's tense. I think he was trying to soften the blow in his own clumsy way." Lucas seemed amused rather than concerned, but Susan was not as forgiving of Giles's quirky behavior. He was a vindictive autocrat hiding behind a bumbling demeanor. He tried to deceive the faculty into thinking he was too inept to use his position to conspire against them, but she was not fooled.

Lucas smiled. "It's fun to gossip about the department eccentrics. We haven't done this for a while."

Susan agreed. "Talking with you always helped me sort things out. I'm still not sure I understand everything that's gone on this year."

Lucas sipped his coffee and scanned the view. "It's so clear today you can see Mount Baker in Washington." Lucas pointed to a distant snow-covered peak, a perfect cone shape hovering over the horizon. Moments passed until finally Lucas cleared his throat. "Susan, I want to tell you something."

"Okay." Susan felt happy to be with Lucas—pleased they were connecting again.

"I'm engaged," Lucas blurted, his voice breaking on the last word.

"You're engaged—to be married?" Susan gasped.

Lucas nodded. "I met Carol at Tranquility Farm. She's getting a counseling psych degree at U of V. She helps during weekend retreats at Tranquility. That's how I got to know her."

"When are you getting married?" Susan asked with disbelief.

"After Carol finishes her degree, maybe next year."

A throbbing lump formed in Susan's throat. "If you met her at Tranquility Farm, you haven't known her very long. You must be very much in love."

"We're on parallel tracks. We both want to open private clinical practices in Victoria so we'll probably open one together. I want to stay here and my future in the department doesn't look promising. It might be a struggle at first, but I think Carol and I could have a good life here—eventually."

"You haven't mentioned love, Lucas," Susan whispered.

"Sometimes you meet someone and you know they're right for you at this time and in this place. That's the way I feel about Carol. We share the same goals and values. You could call that a form of love."

"Your relationship sounds pretty businesslike," Susan persisted. She was venturing into personal territory where she had no right to intrude. But her astonishment at Lucas's news compelled her need to hear details.

Lucas scanned her face. His eyes were filled with regret. At last, he responded, "I could say the same thing about you and Dan. Isn't he right for you now and in this place? Maybe that's more important than romantic passion."

Susan dropped her eyes. Her cheeks burned. "You're wrong, Lucas. Dan is not right for me—not now, not ever. He pressured me to sleep with him, so I did. I was lonely, and I needed his help to get my writing back on track and to set up my lab. The weekend you saw us together I made sure he was too drunk each night to do anything. Dan's back in New York this summer working on another project. When he gets back to BC, our relationship will be one of collaborators—nothing else." She raised her eyes, blinking back tears. Lucas smiled and reached for her hand.

"There's something else I need to tell you," Lucas continued. "Carol wants me to end all my friendships with other women, especially the ones I've—" Lucas stopped.

"The ones you've slept with?" Susan finished his sentence.

"Yeah, the ones I've slept with."

"Lucas, we spent one weekend together. One weekend hardly constitutes a threat to your relationship with Carol," Susan bristled.

Lucas fumbled with his coffee cup. "Let's see if I can explain. Carol and I are involved in a way of life that requires total commitment. Part of the commitment is honesty and respect for your partner's feelings when something in your own life makes them uneasy."

"What you're saying is that past lovers make Carol uncomfortable, so she wants you to stop having contact with them no matter how fleeting the sexual part was—is that right?"

"Yeah, that's the general idea." Lucas looked ill at ease.

"Are you having this same conversation with all the women in Victoria you've slept with?" Susan snapped. Her barb had its effect—Lucas blanched. "I'm sorry I shouldn't have said that, but Carol's attitude is ridiculous and immature. Ex-lovers and even ex-spouses are part of life. If I shunned the men I'd slept with once or twice—" Susan shrugged. "I guess there'd be men friends I'd never see again—which would be my loss."

"I think Carol's concerned about the intensity of our sexual relationship," Lucas murmured.

"Let me see if I understand. You've told her about us, and she's jealous. Even though we don't sleep together anymore, she doesn't want us to enjoy each other's friendship."

Lucas nodded.

"What am I supposed to do around the department? Walk the other way when I see you in the hallway? We're colleagues after all, and we work in the same place—this whole thing is absurd," Susan snarled.

"Carol understands that. She doesn't want me to see you away from the department—that's all."

Susan examined Lucas's face. She saw he was struggling, too. "You've been a good friend to me this year. I'll miss you—that's why I sound so angry. I've loved being with you."

Lucas nodded. "Yeah, me too."

They rose from the table to climb the hill toward the psychology department. Susan searched for something to say. "Lucas, Giles is right. It's only your first year. It might be too soon to assume your contract won't be renewed. The students like you, and Carl Thorndike is on your side. Things in the department probably will work out."

"That's all true, but I'm not going to try very hard to please the department because I'm not sure after this year I want to stay at JDU."

As they approached her office, Susan's resolve crumbled and she whispered, "Lucas, I'm crushed at the thought of not being with you anymore—not just in bed—in any way." She fumbled with the key to open her office door.

"Let's go into your office and talk for a few minutes." Lucas nudged her through the open door and shut it behind them.

Susan turned to face him. "Can I at least give you one last hug, or is that forbidden?"

Lucas laughed and circled her with his arms. "No, it's not forbidden. We're saying good-bye." He kissed her on the forehead. "I told Carol that I love you. That's why she's so adamant that I break all contact with you."

Susan raised her face, and Lucas's lips pressed against hers. Her eyes brimmed with tears. "Lucas, did seeing me with Dan turn you away?"

"No," Lucas shook his head and replied, "I knew a lot of guys like Dan back in Boston. It would be hard for you to work with him without eventually sleeping with him. That's just the way guys like him operate. Like sailors are supposed to have a woman in every port, guys like Dan have a lover in every lab."

Susan sighed and leaned her head against Lucas's chest. She shivered. "Did we ever have a chance, Lucas?"

Lucas sat back on the edge of Susan's desk with his arms on her shoulders. His look was solemn as he stroked the back of her neck. "Susan, I came here to change my life. When I'm with you, I can't escape all of the competitive academic shit I want to leave behind."

"There you go, comparing me to your ex-wife—it's not fair." Susan's throat tightened. She wanted to scream.

"Calm down." Lucas continued his caress. "You're not like Sandy at all. Sandy was sure of what she wanted her future to look like. You're almost as confused as I am—that's one of the reasons I love you—I love your vulnerability. But you're from back east and you have those competitive career values—you can't help it, it's what you were surrounded with in graduate school. Dan fits in, but I don't because I'm going in a different direction. Dan is what you need—you like his energy and the two of you do good work together—and you like that—it's taking you in the direction you want to go right now. Carol's fresh and new to me. She's from BC and she's part of this place—there are no ghosts from the past when I'm with her. She's what I need right now. I hope you understand that."

Lucas kissed her, nibbling at her lips as he put his arms around her waist, pressing her against him. "Are you expecting anyone to drop by your office this afternoon?" he whispered next to her ear.

Susan lifted her arm behind his shoulder to glance at her watch. She managed to make out the time through her tears. "It's after four o'clock on a Friday afternoon. Anyone in the department who's still on campus is in the faculty club drinking by now."

Lucas slipped his hands under her blouse and loosened the clasp of her bra. His hands fondled her breasts, while his thumbs rotated around her nipples, massaging their tips.

"Lucas, I don't think this is allowed under your new relationship guidelines," Susan moaned.

"It's okay—I'm keeping my commitment—we're not seeing each other outside the department." He stood and started to unbutton her blouse. "Should we clear your desk or try the floor?" Lucas asked, grinning.

Susan laughed. "The floor's a better bet—at least there's a carpet."

"I agree," Lucas said. "That way you'll be on top." Lucas dropped his hands to her waist and sank to the floor pulling Susan over him as they stretched out on the rug.

TWENTY-NINE

Susan sat on The Castle veranda. She had avoided the place since the day Lucas told her about Carol. Her sandwich and coffee lay on the table in front of her untouched. Sitting here, she realized the passing months had not dulled the pain. Susan closed her eyes to relive the Friday afternoon in her office. The stark atmosphere was not the best choice for a farewell, but it did not affect their passionate enthusiasm. When they finally reclaimed their abandoned clothes, Lucas laughed at the rug burns on his knees. If she had made love to someone in the past the way she made love to Lucas that day, she would have overturned her life to be with him. But Lucas was right. There were times when other things outweighed the power of sexual attraction, even love. She accepted Lucas's wisdom, but it was not easy. The ache of loss would take a long time to lose its grip.

Her mood made it difficult to deal with the daily phone calls from Dan. "Dan, stop checking up on me. I'm working on my chapters, and I'm very diligent about it," Susan assured him. What she told him was almost true. She was writing, just not that diligently.

"I know you're pulling your weight, Sue. I call you because I miss you and I want to hear your voice."

"Dan, you've so many friends and colleagues in New York it's hard to believe you have time to miss anyone." Out of curiosity and to shift his attention away from her, she asked, "How're your friends at NYU and Columbia? Have you seen any of them yet?"

"Yeah, I have. I think we're definitely going to be the front runners in the market when it comes to textbooks in cognitive psychology—good news for us."

Susan laughed. Dan, predictably, had assessed his academic competition. "Say hello to Howard Lloyd for me if you see him. Tell him I'm doing okay," Susan said.

"Will do," Dan agreed, and then lowered his voice to a whisper. "Sue, I'd like to hear you say that you think of me and miss me, too. I'd like that a lot."

Susan hedged. "I miss your help in the lab. I'm not nearly as good at setting up lab equipment as you are."

"You know that's not what I mean," Dan sounded disappointed. "I really miss our talks. I've told you things about me I've never told anyone before. I have lots of friends here, but it's not the same. When it was just the two of us in BC, things seemed, I don't know, cleaner—more real—less showy. I liked that." Dan's voice turned wistful.

Susan was surprised by Dan's unusual self-reflection, but her experience with his lies stopped her from indulging his sentimentality. She knew he had plenty of diversions in New York despite his mutterings during each phone call. "Don't forget to say hello to Howard," she said as she hung up.

The days of August lay ahead. Most of the faculty had fled the department. The lure of sailing, hiking, camping, and the golf course dwarfed the mundane pursuits of research and publishing for most members of the JDU psychology department. Giles posted a "Gone Sailing" sign on his office door and then disappeared. The few part-time instructors hired to teach summer courses rattled around the empty hallways lined with unbroken rows of closed office doors. Susan followed the progress of a colorful spinnaker on a distant sailboat out in the bay. Probably a JDU faculty member enjoying the sea on this gentle summer day.

"Mind if I join you?"

Susan looked up to see Jim Kracknoy smiling down at her. He had already placed his coffee cup on the table and was settling himself into the seat across from Susan. "You look like you're deep in thought," he said as he lifted the cup to his lips.

"I was thinking about my first year here," Susan lied.

Jim looked wary. "Giles spoke to you about the executive committee's first year evaluation of your performance, didn't he? And you got our letter—eventually?"

"Oh, yes," Susan responded. "I'm pleased it was so positive."

Jim relaxed. "Good, I'm glad Giles gave you our message. He sometimes forgets, or he garbles things and the message from the committee doesn't quite come out as we intended. But he's the chairman, and we must follow the chain of command idea, for better or, in our case, for worse. I hope the formal letter from the committee cleared things up if needed." Jim laughed. "The executive committee is pleased with your performance and with Jack Bernoski. Lucas—well, I'm not so sure. He's had some problems getting his research off the ground, and he seems to have gotten on Otto's bad side. Otto's an important man at JDU, so that hasn't worked in Lucas's favor." Jim became reflective. "I've talked to Lucas, but he seems to be—I don't know—lost in some way—not quite sure of where he's going in his career, what he wants to do. The students like him, though, which is good."

Jim sipped his coffee. Annoyed, Susan snapped, "Considering how the department hired us, sight unseen, two out of three isn't a bad success rate."

Jim looked sheepish. "Well, that's one way to look at it. We did take a chance on all of you." He took a swallow of coffee. "Besides, it's only the first year. The more formal evaluation occurs at the end of the second year, so Lucas has plenty of time to turn himself around—even time to mend fences with Otto. Lucas understands he needs to get his research started. He called me to ask to reassign his office to the old army hut that houses the neuropsych grad student offices. We usually don't like to do that—they're too shabby for faculty—but Lucas insisted. He said it would be better for his research if he was around the grad students all the time. He convinced me, so I agreed."

Susan sucked in her breath. She knew what Lucas was doing. His promise to Carol was in jeopardy if he saw Susan every day in the department, so he was reducing the possibilities they would meet. She felt a twinge of regret. Lucas was protecting them from the attraction they felt by putting physical distance between them. She would rarely see him if his office was in a different building—only at department meetings, and those could be avoided easily. Not seeing each other would make things easier for both, but in the end Lucas had Carol and she was alone.

"I hope you're happy here, Susan. The department has high hopes for you. The dean and president want to turn JDU into a first-rate research university—bright young sparks like you fit right into the plans of the administration."

Susan remembered her conversation with Giles. "Yes, Giles told me the dean wants to turn JDU into an Ivory League university."

"A what?" Jim looked puzzled.

Susan laughed. "Giles meant Ivy League university. He just got confused."

Jim sniggered. "Giles has a tendency to get confused, but that's a good one—I'll have to remember that—Ivory League University." Jim shook his head in resigned amusement. "Well, whatever we turn into, I hope you're happy here."

Susan gave Jim a weak smile. He wanted reassurance, but she wanted honesty. "I'm happy enough, I guess. The book is going well, my dissertation is in press, and I've several experiments set up to run this summer." But, she was compelled to add, "It's just—sometimes I get lonely—I'm far away from what's familiar and the faculty here is not very...." Susan struggled to find the right word. "Interactive."

Jim nodded. "A lot of new faculty members feel that way. I think people move to a place like Vancouver Island because they're not social types—they like the isolation of an island and want to be left alone. It takes time to adjust. I've observed over my years here that the East-to-West Coast transition is actually harder than the adjustment from the States to Canada." His smile was reassuring. "It takes time, but it'll happen."

Susan took a gamble. "Is there any chance the department will get a new chairman?" She did not say that it would make her happier if someone other than Giles was in that position—she thought that would be too much of a risk.

Jim studied her face. "I know a new chairman would help the atmosphere for young faculty like you."

"It would help the dean achieve his Ivory League goals," Susan teased.

Jim laughed. "I get your point—probably Giles has outlived his time. We need someone with outstanding scholarly credentials to give the department some clout, some prestige. We don't need one of the good old boys of JDU anymore."

"I've heard some faculty would like you to be chairman," Susan ventured. "How would that happen? Would there be an internal revolt to oust Giles?"

Jim's laugh was hearty as he shook his head. "No, nothing like that. Giles's term is up next year, and we'll just elect someone else." There was a pause while Jim searched for a response. "I know some faculty in the department, like Carl Thorndike, want me as chairman, but it's not something I want to do. I've talked to the dean, and we'll probably search for someone from the outside. If we can't find somebody, I'll do it on a temporary basis until we do find someone." Jim smiled at Susan. "But you're right—there's general agreement that Giles is not the chairman to lead the department into an Ivory League future. Maybe you'd like to be on the search committee for a new chairman when the time comes. We'll need the perspective of the young faculty—the future of the department."

Susan was not going to reveal her plans to leave JDU as soon as possible after the publication of the book. Besides, she did not want to spoil one of the few positive conversations she had had since her arrival. "Yeah, sure, why not?" she agreed.

Jim looked at his watch. "I have to run—another meeting." He touched Susan's shoulder with a light pat as he rounded the table. "Don't work every day this summer. Enjoy the sunny weather while it lasts, and enjoy Victoria, too." He waved at the view of the bay and the mountains before he turned to walk up the hill.

Susan watched Jim saunter off in the direction of the psychology department. She regarded his receding back for a few minutes, and then threw her uneaten food into the nearest trash bin. Jim's comments about Lucas troubled her. She was the one who was lost, not Lucas. She felt trapped in an unwanted relationship with Dan until they finished the book. She thought it would be a casual, temporary liaison, but he continued to mention divorce and his hope for a permanent arrangement. He called her every day and whined about how much he missed her, but Susan knew the truth. There were too many women in New York, and Dan had too little resistance.

She walked to the water's edge to inhale the salt air. The view of the mountains on the Olympic Peninsula was always a comfort. Her first year at JDU was a success as Jim Kracknoy had confirmed. But her unrelenting loneliness was unbearable today. She wanted to share the view with some-one—with Lucas. Susan turned and walked slowly up the hill to the Angus building. Burying herself in work had to be her salvation, but sadly she had learned this year that work alone would not fill her inner void.

T H I R T Y

"Sue, it's great to hear your voice."

"I didn't think I'd find you home—it's nine o'clock your time—on a Friday night."

Julie laughed. "I have some new actor friends, so I never go out before ten-thirty. That's when the curtain goes down."

"I'm calling to warn you Dan's back in New York this summer. I don't think you'll run into him at the Institute because he's spending most of his time working on a book with Jennifer."

"It doesn't matter where he is. I'm lining up placements to get some supervised clinical experience. I've been in Brooklyn most of this summer." Julie loved intrigue, so she was quick to add, "So Dan is with Jennifer again. How do you feel about that?"

It was Susan's turn to laugh. "The rumors you heard were true. Jennifer's moving to Boston to marry someone at MIT."

"Good for her," Julie hooted. "I knew she'd get tired of the office couch quickie sex stuff after a while." Julie paused. "You didn't just call to tell me about Dan and Jennifer. What's happening with you?"

Susan took a deep breath. She told Julie everything—how Dan wanted the two of them to be a permanent couple—his idea to divorce his wife—the story about Liz Grantley—what Dan said about enjoying the relationship he had with Liz and wanting to repeat it with Susan. She avoided mention of the occult machinations between Dan and his wife. She knew Julie would react to that part of the story with scathing derision and a warning that Dan was a liar on the brink of insanity. Susan entertained that thought herself, but today she felt too vulnerable to tolerate Julie's wrath.

"Dan calls me the love of his life—and now he's phoning me every day from New York to tell me how much he misses me." Susan's voice rose in desperation. "I didn't expect Dan to take this whole thing seriously. He told me he had to keep his marriage together—it was an important value in his family and he didn't want to disappoint his parents. Now it seems he's been dreaming of being part of an academic couple since his graduate school affair with Liz Grantley. He told me things didn't work out with Jennifer. They're better at being friends than lovers."

Julie was calm. "Sue, don't sound so tense. If Dan really wants to be with you, he has a lot of work to do before that happens. Frankly, I don't think he has the courage to change his family life. It would take too much time away from his real loves—himself and his career. The real love of Dan Kavline's life is Dan Kavline, not you."

Susan exhaled. "When I'm rational, that's the way I see it, too. He's much more comfortable publishing papers, designing experiments, and playing with lab equipment. I can't see him going through a divorce. It's not so easy to walk away from three kids and a wife. My divorce was simple, straightforward—no kids and we both wanted to split. Even then, there's a lot of emotion to work through, and I just can't see Dan doing that. From what I know of Mona, I don't think she'll be willing to divorce Dan. The whole thing has the potential for being a real mess."

"Bank on what he told you about Jennifer. It didn't work out in bed, but they still remain collaborators. If by some slim chance he does divorce and he pushes the issue of being more permanent, tell him you want a relationship like the one he has with Jennifer—if it ever gets to that point, but I don't think it will. What happened to that guy in your department who's trying to find himself? Has anything happened between the two of you?" Julie asked.

"He's getting married. He met someone at a therapy retreat, and they're going to start a private practice together in Victoria. He'll probably leave JDU—he's not happy in the department."

"Did the two of you ever sleep together?" Julie asked.

Susan hesitated, and then lied. "No, we're just friends." Her guilt was immediate. She did not like deceiving Julie, but the emptiness she felt at Lucas's departure was tender and she could not face Julie's inevitable inquisition.

"Sue, you need something in your life other than psychology and psychologists. Do something different. I'd urge you to come back to New York for some fun time with me. I love being around actors and so would you. They're so much fun, so spontaneous and unafraid—just what you need. And the guys are really attractive—keep themselves in good shape—nothing like flabby academic men. Given the Dan situation, that's probably not a good idea. He's so egotistical he'd probably think you're back in New York because you couldn't stand being away from him."

Susan smiled. Julie had a real handle on Dan's ego. "Julie, talking with you has calmed me. Sometimes I feel so alone here, and I need the connection with you—and with my old life—minus Paul, of course."

"Sue, there's real irony here. I was worried you were moving to BC because you were in love with Dan and Dan, being who he is, would use you and dump you. You proved me wrong. You've kept your head while he's the one talking about love and marriage."

"Dan may have a dream about a cozy relationship with one of his collaborators—same bed, same department—but it's not the dream for me. At least, not with him."

Julie laughed. "Make good use of the summer. Find another man. Make new friends. Find happiness."

"I do have some good news. I got a positive review from the department executive committee. The assistant chairman told me today that the department has high hopes that new faculty like me will increase the university's research standing, which is the plan of the new JDU president." Susan tried to sound cheerful, but, instead, her tone was flat.

The other end of the phone line fell silent. Finally, Julie said, "Sue, you have what you said you wanted—an academic job in a department with a graduate program—and now a seal of approval on your first year there. I can tell you're unhappy, and I know it's been a struggle for you. Write the book, apply for other jobs, and get out of there and away from Dan. Once the book is published, you'll have the leverage to do that. In the meantime, my advice is the same—have some fun away from psychology."

Susan sipped her brandy and leaned against the kitchen window. It was almost midnight, and the lights of downtown Victoria vibrated against the inky sky. Susan vowed to end her dependence on brandy as a sleeping pill even though insomnia was becoming a habit. The historical novels stacked by her bedside would become her new sleep remedy in place of this addictive fluid that slipped effortlessly down her throat.

She was relieved Julie agreed with her. Dan needed to jump a lot of hurdles before he could pressure her to be part of his plan. Psychologist couples were not unknown. Most resembled Joyce and Ari Petras—a younger woman, usually a former student, with an older man. She and Dan as a couple would fit this cliché. Susan pictured herself in Joyce Petras's place. Watching Joyce navigate the perilous waters of department perceptions convinced her it was not the course for her. Dan in the same department was too much closeness at too great a cost. Susan trusted Julie. Dan would never be able to rearrange his life.

Julie was right on another point. Susan was unhappy, despite achieving what she wanted. She craved professional validation, and she got it today from Jim Kracknoy. The department, at least the executive committee members, was behind her and wanted her to succeed. But her professional success was set against a background of personal agony. Her failure weighed against her success, and the effects of one cancelled the other. Instead of happiness and satisfaction, she felt adrift and hollow.

And then there was Lucas. Susan cringed at the memory of his face the day he met Dan in her office. What was written in the note he discarded as he retreated down the corridor? She would never know. Her friendship with Lucas was not simple, but it was real. Susan could not imagine herself in body work therapy sessions—screaming and drumming—and Lucas probably could not imagine her there either. She could envision Lucas as a researcher, but his cynicism about the demands of academic life would gradually erode the warmth of their friendship. Their time together always seemed destined to be a cherished memory. She hoped her anguish over his loss would lessen with time.

A trace of brandy lay at the bottom of her glass and she examined the dregs hoping for an insight. It was like studying tea leaves for a glimpse into the future. She swirled the brandy in the glass. The drink eased her pain, but it offered no answers. She would have to find them herself, but the way forward was far from obvious. There was work, which was going well—finally—but her loneliness was crushing. Night after night spent alone was leading her toward a despondent abyss. Yesterday, driven by loneliness, she went to The Beaver in a pitiful attempt to feel close to Lucas again. She sat at the same table they shared, and the waiter who served them months before took her order.

"Hi, where's Lucas? I haven't seen him in a while," he said as he dropped a paper coaster on the table.

"He's probably on Quadra Island with his fiancé," Susan answered.

"Lucas is getting *married*. I didn't know that. From the times he was in here," suddenly the waiter hesitated, "ah, he looked pretty committed to the single life."

Susan's face fell. She did not want to hear about Lucas's social life. The waiter looked regretful. "Hey, listen, I'm getting off shift. Let me buy you a beer." He shuffled to the bar to pour the two pints, returned to the table, and sat down introducing himself as Greg. "Where did you meet Lucas?" he asked.

"At JDU." Susan sipped the cold beer, not liking the taste much.

"Yeah, I know Lucas is a professor there. I went to JDU—graduated last spring with a political science degree—couldn't bring myself to leave Victoria just yet. I'm from Manitoba, and I really didn't want to go back to the cold. Eventually, though, I think I'll apply to law school somewhere back east. What are you studying?"

Susan was surprised, then realized she was probably not much older than Greg. It was a logical mistake to make—to assume she was a student at JDU not a professor. She started to correct him, then stopped herself. Why not continue the charade? Greg was athletic, not bad looking with his short-cropped blond hair. He probably played rugby at JDU—he looked like a rugby player. Maybe he worked in a pub because the work involved beer. Susan read somewhere that rugby players loved their drink. If she wanted to invite him home, it was more promising to let him think she was a student. "Psychology—I'm studying psychology."

Susan sighed and poured the last of the brandy into her glass. It was pathetic to fake an identity just to up the chances of companionship—of sex. Ashamed, she had finished her beer, said good-bye to Greg, who told her the nights he worked and asked her to stop by again. Desperation would probably lead her to accept his invitation, and she gulped her brandy to banish the thought. The no-commitment sexual arrangements at the Institute were fun, but she was hesitant to dive back into that life. It felt like a behavioral regression. She thought of Julie and her actor friends, and remorse combined with envy swept over her. She could be in New York with Julie instead of here in Victoria compelled by loneliness to lie to undergraduate political science majors.

Susan sat on her bed and picked up the book on top of the stack on the bedroom floor. She grew anxious thinking about Dan's return at the end of the summer. The writing was almost done, and she needed a strategy to keep Dan focused on the publication of the book. Being with Lucas ruined her ability to endure Dan's paltry version of intimacy. She would rather have one-nighters with rugby types like Greg. Susan scanned the description of the novel's plot on the back cover. Good, she thought, there is a female protagonist who triumphs over adversity—just what she needed—a lesson in fortitude even if it was a fiction.